Killer Comfort Food

By Lynn Cahoon

The Farm-to-Fork Mysteries

Deep Fried Revenge
One Potato, Two Potato, Dead
Killer Green Tomatoes
Who Moved My Goat Cheese?
Novellas:
Penned In
Have a Deadly New Year

The Tourist Trap Mysteries
Guidebook to Murder
Mission to Murder
If the Shoe Kills
Dressed to Kill
Killer Run
Murder on Wheels
Tea Cups and Carnage
Hospitality and Homicide
Killer Party
Memories and Murder
Murder in Waiting
Novellas:
Rockets' Dead Glare
A Deadly Brew
Santa Puppy
Corned Beef and Casualties
Mother's Day Mayhem
A Very Mummy Holiday

The Cat Latimer Mysteries
A Story to Kill
Fatality by Firelight
Of Murder and Men
Slay in Character
Sconed to Death
A Field Guide to Homicide

The Kitchen Witch Mysteries
Chili Cauldron Curse

Killer Comfort Food

A Farm-to-Fork Mystery

Lynn Cahoon

LYRICAL UNDERGROUND
Kensington Publishing Corp.
www.kensingtonbooks.com

LYRICAL UNDERGROUND BOOKS are published by

Kensington Publishing Corp.
119 West 40th Street
New York, NY 10018

All Kensington titles, imprints, and distributed lines are available at special quantity discounts for bulk purchases for sales promotion, premiums, fund-raising, educational, or institutional use.

Special book excerpts or customized printings can also be created to fit specific needs. For details, write or phone the office of the Kensington Sales Manager: Kensington Publishing Corp., 119 West 40th Street, New York, NY 10018. Attn. Sales Department. Phone: 1-800-221-2647.

Lyrical Underground and Lyrical Underground logo Reg. US Pat. & TM Off.

First Electronic Edition: January 2021
ISBN-13: 978-1-5161-0991-3 (ebook)
ISBN-10: 1-5161-0991-0 (ebook)

First Print Edition: January 2021
ISBN-13: 978-1-5161-0992-0
ISBN-10: 1-5161-0992-9

For my middle school librarian who allowed me to hang at lunch and unbox and prep new books for the library. My first venture into the book world.

Acknowledgments

River Vista, Idaho, is made up of all the good things about the real small town where I lived from third grade. The odd thing is, I was brought home from the hospital to a small farmhouse on a dairy farm just about a mile away. If we hadn't lost my father, I would have grown up in the same area, gone to the same schools, with the same kids, but I would have been a totally different person. Would I still love reading as much? Would I still have read *A Wrinkle in Time* and put myself in the character's shoes? I don't know. But I'm who I am now because of my childhood. The good and the bad. Now I realize the definition of both of those words is up to me.

Kensington, Esi, and all—You rock.
Enjoy your trip to River Vista.

Chapter 1

Angie Turner stood in the back of the banquet room of the County Seat, watching as her friend and partner, Felicia Williams, led the cookie baking class. It was the last class they'd scheduled for the Christmas season. Of course, it was past Christmas, but the class had been so popular, the room was filled to capacity, even on a wintery January Saturday. Or maybe *because* it was a cold Saturday. With the weather in southwestern Idaho turning to snowy days, local cooks were still enjoying the fun of turning on the oven during the weekend and creating some baking magic.

Angie's thoughts were already turning toward spring and what she wanted to plant this year. Which brought her to the thought that had been keeping her awake for months now. *What is going to happen to Nona's farm?* She hadn't heard from Jon Ansley, the lawyer working for Taylor Farms and the soybean project, for a few weeks now, but that didn't mean the guy had gone away. They already had one of the nearby farms locked into a contract. And her elderly neighbor, Mrs. Potter, was weakening. Especially with the last, very-crazy-large, offer. Angie couldn't blame her—getting that kind of money out of her farm would set her and her family up for generations.

Angie didn't want to sell. The house, the barn, the land, held memories for her. Good memories. Like the snowball cookies Felicia was demonstrating for the packed class.

She turned and left the room, knowing she wasn't needed there. But where to go? The County Seat's kitchen was deep into prep for that night's service. If she went in there, her second in command, Estebe Blackstone, would just frown at the intrusion to his time and put her to work. Instead, she grabbed her coat and headed outside, jaywalking across the street to the city park.

Traffic on the cold winter Saturday was light. The people who lived in the surrounding subdivisions typically went to a larger town for their weekend chores like shopping and dry cleaning. River Vista was changing from a dying agricultural town to a more boutique small town. The dance studio that had opened last month on Main Street was crowded with students hoping to make it big someday. Next to that, a bakery had just opened, and Angie could see the parents from the dance studio making their way into the store for more coffee and a midday treat.

Change was good. Development was normal. She didn't want to give up her family home. Even though the plant would bring much-needed stable jobs to the area. What was the saying: Not in my backyard?

Was she selfish to be fighting the development? She sighed as she brushed snow off a wooden bench where she could sit and watch the activity on Main Street.

A car slowed as it drove past her. The metal swings were empty and silent. The ancient merry-go-round still. The park had three horseshoe pits that were filled with snow over the sand that surrounded the metal poles. The city council had voted last year to upgrade the park with more up-to-date and safer playground equipment, but the funds hadn't been there for the fall renovation. The County Seat had participated in a fund-raiser this Christmas raising money for the now scheduled March renovation. A large trench had been dug to move water lines in October, but the project had been put on hold after the early snowstorm.

Now, with the blanket of snow, the park looked like it had been locked in time. One of the last remnants of the town that used to be. River Vista Days happened every August, with the center of the activities right here in the park. A street dance closed Main Street, and a carnival set up in the parking lot right behind the park. It was a special event for the town, and Angie wondered if, with all the development, it would still feel the same.

Her cell rang. She answered without looking at the caller ID. "This is Angie."

"Why are you sitting out in the cold? You're going to get sick," a deep, smoky female voice asked.

"Who is this?" Angie glanced around her, wondering who was watching her mope.

"Barb. Barb Travis. Come over to the Red Eye. I need to talk to you. Besides, you need to warm up before you freeze to death."

"I'm not cold," Angie protested, but she realized the line had gone dead. Barb Travis, owner/manager of the country dive bar a few doors down from the restaurant, was a woman of few words. She was in her fifties, but she looked like she could toss out any errant cowboy who decided to cause trouble in her establishment. And when Barb spoke, you listened. If you knew what was good for you.

Knowing the woman wouldn't give up, Angie stood and headed back across the street. Her pity party had been cancelled. She needed to let the attorney she'd hired worry about the fate of her home. But, like Barb, Angie wasn't good at handing problems over to others. She knew she needed to find a way out of this mess that didn't turn her home into a parking lot for the plant, or worse, leave her as the sole house hemmed in by industrial development.

She pushed open the heavy wooden doors and stepped into the darkness of the bar. After being outside in the sunny, snow-bright day, it took a few minutes for Angie's eyes to adjust to the bar lit with strands and strands of white Christmas lights. The tree that had been at the back of the bandstand was gone, but Barb had kept the additional lights up all around the room. She spotted the woman sitting on a bar stool, watching her.

"Every time you come in here, it's like you're walking into a strange country. Don't tell me you didn't frequent your share of dive bars when you were in college." Barb's rasp turned into a chuckle, then a cough, which went on a little too long for Angie's mind.

"I'm just not used to the dark anymore. Especially, today, after being outside. The sun sparkles on all that snow, now that it's had time to ice over." Angie moved toward the bar, taking off her gloves and hat and stuffing them into her coat pocket. She didn't look at Barb when she sat down next to her, just asked the one question Angie didn't think she'd answer. At least not truthfully. "How are you?"

"I'm fine. You worry too much." Barb stuffed the tissue she'd used to wipe her mouth into a pocket. "Anyway, I need a favor."

"Anything." Angie smiled and shrugged out of the parka. The bar's heat was on high, and the large room was warming up fast.

"You'll take that back when you hear what I'm asking." Barb pulled out a picture and pushed it across the bar toward Angie.

She glanced down at it. The picture showed a woman with a small girl by her side. They were standing near a sixties Mustang, and both the woman and the girl had on matching dresses and knee-high white boots. The round wire rimmed glasses framed the woman's face, and she had dark hair, long and wavy . She stared at the picture, then glanced at Barb. "Is this you?"

"Guilty as charged. That was taken Easter 1987. My daughter, Sunny, was two."

Angie glanced up sharply. "I didn't know you had kids."

"Just the one. Sunny. She graduated from law school, and then decided her mom's occupation was a little too common for her new friends."

Now Angie didn't like the grown-up Sunny. Not at all. "That reminds me of Felicia's new friends from her yoga group. Several of them have attitude problems. Seriously, people are all the same, no matter what they do for a living."

"You don't have to tell me that. You'd be surprised at who comes into this place for a little drink now and then." Barb took back the picture. "She was a good girl. My sister raised her from the time she started school. I was wild back then, and Sunny was unplanned. Karen couldn't have kids. It just made sense. At least on paper. In Sunny's eyes, I became more like an aunt than her mother. Karen's husband was a big shot lawyer in Boise and handled the adoption quietly. I should never have signed those papers. It was easier that way. I'm not sure she even remembered our time together. Don't think badly of her. Or of me."

"Sorry, I'm partial to the underdog in a fight. I would do anything to be able to talk to my mother, or my Nona, just one more time. Surely your sister has told her the truth by now."

"I don't think Sunny remembers she had a life before Karen was her mom. My sister died a few years after Sunny graduated from high school. Her husband remarried, and they didn't want me confusing the issue. I didn't even get an invitation to Sunny's wedding." Barb sipped on her coffee. "They said they mailed one but it was returned because it was an old address. I was running with a hard crowd at the time. I wouldn't have fit in anyway, especially not as the mother of the bride."

"It's never too late to change the future. We don't have infinite time to make things right." Angie shook her head. "But this isn't about my wishes and dreams. You needed my help with something?"

Barb pulled out another picture. This one was clipped from a newspaper. It was a wedding announcement. "I'm sorry. This is the most recent picture I have of Sunny."

Angie set the picture down on the bar, but only glanced at it. She needed to get back to the restaurant. Service was starting soon, and she had a lot to get done before the doors opened. "I'd love to stay and chat with you for a while, but I have to open the restaurant. This is going to sound shorter than I mean it to. What do you need?"

"Sunny's missing. She always sends me, her aunt, a Christmas card, and she didn't this year. I went by her house over in that new subdivision just north of town when her husband was at work, and no one's there. My little girl has disappeared, and I think he's behind it."

* * * *

Felicia was cleaning up the banquet/training center when Angie got back to the restaurant. She looked up when Angie walked in, immediately setting down the towel she was using to wipe down the table, and made her way over to Angie. "What's wrong?"

"Coffee first, please." After Felicia had poured two cups of coffee, Angie told her what Barb had said. "I just can't wrap my head around it. Barb must be out of her mind with worry."

"Why doesn't she go to the police?" Felicia sipped her coffee and glanced at her watch.

Angie knew it was almost time to start the final prep for service. They didn't have time for this. They didn't have time for the head chef to be freaking out. But she was. And Angie needed to tell someone else Barb's story before she could just go on with her day. "She did. Sheriff Brown took a missing person's report, but the husband said she'd gone off to visit her mother. Since Karen's dead and Barb hasn't seen her, his story doesn't hold up. Unless he's talking about the stepmom, and apparently, she lives here in Boise. Allen's looking into the husband now."

"I have a bad feeling about this. What if he killed her?" Felicia's gaze moved to a spot on the wall that would show her the Red Eye if she'd had X-ray vision. "He must know something to lie like that."

"Or Sunny lied to him." Angie nodded to the waiter, who peeked into the room and then disappeared. She stood and moved to the doorway. "You're needed out front, and I need to get in the kitchen. We can talk about this later. But thanks for letting me vent. I'm not sure I could have held that in for the entire service."

Felicia fell in step with Angie. "I'll finish cleaning this room tomorrow."

"I feel bad not even staying for the end, but how did the class go?"

"You were here for most of it. I saw you in the back. You tell me?" Felicia turned off the lights to the room. She carried a tin of cookies out of the room with them.

"They were engaged, making notes, and chatting with each other. It sounds like it was wonderful." Angie turned toward her office. She needed to drop off her coat and get on her chef's whites. "You're an excellent teacher."

"Yeah, but this group knows me from yoga. They're easier to talk to, I don't have to put up a confident face." Felicia took the coffee cup from Angie and put both into a dishpan. "Go have a great service. We'll talk about everything either tonight, or if we're too beat, I'll come out and make you breakfast tomorrow. I'm needing a Dom fix."

Dom was Angie's year-old Saint Bernard. He adored Felicia almost as much as he loved Angie or Ian, Angie's boyfriend. Angie tapped on the tin. "Is that what you're doing with the cookies? Bringing them over to the house?"

Felicia shook her head. "I think now I'm dropping them off at the Red Eye. Poor Barb, she must be going out of her mind. Sugar will help keep her calm."

"Have you not ever heard of a sugar high?" Angie stared at Felicia, not believing what she'd just heard.

"Don't judge. When I'm worried, I eat. I know you have the same bad habit. I just want Barb to know we're here for her. Just in case." Felicia glanced at the clock. "I'm going to have Tori get the staff working on the dining room, and then I'm popping out. I'll be right back."

Angie made the turn into the kitchen, leaving Felicia to handle the front of the house. Her friend was a top-notch pastry chef as well as being amazing at running the front of the house. And she had a heart of gold that seemed to carry the weight of her friends' burdens. Angie was surprised that Barb hadn't asked Felicia for the favor, rather than her.

"Why are you looking like someone stole your milk money?" Estebe stood by the chef table watching her. "Is there something wrong?"

At Estebe's question, she felt the gaze of everyone in the kitchen land on her. They'd be worried about the restaurant. About their jobs. About their scheduled hours. Angie needed to put Barb's issues away and clear the kitchen from any negative energy. There was enough time outside of service to worry about what had happened to Sunny Travis. Angie didn't need to upset her kitchen family.

"No worries at all. I'm just thinking about the farm and this soybean plant." Angie hoped the lie would ease their fears. "I mean, seriously, if someone was going to run me out of my home, why couldn't it have been for a winery or a bakery? I like bread."

A smile creased Estebe's face, showing the lines already forming. "And you like wine. Do not bring tomorrow's worries into today. Let them stay in the future."

A Nona-ism if she'd ever heard one. "My grandmother used to say something similar. You're right. I'm putting it away. How is prep going?"

"Estebe wants to change my appetizer recipe," Nancy called out. "He thinks every recipe needs a potato element."

"It is Idaho," Matt quipped.

"I like my bruschetta just the way I designed it. With toasted French bread." Nancy nodded to Matt's station. "You have a lot of chopping left to do. I think you should keep your head down and out of this conversation."

Smiling, Angie went to the sink and washed her hands. She greeted Hope and Bleak, who were washing pans from the prep work. When she had a clean apron on over her chef coat, she moved back toward Estebe. "What can I help you with?"

After it started, dinner service moved liked a well-rehearsed dance. *This is why I love being a chef.* Angie finished wiping a plate and handed it to the waiting server. Felicia stepped into the kitchen. "Who wants to meet the chef tonight?" Angie asked. "Tell me it's a kid rather than some politician. I love chatting up the kids. They don't have any secret agenda."

"Actually, they wanted to talk to Nancy. It's a couple, and the man says he knew you from before?" Felicia frowned as she delivered the message. "If you want, I can tell him you're too busy to leave the kitchen."

"No need. I wonder who it is? Probably someone from high school. I graduated from Nampa High. It could be any of the old crew." Nancy stepped away from grilling. "Matt, cover me for a bit. That steak is just about ready to flip. And I just put on the chops."

After Nancy had explained what she was working on, she stepped away from the stove and paused at the doorway, where there was a small mirror hung on the wall. She wiped her face with a towel, then threw it in the laundry bin to the side of the room. "Probably some guy I dumped. I hope he's not here to make amends."

Angie followed her out of the kitchen. "I need to see this. I don't think I've met any of your friends. You're always so busy working, I don't get to see you off the clock."

"Well, don't judge me for my high school friends. I didn't come into my own until college." Nancy grinned at Angie and then scanned the room. "I don't see anyone I know…"

Angie knew exactly when Nancy recognized the guy. And it didn't seem like it was an old boyfriend. If Angie didn't know better, she'd think that Nancy was going to bolt out the back door. Angie put a hand on her chef's arm. "What's wrong, who is it?"

Instead of answering, Nancy stepped out in the dining room and walked directly toward the table where a man sat, smiling at her. The woman at the table didn't look up, not once.

"Charles, what are you doing here?" Nancy demanded. "I thought you were in Napa Valley now."

"I move around a bit. Business, you know." He stood and leaned over to kiss her on the cheek, but Nancy shuddered and backed away from him.

"Well, you can just move your way out of this town and out of our lives. There's no way I'm going to let you see the kids." Nancy's eyes were black. Angie stepped up and stood between the two.

"I'm Nancy's boss. I'm afraid if you two have problems, you're going to have to leave. I can't ruin the mood for my other diners just because you have issues with my chef." Angie hoped her voice sounded as authoritative as she wanted.

"Sorry, we haven't been properly introduced." He turned to Angie, ignoring Nancy to his left. "Angie Turner, you are lovelier than the photos from your newsletter articles when this place opened."

"I'm sorry, you're still going to have to leave, Mr...." Angie held her hand out toward the doorway. "And don't worry about the meal, we'll comp it."

"That's kind of you." He held his hand out to his dinner companion. "Come, Jane, I feel like we're not welcome here."

"Yes, Charles." The woman stood, tucking her purse under one arm. She didn't argue, didn't mention that she hadn't eaten much of her meal. She just stood and followed him to the coatrack.

Angie put a hand on Nancy's arm. "Go back to the kitchen."

Nancy nodded, then shot daggers to the man's back. "Don't trust him."

"I'm just going to make sure they get out the door. We'll talk later." Angie smiled, nodding to the kitchen. "You need to get back before Matt burns something."

"He wouldn't dare." Nancy's eyes narrowed, and she started back to the kitchen, only looking back once at the exiting couple.

Angie stepped over to the hostess stand and watched while the man held out a nice wool coat for his date. He shrugged into his own coat, then nodded to the door. "Go ahead, I'll be out in a second."

Once the woman was outside, he turned to Angie. "There are two sides to every story."

"I don't really care, Mr...."

He paused and looked at her carefully. "She didn't tell you who I am, did she? I'm Charles Gowan, Nancy's ex-husband."

Chapter 2

After service, Nancy rushed out the back door, her coat and bag in hand. Angie watched her leave as she finished sending out the last plate.

Angie glanced at Estebe. "Do you know what's going on?"

"Not a clue, but Nancy is scared. I've never seen her frightened before." He shook his head. "She said she needed to check on the kids, so I told her to leave as soon as she was done with service. I am worried about her."

"Me, too." Angie sent up a wish for safekeeping for Nancy and her family as the crew went about the business of cleaning up after the last service of the week.

Angie was still thinking about Nancy when she arrived home that night. Dom sat at the kitchen door, waiting for her to set her bag on the table. Then he danced around until Angie acknowledged him. She locked the door, throwing the dead bolt as well, then sat on one of the kitchen chairs and leaned down to give Dom a big hug. "It was crazy at the restaurant tonight, big guy. Barb's looking for her daughter and wants me to help. Then Nancy's ex-husband came by and upset her. Lots of emotion flying around tonight."

Dom stared at her with his big brown eyes. He woofed, then licked her arm. Angie translated that to, *I'm glad your home, let's cuddle on the couch and eat popcorn.* Or he could be saying that she worked too hard and took on too many problems from other people. Either interpretation would be spot-on, but she thought the scenario with the popcorn was probably more her dog's style.

She was worn to the bone but too wound up to sleep yet, so she followed Dom's unspoken suggestion, pouring a glass of wine to go with it. Then they watched reruns on the cooking channel until her eyelids started drooping. She'd solve mysteries tomorrow when she could actually think.

Sunday morning, she smelt the coffee and some sort of cinnamon bread baking before she even got out of bed. Dom had already left to join the visitor in the kitchen. Felicia was probably working on some ideas for the next cooking class. She could entertain herself for a bit. So Angie showered and got ready for the day before going downstairs.

Felicia looked up from her laptop when Angie came into the kitchen. "Good morning, sleepyhead. I take it you and Dom had a late night watching television."

"What gave me away?" Angie poured herself a cup of coffee and sat at the table.

"The two bags of microwaved popcorn in the trash. Typically, you only need one to wind down." Felicia turned the laptop toward Angie and pointed to the screen. "This is Nancy's ex-husband, Charles Gowan. From his website and his own press, he's a hotshot developer in northern California. She's been working three jobs just to get by and get out of the debt he left her with, and he lives in a mansion on top of a vineyard. Not sure if he owns the vineyard, too, or if it's just a great photo op."

"What a jerk." Angie sipped her coffee. "Did you know he was rich?"

"No. I figured he was some deadbeat. I wonder why Nancy's attorney didn't go after him." Felicia sighed. "I can't believe someone would be that vindictive."

"Maybe there were other reasons Nancy didn't want him in her life." Angie reached down to rub Dom's ears. "I should go feed Mabel and Precious."

"Already done." Felicia turned the laptop back and started working again.

"Thanks, but did you make sure their water wasn't frozen over?" Angie stood and glanced out the window. Mabel, the lone black and white hen from Nona's flock, was digging at something in the garden.

"No, because I didn't feed them. Ian was here when I arrived. He said to tell you good morning when you got up and that he was going to lunch with the family after church. You could meet them at the café in Meridian at twelve thirty if you wanted." Felicia didn't even look up from the laptop. "You have that boy well trained."

"I don't have him trained," Angie protested. "He just knows I work late nights when the restaurant is open. He stops in to feed them because he worries about the animals."

"Okay. But Estebe wouldn't do that for me if I wanted to sleep in." Felicia grinned. "Which is one of the reasons I'm leaning on getting a cat. They're very independent. Not like a pet goat."

"I didn't set out to have a pet goat," Angie protested, but she saw the humor in her friend's eyes. "And you might want to hold off on the cat until we know that I'm not moving into the apartment with Dom, Precious, and Mabel."

"You're not losing the farm. That lawyer you hired is going to figure out something." Felicia stood and crossed the kitchen to stand next to her at the sink. "No worrying. Not yet. Save your worry for tomorrow."

Angie stared out the window for a few minutes, hearing the words echo in her head. First Estebe, now Felicia had used a version of one of Nona's favorite sayings to comfort Angie. It had to be a sign. Wherever the words were coming from, they were comforting.

The bell went off on the oven. "Cinnamon rolls are done. These are a make-the-night-before version I wanted to teach in our next class." Felicia moved over to the oven and opened it. The smell of fresh baked rolls and sweet cinnamon and sugar filled the room.

Dom lifted his head from his bed, took a big sniff, then Angie could have sworn he smiled as he lay back down to go to sleep. Her dog loved the kitchen and the food smells that surrounded him as he slept. One more reason she couldn't sell. This was Dom's home as well as hers. She needed to protect it. She turned her attention back to Felicia, who was dishing up the cinnamon rolls.

"I hope the weather is going to be fairly reasonable today. After this breakfast, I'm going to need to take Dom for a hike." She paused at the fridge. "You want some orange juice, too?"

"Of course, and there's bacon in the microwave. It should still be warm." Felicia set the plates on the table and grabbed silverware. "I was going to make a baked apple salad, too, but I got lost in the research on Nancy's husband."

As they sat and ate, a thought came to Angie. "Did the research you found say why he was in Idaho? I would think he'd be too busy with his new California life to mess with anything here."

"Could be a new upscale development going in over outside of Eagle. I heard they're expanding State Street coming out of Boise to eight lanes to accommodate the traffic into downtown." Felicia glanced at the laptop. "Do you want me to keep looking?"

"It can wait until after brunch. I really wanted to talk about next month's class. Do we have everything planned out?" Angie bit into the crunchy, thick bacon and almost groaned. This was why she bought everything local. The pork was from a processing plant between here and the river, and the bacon they made was thick and meaty. She didn't understand how anyone used the paper-thin stuff from the grocery store.

"Earth to Angie, did you hear me?"

"I was lost in the taste. Sorry. Let me refocus right after I finish this slice." Angie ate the last bite of bacon, then smiled at her friend. "Go ahead, I'm listening."

"You and your food. I swear, you love eating more than anyone I've ever met." Felicia laughed but then started listing off the recipes that they would be teaching the next week. Angie would be joining her in this class to give the group two different perspectives on food preparations. Felicia had gotten a lot of her yoga class members to sign up for multiple classes. They were stay-at-home moms with more time and money than activities.

After they'd approved the class and decided who would teach what recipe, Angie made some notes in her planner. Then she refilled the coffee cups. Sitting down at the table, she pulled out the picture of Sunny. "Do you know her? Is she in your class?"

Felicia's eyes widened. "*This* is Barb's daughter? Of course I know her. And you do, too. Well, you know her husband."

"I do?" The picture had only shown Sunny's face to the front. Her groom had been turned to the side when they walked down the stairs of the cathedral. He had dark hair, but she couldn't see his eyes. "How do I know her husband?"

"That's Susan and Jon Ansley. You met him on the hiking trails—he's the one who's been handling the soybean plant development legal pre-work. Didn't he tell you that his wife had died?" Felicia started keying on the laptop, looking for something. She turned around the screen again when she found what she'd been looking for. An article from the *Statesman*. "Local wife goes missing. Husband is offering a large reward for her whereabouts."

"That was her? I mean, I think he said his wife had died." As Angie thought about it, maybe he hadn't. He'd said the dog was his wife's, and she couldn't remember the rest. She'd been so mad that Ansley was trying to force her out of her home, she hadn't thought about what he'd said for a while. "I don't remember exactly."

"You should call your attorney. If Jon is under suspicion of killing his wife, I can't see how he'd be able to broker this deal."

"Maybe she did just leave." Angie spun her phone on the table. "You want to go into town with me tomorrow?"

"Why?"

"I'm going to go talk to Jon Ansley and ask him about his wife." Angie picked up her phone, scrolling through the emails. When she found the last one from the law firm, she blew up the address. "His office is in one of those new buildings on Overland by the theaters. Most of the established offices have places downtown to be closer to the Statehouse."

"Better for us. Traffic downtown is a nightmare." Felicia picked up her plate and rinsed it in the sink. "You want me to do the dishes before I leave?"

"No, I'll mess with them when I get back from running with Dom. I'll call when I'm heading into town tomorrow. Do you want me to pick you up at the restaurant?" Angie glanced around the kitchen, making sure everything was put up and out of Dom's reach.

"Sounds good. I'm leaving to go over to Estebe's soon. He's making me a late lunch."

Angie glanced at her friend's yoga pants and BSU sweatshirt. "Have fun."

"Don't look at me that way. I'm stopping at the apartment to change into jeans. They will be warmer than these sweats." She waved and then leaned down to kiss Dom.

"I wasn't saying anything," Angie protested as Felicia walked outside.

"Whatever." Felicia held her hand up in a wave and then closed the door.

"I think our friend is in love," Angie said as she and Dom sat alone in the kitchen.

He woofed his answer, then stared at his leash.

"I get the point. Let me just run up and change into warmer clothes." She ruffled Dom's fur and ran up the stairs. Her life was good. At least for the time being. And that was all she could think about today.

* * * *

The next morning, when Angie got ready to leave, Dom sat in front of the door. She'd taken Felicia's advice and had changed into jeans and a sweater. Dom woofed when she came down and turned to stare at his leash.

"Sorry, guy, I'm heading into town for a bit. You stay here and guard the castle." She gave him a hug and watched as he went back to his doggie bed and lay down, his sad brown eyes staring holes into her.

She grabbed her tote and her keys. "Not going to work, buddy."

When she locked the door, she heard the short whine of protest. She felt bad, but she didn't want to leave him in the car, and usually law offices didn't have pet-friendly policies. As she drove into River Vista, she thought about what she wanted to ask Jon and how she could keep it professional. He already knew she didn't like him after a kind of heated exchange at the first community meeting. Unfortunately, she was the only voice of dissent against the moneymaking plant. Building the plant meant jobs, not just in the building phase, but later, in running the plant. Most of the locals loved the idea, so her protests had been a lone cry in the wilderness. Until she'd hired an attorney to handle amplifying her voice.

The Bluetooth speaker picked up a call, and Angie decided to take a chance. "This is Angie."

"Angie? This is Maggie Brown. Allen's wife? I was wondering if you could stop by today. I'd love to chat with you a bit."

"Maggie, thanks for the offer, but I'm swamped. In fact, I'm on my way into town, then I have to work on some menu planning." Ten to one, Ian's aunt wanted to talk about the non-scheduled wedding that would follow the not-yet-happening engagement. Ian needed to handle this rather than her. "Maybe we could do lunch later this month?"

"That would be lovely, but I really need your insight soon. I was hoping we could talk today while school was in session. Bleak, well, she's being difficult." Maggie sighed. "I know I shouldn't bother you, especially since you did so much by giving her a job, but I don't know what to do."

Angie thought she heard tears in Maggie's voice. Guilt, it always worked on her. Angie glanced at the clock. By the time she got back to town, it would be after noon. Maybe she could stop in to see Maggie after she updated Barb? "Look, I can't promise anything, but if I can, I'll stop by this afternoon. What time does she get out of school?"

"Three. And by the time she gets home, it's always closer to four. I don't know what she's doing during that time, but I'm worried." Maggie paused. "And it would be better if you didn't mention this to Ian or Allen. I don't want them getting the wrong idea and scaring the girl."

Angie groaned. Keeping secrets wasn't one of her best skills. And she really didn't want to hone in on her sweet boyfriend, especially when it came to his family. "You're asking a lot."

"I know. But I'll see you this afternoon."

The line died before Angie could tell Maggie that she wasn't going to keep a secret from Ian. So was that implicit agreement? She wondered how the legal system felt about that fine distinction. All she had agreed to do was to talk to Maggie. She'd tell her flat-out today that she wasn't going to lie to Ian or his uncle. With that moral line drawn in the sand, she pulled into the parking lot behind the restaurant next to Felicia's car to wait.

A knock sounded on her window, and she turned away from watching the door. Ian stood outside her car.

Angie rolled down the window. "Hey, handsome. What are you doing hanging out in the alley?"

"I would ask you the same thing, but I'm wise to your ways." He shook his head. "I can't believe you're doing this."

Angie froze. She hadn't even talked to Maggie yet. How had he known? She turned down the radio. "Look, I don't know what you think you know, but…"

"It's obvious, you're going into town to check out the animal shelter, right?" He nodded to the doorway. "Felicia's been talking about getting a kitten, and you're enabling her."

Angie smiled but felt a little sick. If this was how she felt by even thinking of keeping something from Ian, there was no way she could keep Maggie's secret. She'd just have to tell her when she got to the house. And if that meant Maggie didn't want to talk to her, well, that was a blessing in disguise.

"Actually, no. We're going into town to talk to the guy who wants to tear down my house." She rubbed her face. "And before you tell me it's a bad idea, I already know that. But I just found out that Barb's daughter is missing and…"

Felicia climbed into the car. "I need to be back by noon. Estebe is taking me out for lunch at a new place near the winery."

"Sorry, I've got to go." Angie reached out and touched Ian's face with her gloved hand. "Don't worry, we'll talk later."

"Call me as soon as you're heading back. I'd like to hear the rest of this story." He squeezed her hand. Then he added, "And I'd like to know the two of you are safe."

As they drove out of the parking lot, Felicia glanced back at the place where Ian was still standing, watching them leave. "Don't tell me you told him what we're doing."

"Kind of." Angie didn't look back as she turned out onto the road that would lead to the highway. She glanced over at her friend, who was digging through her purse. "Do you know what's going on with Bleak?"

Felicia's head snapped up. "No. What's going on?"

Angie focused on the road ahead. "I have no clue, but I've been asked to the Browns' house to talk to Maggie about it. And sworn to secrecy, at least where Sheriff Brown and Ian are concerned, so you can't say anything. I just thought if there was something happening, you might have seen something."

"She's doing a great job as a hostess. I'm not sure she's going to want Hope's dishwashing job this summer. She's really good with people." Felicia sat back in her seat. "She's been so happy, chatty about school and the kids. I can't imagine anything is going on that's worth this kind of angst."

"Maybe Maggie's just overreacting. She hadn't raised a kid before, and now she gets a teenager as her first try as a mom." The Browns had taken on permanent foster care roles for the teenager, whom Ian had found sleeping in the alley last summer. He had convinced Angie to hire her even before they'd known the whole story about why she'd left her Utah home. "I don't know that I'd be a great mom, especially if I got a kid who could talk back. I wasn't the easiest kid for my grandmother to raise. At least until I discovered I loved cooking."

"And the rest is history." Felicia smiled, then turned to look out the window. "Bleak will be fine. She has a village of people who care for her."

Angie drove toward Boise and her next problem. Bleak would be fine. And she was going to keep the farmhouse. Good things happened to good people.

That was her mantra for the upcoming days, and no one was going to mess with it.

Chapter 3

No one sat at the reception desk when Angie and Felicia walked into the law office. A low hum of canned music flowed through the room, and a sign directed visitors to the offices at the left. A wooden door had been propped open, and after giving Felicia a shrug, Angie made her way into a large room with a lot of desks in the middle. On all four sides, offices with glass walls and doors circled the room. One woman nearest the door looked up from her computer and asked in a bored tone, "May I help you?"

"We're here to see Jon Ansley," Angie said, trying to ooze confidence into her tone. She didn't want to be asked why or challenged.

Surprisingly, the woman only pointed to the left and said, "Third door on the left. If he's there."

"Thanks." Angie met Felicia's gaze, but this time her friend shrugged. For a law office, they didn't protect their lawyers very well. The last time Angie had been in a law office had been downtown, where she'd been read Nona's will. That guy had the receptionist *and* an assistant you had to get through before you got to talk to the busy attorney.

At the third door, they paused, looking in on a man filling a box with pictures and coffee cups. He paused, sensing their presence, then sank into his desk chair. "Go away, Miss Turner. Even if I hadn't been put on administrative leave, I wouldn't be able to talk to you without your attorney being present. I'm sure the firm will assign someone new to handle the soybean plant's interests soon. You can tell him your sob story."

"Nice to see you, too, Jon." Angie decided to ignore his command and stepped into the office. She took one of the photos out of the box. "This is your wife, Sunny?"

"Susan. She never did like that nickname her mother saddled her with." He took the picture frame back from Angie and returned it to the box. "Why do you want to know?"

"Her birth mother's worried about her." Angie let the words settle in and watched his face.

He leaned back in his chair and rubbed a hand over his face. "What are you talking about? Her birth mother's in Canada. Don't tell me you know people in Canada?"

Angie saw confusion on the man's face. "You said your wife was dead. The first time we met at Celebration Park, you told me she died."

"I don't think I ever said the word 'dead.' Timber misses her. Although if she wasn't dead, Susan would have never left that dog with me for this long. She loved the dog way more than she loved me." He stared at them. "So, you're not here to talk about the land purchase? Taylor Farms offered you a great package. Twice what the actual land is worth, plus relocation money. You could buy a new place in a great neighborhood for that."

"I like my house. I don't want to sell." Angie slipped into one of the chairs and pointed to the other one for Felicia to join her. "And that's not why I'm here. So, your wife isn't dead? You know that?"

"Of course I know that." He took out a pack of cigarettes and lit one. He grinned. "I always wanted to do this. They can't put me on administrative leave twice."

Felicia frowned at him. "Your smoke isn't just an health hazard for you. We're in the office too."

"And again, I'm asking why. Sorry I'm not making it hospitable for you." He took a drag from the cigarette and continued to watch them.

"Her birth mom actually lives in River Vista. She's worried about Sunny, I mean Susan," Angie blurted out.

He frowned, sitting up and crushing the cigarette on the glass-topped desk. "That's not possible. Susan's note said she was going to stay with her mother. Her birth mother. She was adopted. She told me the family was from Canada."

Angie studied him. She thought he was being truthful. But on the other hand, lawyers lied. All the time. This could just be one of the stories he told himself. "When was the last time you saw her?"

"December twelfth. It's been hard. When I met you at the park, I told you a sob story to get you to talk to me. Then, when she really left, I just thought she was mad. That she'd come home eventually. She always was running off in a tizzy. I was working a lot on this Taylor Farms deal, and she wasn't happy." He stared at her. "Her mom thinks I killed her? Is that why I was put on leave? Because people are asking questions about the wife killer who works as a lawyer?"

"I don't know." Angie was starting to feel bad for the guy. But on the other hand, it could all be an act. "Look, I told her mom I'd see what I could find out. Where would she have gone if she isn't…"

"I have no clue." He picked up the picture again.

"I just want to be able to tell her mom that she's okay. That she's safe," Angie pushed. No matter what she thought of the guy based on his attorney work, Barb needed help, and she needed to get on Jon's good side. "Can you think of anywhere?"

"There's one place. We have a cabin in McCall that I thought maybe she might be holed up at. I was going to take some time next week to check there, since I don't have to work." He glanced around the room, his eyes darkening. "Anyway, I was going to go see if she was there and at least take Timber up with me so she could have the dog. She loves that dog."

"Let us know what you find out." Felicia touched Angie's arm, and they moved toward the door. "Jon, I hope you find her."

"Me too." He sank backward in his chair and started to cry.

Angie and Felicia made their way to the exit, not talking or looking at each other.

After they left, Angie started the car and watched the building. "What do you think?"

"I think he was so wrapped up in this Taylor Farms deal he might not have noticed when Sunny left. And after she did, he used the time to get deeper into work, since he assumed she'd come home. And now…" Felicia picked up her phone and texted someone.

"What are you doing?" Angie backed the car out of the parking spot and aimed her car back toward River Vista. If they left now, Felicia wouldn't miss her lunch date with Estebe.

"One of the yoga moms was close to Susan. I'm seeing if I can take her out for coffee tomorrow. She might have some gossip about what happened or at least how the marriage was before Susan left. A lot of times the best friend knows way more than the husband when a marriage is going downhill." She sent the text and got one back before she could put the phone away. "Tomorrow at ten at the library in Meridian. Do you want to come?"

"She doesn't know me."

Felicia grinned. "That's never stopped anyone from gossiping. And this group of women love their gossip. It's like a recreational sport."

"Send me the information, and I'll put it on my schedule for tomorrow. Today, I have to go back to Barb and tell her I didn't find anything."

"Yet," Felicia added.

Passing a slow-moving car, Angie glanced over at her friend. "What do you mean?"

"I mean you haven't found Sunny yet. You've only been looking into this for less than half a day. Be gentle with yourself. Besides, you still have to go talk to Maggie. You need to up your game if you're going to face the sheriff's wife. Everyone I know tries to stay away from her. And that's when she's in a good mood."

"Maggie's a nice woman. A little intense at times, but nice."

"Whatever. Let's get this cleaned up before Bleak takes off and there are two missing daughters in the wind."

Angie parked behind the restaurant. Felicia went in to get ready for her lunch date. And Angie headed over to the Red Eye, wondering if Barb would even be inside. She could walk the two blocks to the Browns' house just a few blocks away from Main Street. Bleak could not only walk to work, but also to school and any of the after-school activities. She'd told Angie she was saving for a cheap car so she could drive back from the dorms and still work for the County Seat once she went to college. It seemed like once she'd hired someone, they never wanted to leave the job. They must be doing something right as an employer.

She pulled on the back door of the saloon that led out to the alley where she stood, expecting it to be locked, but the door swung open easily. Angie walked through the narrow hallway past the bathrooms and the storage area. The smell of stale beer and cigarette smoke was stronger here, mostly because of the confined space. She wondered if it would ever leave, even though smoking inside had been banned for several years now.

Barb sat at the bar, probably on the same stool she'd been on Saturday. She waved Angie closer, seeing her without even turning her head. "I didn't expect to hear from you for a while."

"I went into town today to see Jon Ansley." Angie sat on the stool next to Barb and watched her reaction. A tiny flicker of hope filled the woman's eyes but was gone before Angie could believe it was even there.

"Oh. What did that weasel say?"

"Not much. He was packing up his office."

That got a reaction, and Barb turned to stare at her. "Don't tell me he's leaving town. We'll never find Sunny if he leaves."

"No, he had been put on leave. And he wasn't happy about it. But he seems to think Susan, I mean Sunny, is alive and just mad at him for working too much."

Barb's shoulders dropped. "You believed him?"

"I don't know. Maybe. He did seem concerned, but then again, he's a lawyer." Angie rubbed the edge of the wooden bar where it had been burned too many times with cigarettes then varnished over. "Felicia and I are going to talk to Sunny's best friend tomorrow. One interesting thing came up, though."

"What was that?" Barb didn't even look up from her paper.

"Jon said he thought Sunny had gone to Canada to find her birth mother."

Barb turned her head away and stood up, turning off the lights in the front bar. "You can't believe a word that man says."

"Are you from Canada?" Angie asked.

Barb didn't answer. "Look, I've got an appointment this afternoon in town. I'll talk to you later. Thanks for checking on Sunny. If you hear anything else, let me know, okay?"

Angie followed Barb out and paused just outside the door, hoping to get something else out of her, but the woman locked the bar, then went and got into her newer Mustang. The woman had a type, at least in cars.

After Barb drove away, Angie reluctantly walked toward Sheriff Brown's house. She had to tell Maggie that no matter what, she didn't keep secrets from Ian. If she wanted this issue with Bleak to be kept quiet, she would just have to not tell Angie. She knocked at the door. She decided she wouldn't even step inside until that was clear between them. The door swung open a crack, and Maggie peeked outside. When she saw it was Angie, she opened the door wider and without a word, pulled her into the house and closed the door behind them.

"It won't do if Mr. Stephenson sees you. I swear, that man is more of a gossip than any woman in the world. I can't take my own garbage cans inside without it being a big deal around the mens' group at church about Allen not doing his husbandly duties." Maggie nodded to a hallway. "Let's talk in the kitchen. Do you want some coffee?"

"Maggie, I'm not sure I'm staying," Angie said, but the woman had already disappeared deeper into the house. She mumbled to herself, "I guess coffee couldn't hurt."

When she got to the kitchen, she saw Maggie had been making cookies. It looked like a cookie factory had exploded in the updated room. The breakfast nook had a small table that wasn't covered in trays of cookies.

Maggie handed her a cup and saw her looking around. She pointed to the small table by the wall. "We can sit over there. When I get nervous or upset, I bake. The good news is, with Bleak in the house, this will disappear before they go bad or I have to take them to the church. Do you need cream or sugar?"

Angie shook her head. "Black's fine. Look, Maggie, I need to say something."

"Of course you do. Everyone loves Bleak. I did tell you that when I invited you over, right?" Maggie sat at the small table and frowned. "I'm sure I told you. I wouldn't have just told you to comply. It's not like I have a speck of compelling power in me. Well, I guess being married to the police chief does give me a bit of credence here, but not much."

"No, I meant about keeping our discussion a secret from Ian and Allen. I just can't promise that." Angie sipped her coffee. It was just the way she liked it. Hot and dark roasted. "If that means we can't talk, I'll just have coffee with you and we'll not talk about Bleak. It's up to you."

Maggie stared at her for a long time. Finally, it appeared she'd agreed with Angie's terms. "Okay. I understand your position. I'm just so worried about Bleak. I have to talk to someone, and well, Allen's official position can get in the way of frank discussions."

"I get it. And if it doesn't need to be an Ian discussion, I'll hold back. Just don't ask me to keep things from him. I don't want to damage our relationship over a lie."

Maggie patted Angie's hand. "You're a very nice girl and perfect for our Ian. I won't put you in a bad spot. Anyway, I found one of Bleak's notebooks in her room last week, and she had written all this stuff about southern Utah. Like places runaways could stay and how far it was to Las Vegas and the towns in between. You don't think she's planning on taking off again, do you? She seems so happy. And I just got her weight up to normal. She was so thin when she came to live with us."

"Bleak seems happy at work. Felicia was saying she's excellent at the front of the house. She's a hard worker, and she's talking about working full-time next summer and looking forward to our next retreat. I don't think she's planning on rabbiting anytime soon." Angie thought about their last family meal at the restaurant. Bleak looked normal, chatting and teasing, and eating with the group. "I'll make sure Felicia keeps an eye out for her, but if it's just this, maybe she was thinking about visiting her family."

"You know, if she goes back, they'll force her to stay—or worse." Maggie shuddered. "I can't imagine what her life had been like before she left."

Angie thought about Bleak's aunt and the extreme measures the woman had gone to last summer to bring the girl back into the fold. "Look, I'll talk to Hope. If Bleak's planning something like this, she'll know."

"Would you please?" Maggie's hand shook a bit as she lifted her cup to her lips to sip. "I'm not sure what I'd do without her."

Angie studied the woman in front of her. "Look, maybe you should just come out and ask her. She'd tell you."

"And then I'd have to admit I was reading her journal." Maggie shook her head. "I don't know much about this mothering thing, but even I knew that was a line I shouldn't have crossed. Who knows, maybe she just put that in there to see if I am reading her stuff? She could be testing me."

"That wouldn't surprise me," Angie admitted.

A door opened in the front, and Maggie's eyes widened. She glanced at the clock and whispered, "She shouldn't be home yet."

"Maggie? Are you here?" A man's voice boomed through the house. "I'm heading out on a call and don't think I'll be home for dinner."

"We're in the kitchen, Allen," Maggie called back, clearly relieved it was her husband and not Bleak. She turned to Angie. "Can you just be here for coffee?"

Angie nodded. "Talking about Bleak is normal, right? We both care about her."

"Some kid found a body of a woman out behind the park. Poor kid, he was sledding down the dirt hill where they were redoing the water lines, and…" Sheriff Allen Brown stopped short at the doorway to the kitchen. He stared at Angie. "Crap, you said 'we' were in the kitchen. Angie Turner, I didn't expect to have you here in my house today."

"Are you telling me I can't have visitors?" Maggie stood, her dark eyes flashing at her husband.

"Of course not, dear, I just wasn't expecting anyone. I should be more careful what I say when I come home." He walked over and gave his wife a kiss. "I'm hoping you could keep this under wraps, at least until we find next of kin."

"Look, Allen, I don't want to even know this…" Angie paused, a thought crossing her mind as quickly as her hand flew up to her lips. "Oh no. The body isn't Susan Ansley, is it?"

"How did you know about Susan being missing?" His gaze bore into her.

"Barb asked me to try to help her find her daughter. Sunny is Susan Ansley. And before you find out and question my motives, Felicia and I went to talk to Jon Ansley about what happened to his wife." Angie sighed. She knew telling the truth up front was better than waiting and trying to explain, but she hated the look that River Vista's sheriff was giving her right now.

"Sometimes I wonder what evil I did in another life to deserve you moving back into my town and ruining my life." Allen went to a drawer and pulled out a plastic baggie. He then filled it with cookies.

"Allen, that's not nice to say to Angie." Maggie stepped closer to her, showing girl-power solidarity.

"May not be nice, but it's true. Let's just hope this woman isn't Susan Ansley for all our sakes." He nodded to them and stepped out of the kitchen. "Don't wait up for me."

After the door had closed, Maggie turned toward her. "Now tell me what you know about Susan. You need to be covered just in case this woman is dead in my husband's crime scene."

Chapter 4

By the time Angie got up the next morning, she hadn't heard if the body had been identified. She turned on the television as she made coffee, but there was only a short mention of the discovery and that further information was being held until next of kin was notified. She pulled on her coat and work boots and headed out to the barn. Mabel was inside, the cold morning too much for her. Felicia had bought her a sweater, but Angie hadn't put it on the old hen, worried it would cause a heart attack when they caught her to put it over her head.

"If the weather gets any colder, though, I might just chance it," Angie told the hen as she spread feed down on the ground for her and refilled her water. She took a bucket over to Precious's pen and refilled the water trough. Her water trough was heated so the water didn't ever ice over.

The black goat nuzzled her hand. "Good morning to you too, Miss Precious." Angie filled the food trough with the corn mixture the goat loved and added a bit of hay for later. "What's going on in the goat world today?"

With a bleat, Precious rubbed her head against Angie's hand one more time, then ran to the food trough.

"That's my girl." Angie laughed. "It's all about the food, right, Precious?"

Angie had gotten Precious when she was just a baby, when the goat's mother had been killed by coyotes. She'd found her up on a hiking trail in Celebration Park, and the goat had followed her back to the car, much to Dom's displeasure. So now she had a Saint Bernard, an elderly hen, and a young goat for her private zoo. If she got to keep the farmhouse.

She pushed the worry aside. For some reason, she'd been pulled into too many worries this week. She decided to call Barb and see how she was holding up. She had to be worried sick.

Finished with the chores, once she got back into the house, she poured a cup of coffee and put a breakfast casserole into the oven. Felicia had left a new one to try in her fridge the last time she'd come over. And with the brunch workshop this week, Angie needed to get the review back to her friend so she'd know whether or not to keep it on the menu.

She dialed Barb's number and put the phone on speaker. A tired voice answered on the fourth ring. "What do you want this early?"

"Oh, sorry, I didn't think you'd still be sleeping. You didn't open the bar last night, did you?"

"No, but my sleep schedule is all messed up because of the four nights I close at two. What do you want?" Now she just sounded grumpy.

Angie thought about her question. If no one had told Barb about the body, she'd be the one breaking the news. But if they had, Barb should know whether it was her daughter or not.

"Angie?" This time the voice was quieter, softer.

"I was just wondering if you'd heard about who was found in the park." Angie cringed—that hadn't sounded as gentle as she'd hoped.

"It's not Sunny. Sheriff Brown called late last night to tell me." The words were released like a breath. Then she laughed. "Hell, I'm not sure if I wanted it to be her, just to stop the wondering, or if I wanted my sweet girl to be alive somewhere, not realizing how many people were worried. I'm a bad person."

"You aren't. You're scared and worried." Angie let out a deep breath. She'd thought it might be Susan Ansley's body too. "Did he know who it was?"

"No. At least he didn't tell me. The woman was younger than Sunny, dark hair and five-foot-nine. Some other mother is grieving today. I'm still in limbo." She sighed. "Look, I need to try to get some more sleep or I'll be a mess tonight. Thanks for calling to check on me."

Angie couldn't think of a response, but then she didn't have to as she realized Barb had already hung up on her. She glanced around the kitchen. Tomorrow she'd have to go in to work and start her week. Today, she was home and her mind was a tangle of worry. Everything was jumbling together, and the best thing she could do for that was cook. She took her coffee cup over to the built-in bookshelves in the kitchen that held all her cookbooks and ran a finger across the spines. She definitely wanted to bake something, maybe make a casserole or some soup. Her breakfast still had twenty minutes before it was ready, so she had plenty of time to find a few new recipes to try out.

Her finger stopped on a small black spine. Maybe this was another of Nona's recipe books. Angie pulled it out and opened the cover. Not a cookbook, but a journal. And the writing wasn't Nona's. She closed it and found a name written on the front cover. *Property of Kathleen Corbin.* *Turner* was added in another color of ink.

This was her mother's journal.

She took the book and her coffee back to the table. As she read the first entry, Angie realized the words had been written when her mother was a teenager. Angst about entering high school. What classes to take. What career to focus on. Her dreams. Angie read the first five entries, then set the book away when the oven beeped, telling her the casserole was done.

Her mom had gone to school in River Vista too. She'd attended the old high school, though. The building had been torn down and Ian's farmers' market took up the parking lot on most weekends. Angie had gone to the new high school, which had now been turned into a middle school and another new high school had been built. Generations after generations of families had lived and loved in River Vista.

Angie ate her breakfast, staring at the book while she did. When her phone rang, the sound made her jump, she'd been so lost in thinking about the girl who'd turned into her mother and how much they'd been alike.

"Hey," she answered the phone, still thinking about the treasure she'd found.

"Hey yourself." Ian paused. "Did I catch you cooking?"

"Actually, no. I haven't started yet. I'm just eating breakfast, why?" She glanced down at the plate and was surprised to see the food already gone. She'd been so lost in her thoughts she hadn't even realized she'd eaten.

"I was checking in to see if we're still on for tonight. I hear you've had a tough weekend." His voice was calm and warm. One of the reasons she loved the guy. He knew just how to deal with her moods.

"I'd love to see you. Did you make reservations?" Angie liked researching where she was eating beforehand so she could glance at the menu and not get lost in the choices when she arrived.

"I did. We're going to Canyon Creek. I saw Sydney in Boise last week, and she mentioned how much she'd like to show you their menu this season." He paused. "That's okay, right?"

"I'd love to chat with Sydney tonight." Angie realized she meant it. "And you."

"I don't mind playing second fiddle to a talented chef like Sydney." He laughed as she tried to take back the order of the words. He cut her protests off. "I've got to go. Allen wants to talk to me about Maggie. He's worried about her."

"She called me yesterday, and I went over to have coffee with her." Might as well say it up front, Angie thought.

"Really? That's a good step. Last time we had dinner together, Maggie was so worried about cooking for you she burned everything. Maybe our next dinner there will be at least edible."

"She seems to be warming up to me." That felt like a distraction from the truth, even to Angie.

"You can't know how happy that makes me." He said something to a person in the office. "Allen's here. I'll see you tonight."

"Tonight," she agreed, but then found herself talking to dead air again. Didn't anyone say goodbye anymore?

Angie took her plate to the sink and put the leftovers away. Then she set her mother's journal back on a shelf behind her kitchen desk. One place where Dom couldn't find it and chew the covers as well as some pages. Then she grabbed two recipe books and started making a list for her mise en place. Hopefully cooking would do the trick.

By lunchtime, she had a sausage and white bean soup bubbling on the stove. Two loaves of sourdough bread set on the counter cooling, and Angie had set aside her starter to develop for the next time she baked. She wrote down the recipes in her journal with notes on where she'd found the original recipe and what tweaks, if any, she'd made to it. Most of the time, she'd made major revisions. Or she would have by the time she'd tested the recipe two or three times. The next time she wanted to make a red sauce with the soup, not as thick as a chili, but giving it more of a tomato base to add even more flavor. Sometimes the tweaks made it better, sometimes not. But you never knew until you tried. She closed the journal and set it aside, next to her mother's. Angie hadn't kept a diary during high school. Too much angst to deal with as a teenager. Especially one who had lost her parents so young.

She wasn't hungry yet, but she knew she needed to eat. Dom stared at the bread, hoping for a slice just for him. Instead, she slipped on her tennis shoes and grabbed his leash. She needed the exercise as much as her dog did. "Come on, Dom, let's go for a walk."

A backpack with two bottles of water and a couple of doggie treats, along with another collar and another lead already packed, sat by the back door. Angie added her set of keys to the bag and her wallet, and they were ready to go.

When she and Dom were finishing their walk and heading toward the parking lot, a familiar dog bounded up to greet them. Angie glanced up at the man on the other side of the leash. He looked pale and gaunt. "Mr. Ansley, how are you today?"

He looked at her like he didn't recognize her. "Oh, Miss Turner. I should have expected to see you here. Did you come to throw salt into the wound?"

"Not sure what you're talking about, but I'm here to walk my dog." Angie moved to the side to let him and Timber pass.

He rubbed his face. "Look, I'm sorry. It's been a bad couple of days. Did you know they found a body?"

Angie nodded. "I heard yesterday afternoon. I'm glad it's not your wife."

He barked a laugh. "I should have known you'd have all the details, not like those people in the grocery store. They look at me like I'm a serial killer or something. You just hate me because of the land deal."

"I don't hate you." Angie thought about what she'd just said. "Okay, so maybe I hate you a little. I really don't want to move, and the company you're representing is making that an issue."

"The company my firm is representing. I'm on leave, remember." He smiled, but the emotion didn't hit his eyes. "I just wish life would go back to the way it was before I took on this project. Susan would be home, griping about the women in her yoga class, she'd be taking care of Timber, and I'd be working too many hours."

"Susan didn't like you working for the Taylor Farms account?" Angie glanced down at Dom, who was ignoring Timber and his attempts to play.

"She thought it was slimy, especially since I was doing the recon before anyone was offered contracts on the land. She thought the company should take over the land where the old meat packing company used to be." He shrugged. "She really didn't like me talking to your neighbor and her granddaughter. She said that was why lawyers had a bad name, trying to get the cheapest price for land that had been in the family for years."

Timber, bored with Dom's unwillingness to play, pulled on his leash.

Angie smiled. "Someone wants to get going."

"Yeah, he's been locked up in the house too long. I guess my time off will give me time to get him out and about"—he glanced up at the sky—"as long as we don't get another snowfall soon."

"Have a good walk. And I'm glad it wasn't Susan." Angie moved toward the car.

He turned to watch her; she could see him still standing there. He left as soon as she reached the car. Had he been waiting to make sure she got into the car safe? Great, now even the bad guys in her life were watching out for her. She drove home, thinking about mothers and daughters.

Ian showed up at the house right at six. He was nothing if not a man of routines. But that wasn't a bad thing. Angie had made him a basket to take home with him. Two quarts of the soup, one almost frozen and one from the fridge, along with a loaf of the bread. Her next-door neighbor, Mrs. Potter, was in California for the winter, and her granddaughter, Erica, hadn't come back from winter break yet. They were typically the recipients of Angie's testing days, as long as the recipes turned out tasty. Angie could count on Ian taking some of the product off her hands since he wasn't much of a cook and had lived on ramen and SpaghettiOs before they'd started dating. The good thing was, since she worked four nights a week, she didn't usually have to cook much at home unless she was trying out a new recipe. With what she had in her freezer, and Ian taking her out for dinner dates, she probably didn't need to cook for months. If she didn't want to. The problem was, she loved to cook.

She nodded to the basket. "You should put that in your truck just in case Dom decides to sample the soup I made this morning."

"Dom wouldn't do that, but I'll put the food in the back cab of the truck. I'd hate for him to be tempted."

A short whine came from the side of the room where Dom lay on his bed. Ian laughed. "I hear you, big guy. I'm moving it out to the truck now."

When he didn't come right back in, Angie glanced out the window. Ian was coming back from the barn, clapping his hands together to get rid of the dust from the goat food. Ian probably fed her crew more often than she did lately. Especially on nights when she was working late. Precious was in love with him, that was a definite. Angie knew Dom's loyalty was divided. Only Mabel wasn't affected by Ian's charms. Mabel didn't seem to like anyone, including Angie.

She checked Dom's food and water and grabbed her cell phone, tucking it into her small purse, which she slipped over her shoulder as a crossover bag. She liked the fact she could carry her wallet, keys, and a bit of makeup in a purse that she didn't have to mess with or worry that she'd set down somewhere. It stayed on her body. And bonus, her phone even fit inside the zippered compartment.

She stood at the door, waiting for Ian.

When he came inside, his gaze dusted over her body. "You look amazing."

"Thanks. I can clean up nice with a little forewarning. Besides, I'm excited to talk to Sydney. I haven't seen her since the baby arrived." She laid a hand on his chest. "You look great too."

"I try." He held the door open. "Ready?"

"Be good, Dom. Stay away from the furniture," Angie called out as she left the house.

Ian waited for her to lock the door, then took her arm and led her to the truck, opening the door for her. "You know that kind of goodbye could be giving him ideas."

"Dom's not like that. He likes to think up new and surprising ways to tear up the house while I'm gone." Angie climbed into the truck and waited for Ian to start the engine before speaking. "So, I told you I went to see Jon, the lawyer yesterday, right?"

"Yes, and you were supposed to call me and let me know you were back in town, but since Allen saw you at the house, I let it go." He pulled onto the highway. "How'd that go?"

"Not well. He's claiming Susan just left. That she went to see her mother in Canada." She adjusted the seat belt so it wouldn't pull against her neck. "Apparently his bosses don't like him being looked at as a stone-cold killer, so they gave him some time off."

"Does this help your case against the soybean company?" Ian turned the stereo down that had been playing classical music in the background.

"I don't think so, but maybe." Angie sighed as she looked around the fields that surrounded her home. "I hate to think all of this might be gone. Especially since there's a better alternative closer to town."

"What's that?" Ian turned down another back road that would lead them to River Vista, where they would pick up a larger, four-laned road that would take them to the freeway.

"There's an old meat packing plant that's been abandoned for a while. I guess it was in the running, but with the owner of the one plot of land in jail, they're getting this area for cheap, even if I raise the price on what I want for the farmhouse. The area is prime for development. Mrs. Potter doesn't have family who wants to keep the family farm. I'm leasing out most of my land to a local farmer. And you know Kirk Hanley needs to sell that forty acres next door to pay his lawyer bills for the next appeal." She shook her head. "Anyway, I saw Jon today at the walking path."

"Another reason I really hate you going there." Ian shot her a look. "Fine, I'll take off my worried boyfriend role. What did you talk about with the possible stone-cold killer?"

"I don't think he killed Susan. He's missing her too much. And he's taking care of the dog. Who would do that if they killed their wife?"

Ian stared at her. "The only reason you don't think Jon Ansley killed his wife is because he's being nice to the dog? The dog that he left off the leash the first time you saw him?"

"Okay, so it's a stupid reason, but no, I still don't think he killed her." She adjusted her purse closer to her. Her reasoning sounded stupid even to her ears. "What did Allen say about the woman they found? Do they know who she is?"

"They don't. They have her details out and a BOLO going, but so far, she doesn't match any missing persons and he didn't get a match from the fingerprints. At least not yet. Allen's pretty frustrated by the whole thing. Especially since the media wants to connect this with the Ansley disappearance." He glanced at her. "So, why are we talking about death and murder on our date night?"

"Just small talk." She thought about Bleak. No need to bring that up unless Ian did. "And how did your day go?"

"Nice change of subject, kind of. It's a bit slow at the office. I was wondering if you wanted to take a short getaway with me next month. We could go south. Somewhere a little warmer. I was thinking Sedona?" He glanced at her, hopeful.

"I wouldn't be able to go for a full week. Estebe's out the first week of February on some men's trip with his Basque group. Nancy, well, she's got a lot on her mind right now, and I'd hate to push her into a head chef role before she's ready. I could go on a Sunday and come back the following Wednesday." She thought of her calendar, checking for any other appointments she might have. "What about the next week?"

"Let me see if I can move some meetings tomorrow." He nodded to her purse. "Check your appointments now. I don't want something else to come up if I move these and we still can't go."

Angie smiled and pulled out her phone. "Man, you're never going to let me live that down, are you?"

"I had two hundred in a deposit I almost lost because you couldn't go to San Diego last minute. I'm not made of money here. I'm basically working for a charity." He grinned. "And no, it gives me great pleasure to tease you about your mistake, so sue me."

Last year, Angie had bailed on an impromptu getaway after assuring Ian her calendar was clear. They'd had a catering gig the same week, so she had to cancel. "You should be thankful that I can even take time off. Typically, when I start up a new venture, it takes years to get this solid of a kitchen staff trained. I'm so lucky."

"You have good people working with you." Ian passed the River Vista outskirts sign and slowed down as he drove through town. No one was out on the streets, not in this weather. The dance school only did night classes on Wednesday, and the bakery closed at three on weekdays. The only cars in this part of town were driving through or heading to the gas station. A lone police car sat at the back of the park, crime-scene tape flapping in the breeze.

"They still have the place blocked off?" She pointed over toward the park.

"Investigations take time." He stepped on the gas and headed out of town toward the highway. "And we are not talking about it anymore."

Chapter 5

It took a while, but by the time they'd reached Copper Canyon, Angie and Ian had fallen into a discussion about places they wanted to travel to and why. When he opened the door for her, he leaned down to kiss her. "Thanks for changing the subject. Sometimes I think all we talk about is tragedy. I'd like tonight to be about hope and joy, not pain and hate."

"I'm assuming you're meaning the emotion hope, and not my newest chef." She grinned at his reaction. "Calm down, I'm just teasing you. I agree. I think we should focus on the happy stuff. But if your uncle spills any interesting tidbits, I expect you to fulfill your duties as my boyfriend and tell me all the good stuff."

"You're impossible." He kissed her again. "Let's go see what Sydney's been up to." He took her hand, and they strolled into the restaurant. When he gave the hostess his name, the woman grinned.

"Come this way. You two are going to enjoy the chef table. Our head chef is quite the character." She led them through the dining room and back to the kitchen.

Angie glanced at the wall of French doors that led out into a patio. She pointed them out to Ian. "I'd really love to do that, but then I'd have to tear up our parking lot, get a waiver from the city to block the alley, and build a garden. Not to mention that our dining room is on the front side of the building. We don't have a wall to work off of."

The woman glanced at the patio area, then back at Angie. "I'm sorry, maybe I should know you? Are you a local chef?"

"She is." Ian put a hand on Angie's shoulder. "This is the head chef and mastermind who opened the County Seat in River Vista."

"Oh my, I should have recognized you. I've been studying your career in school. I'm trying to decide whether I want to stay in hospitality or move into more of a chef role. Do you have any suggestions?"

Angie smiled, feeling trapped. She always dreaded when young people asked for advice. What did she know about which fork in the road to take? "If I were in your shoes, I'd figure out where I wanted to be in ten years. As soon as I'd answered that question, the rest fell into place. Including knowing what role I wanted to play and the people I wanted in my life. I knew I had something magical inside me. Now all we have to do is make it through the first five years. Then we'll know if the County Seat's going make it."

The woman held the door to the kitchen open. "You must be really jacked about the soybean plant being built out there. I swear it's going to bring in so many jobs, the area won't know what it did without it."

"Not if I can help it," Angie murmured.

"Excuse me?" The hostess leaned closer, apparently thinking she hadn't heard Angie's words correctly. Then she grinned at someone across the room who was blocked from Angie and Ian's view. "Anyway, here's Sydney! Enjoy your meal."

The hostess waited for her boss to greet the new arrivals, then disappeared into the dining room again.

"You handled that tactfully," Ian whispered in her ear.

Angie shook her head. "Actually, I need to stop reacting. They don't know what's at stake for me. They just have the community's best interest at heart."

Sydney paused a little way away, frowning. "Is something wrong? Did Di say something inappropriate?"

"No, we were just carrying on a conversation from the car." Angie stepped forward and kissed Sydney on the cheek. She glanced at her friend. "Look at you. No one could tell you just had a baby."

"Six months ago. And I've been working out since my doctor gave me the okay." Sydney patted her stomach. "I love Brooks, but being pregnant was horrible. I can't believe people have more than one kid."

"You look amazing." Ian gave Sydney a kiss, as well. "So glad we could stop by tonight."

"I'm the one who's excited to have you. I've got some new menu items I'm dying for you to try. I think your work with Farm to Fork is so important. I'm doing my best to replicate the local sourcing." Sydney waved over a waitress who had been at the side of the kitchen. "Katrina will get your drinks while I go get your first appetizer."

"'First'? As in many?" Angie laughed. "I'm glad I didn't eat much for lunch."

"I hope you're right, because we've got a full menu ready for you to taste." Sydney moved toward the cook line as Ian and Angie got settled at the table.

They ordered water and a glass of wine and watched the kitchen work around them. Ian took her hand. "Before I met you, I wasn't even curious about how a home kitchen worked, much less a fine dining experience. I was all about the food supply chain, but not about the meals that the food could create."

"It's more than just the actual meal. It's the experience of eating and tasting and being together. That's why I cook and why I have the restaurant. You've seen us in action. We like feeding people." She smiled at him. "I'm glad you're seeing the rest of the story now."

They ate plate after plate as Sydney brought them over and explained the story behind each recipe. By the time they had the Canyon Creek's specialty dessert, a baked potato made totally out of ice cream, Angie didn't think she could eat another bite. Sydney sat down with her own dish and a cup of coffee. "The crew can handle a few orders while I take a break with you. I've been on my feet all day, and after taking off six weeks with the baby, even cramping feet feel glorious."

"It's nice to work." Angie took a spoonful of the ice cream and almost melted at the strong vanilla flavor. "Everything was wonderful. Thank you for sharing your chef table with us."

"Not a problem. I'm going to come over some Wednesday. Just as soon as I get this new sous chef up to speed. You're so lucky you have such a stable crew."

"I am. I totally agree with you." She smiled and took another bite of the ice cream. She was too full to eat, but she couldn't stop eating this faux potato.

"Wasn't that woman's body found near the County Seat?" Sydney leaned closer to the table.

"Across the street at the park. Of course, anywhere inside River Vista city limits would be close. We're a small town, not like Boise." Angie set her fork down and took a sip of coffee. "It's just so sad."

"I know the woman who disappeared last month. She was in my women's empowerment group. We work with underprivileged women and support the crisis center and other local causes. She was chair of the upcoming Winter Cotillion that's happening next weekend. I can't believe she's not going to be here to enjoy the party." Sydney kicked off her shoes and tucked her foot under her leg as she leaned back to finish the ice cream. "She didn't seem like the type to just take off. When they found that body... well, I thought the worse."

Angie nodded. "I can see why. Things like this don't happen in River Vista. Or in Boise, for that matter. We're a quiet community."

"Well, it's been getting worse. Like the thing last summer at the fair. That was crazy." Sydney turned to the cook line and frowned. Two chefs were talking in hushed tones. "I think something went wrong. I need to get this."

Angie stood. "And we need to get home. Have Di print out our bill, and we'll get out of your kitchen."

"You're kidding, right?" Sydney came and gave Angie a hug. "Tonight's on me. Thanks for the feedback on the menu. I think you should be charging me for your expertise."

They said their goodbyes, and as Angie settled into the truck, she thought about Susan. Why *had* she left town? Or was she still around—in body at least?

A few miles in, Angie realized Ian was taking the back roads back home. Depending on the time of day, sometimes back roads were quicker than going onto the freeway. The area just kept growing. She turned to Ian, who smiled and took her hand. "Sorry I've been quiet."

"You're thinking about Barb's daughter, aren't you?"

When she nodded, he sighed. "Sometimes getting involved in these things isn't safe. You've got to know that, right?"

"I just can't sit there and let Barb worry forever about what happened. I care for her, even if she is the grumpiest bar owner in River Vista." Angie squeezed Ian's hand. "And you wouldn't like me so much if I just let the world go by without trying to help."

"I just don't see what you can do in this case."

Angie stared out the window, watching the buildings, then the fields, go by as they got farther into the country. Finally, she answered Ian. "I'm going to a Winter Cotillion next Saturday. Want to be my escort?"

* * * *

When she'd gotten home that night, she took a chance that Felicia was part of this committee, or if not, that she knew how to get tickets. Then she called Estebe and asked if he'd hold down the fort as head chef while she took a Saturday night off. The hesitation in his voice told Angie that he suspected she was doing something she probably shouldn't be. So she lied and told him that Ian wanted to go to the dance/dinner because of his connections with the group. The excuse sounded totally fake, at least to Angie's ears, but Estebe seemed to buy it.

And she had the night off.

This wasn't family meal Wednesday, so she didn't go in to work quite as early as she would next week. They hadn't changed the menu for a couple of weeks, so it would be a standard night. No surprises.

Bleak stood leaning on the wall outside the office when Angie arrived. And the no-surprises theme went out the window. "Hey, Bleak, what's going on? Are you sick? Do you need the night off?"

"I'm not sick, and I don't need time off." Bleak waited for Angie to open the door, then she crossed the room and slouched into one of Angie's visitor's chairs. "But I do need to talk to you. Privately, without you telling anyone else."

Inside, Angie groaned. Had Bleak found out about Maggie's conversation with Angie? Was this why she was putting on the gag order? She took a deep breath and accepted the terms of the conversations. If Bleak was ready to tell someone what was going on, she could be that person for her. And still keep her best interests at heart. She shut the office door. "As long as I don't feel like you're in legal trouble or not safe, I'll keep the promise."

Bleak seemed to consider that qualifier, then nodded. "Look, Allen and Maggie are the best. But if I tell Allen, he's going to have to do something. And Maggie? Well, she just wouldn't understand. That woman is so sweet. She's lived a charmed life. She and Allen dated in high school. Actually, she used the word 'courted.' They didn't have sex until they were married. Can you imagine?"

Angie smiled. She knew that the abstinence curriculum was taught by the local school district. With Maggie and Allen's strong religious views, it didn't surprise her, but Bleak had grown up in a different world. Way different. "I really don't want to talk about Allen and Maggie's sex life, if you don't mind. You know I'm dating their nephew."

"Sorry, I just needed to explain why I needed to talk to you rather than Maggie. She'd never understand, and I need some advice about what to do."

"What can I help you with?" Angie opened the conversational door. She might regret this later, but maybe Bleak just wanted to talk about work stuff. Felicia should be the one she was talking to; maybe Angie could call in her friend before Bleak went too far, but she stopped her hand from moving to the phone. Bleak had trusted her. She was just going to have to live up to that trust.

"I heard from one of my nieces at home. My aunt is being charged with attempted kidnapping, and they want me not to testify. It will take her out of the house, and she's the only one who's working. My uncle, well, he's busy with the farm." Bleak dropped her eyes. "If she goes to jail, they won't have any money."

"You know your aunt's actions aren't your fault, right?" Angie felt for the girl. She was too young to be carrying this kind of weight on her shoulders. She should be thinking about prom and football games, not who was going to feed her relatives.

"I know. And she should be punished. But on the other hand, the church lessons are all about forgiveness. I'm so confused." Bleak looked like her name, miserable.

"I don't think you have to make a decision now. There's going to be a lot of pre-work for this trial and lawyer things. You have some time to decide how you feel. And if you want to testify, or if you don't, it won't change the way Maggie and Allen feel about you." Angie smiled, "Or the way your work family feels. We're here to support you in whatever you decide. But it's your decision. Not your aunt's or any of us here. It's what you want. You were the victim."

"I feel bad for her."

"You wouldn't be human if you didn't. This has proven how strong you really are." Angie decided to change the conversation's tone. "Hope tells me you've been asked to the winter formal. Are you going?"

Bleak's face turned bright red. "I don't know yet. Ty is a drummer. He's not one of those band geeks, but he's passionate about music. I guess he's cool."

And I guess you're a little bit in love with him. But Angie didn't say that out loud. Instead she glanced at her watch. "Getting close to time for prep. Are you okay?"

Bleak nodded. "It helps having your opinion. I know you don't have a vested interest in either side."

Angie stood, following her out of the office. "You're wrong there. I do have a side. I want you to be happy, no matter what the choice is. And I'm here to support you, no matter what you decide."

Bleak glanced back over her shoulder and smiled. The emotion behind it was so rare and true, Angie had to take a short breath. "Thanks, Angie. I love working here."

Angie stayed at the chef table long after service had ended. Felicia came in and sat next to her, putting her feet up on a chair. She groaned as she wiggled her bare toes. "Maybe I need to rethink wearing heels for service."

"The dining room already empty?" Angie glanced up from the laptop where she'd been searching for any information on the internet about Susan Ansley.

"Almost empty. Jeorge is still serving a few stragglers at the bar, but I told them they need to drink up and head out before our eleven p.m. closing time. They're probably going over to the Red Eye. I'm not sure they want to stop drinking yet." Felicia shook her head. "Now, I can party as hard as most, but on a Wednesday night?"

"They are friends of Jon Ansley from his law office." Estebe put a bowl of potato and leek soup in front of both Angie and Felicia. Then he went back to the stove to get one for himself. "They came in when the restaurant had just opened and sat at the bar until their table was ready. I recognized that Jon from the stories from the news. His buddy said it was a kind of going-away party, but that he'd bounce back."

"When did you talk to them?" Felicia held her spoon poised over the bowl, staring at Estebe.

"I told you. Before service started. Jeorge already had the bar open, so I let them inside to wait for their reservation." Estebe focused on his soup. "I didn't see the harm."

"I just hate for people to drink their dinner." Angie shook her head. "Not our problem, as long as they're not too drunk."

"Actually, now that I think about it—" Felicia ate the bite from her spoon, then used it as a pointer to emphasize what she was about to say. "Jeorge said they've been nursing the same mixed drink for the last hour since they came over from their dinner table. I guess they aren't out partying, more like just talking."

Angie stared at the door to the dining room like she could see through the wood. "I wonder if they were talking about the soybean plant."

"It makes sense. Even though Ansley's off the project, he'd want his firm to do well with it." Estebe nodded. "Although I think it's a little callous to be making plans for destroying Angie's farmhouse in her own restaurant."

"Yeah, but it's close to Jon's house." Angie stood and strode to the door.

"Where are you going?" Felicia called after her.

She didn't turn around but paused at the door. "To see what they know about the company who wants to buy my property and if they'd even considered a new site. If I could get it in their heads that plan B is less of a hassle, maybe they'll just go away."

But when she reached the bar area, it was deserted, except for Jeorge, who was filling out his post-shift inventory sheet. He started as she sat down at one of the bar stools. "Ms. Turner, I didn't expect to see you tonight."

"Oh? Why not?" She moved some of the happy hour menus away from the cash register and more to the end of the bar.

"I just mean, you usually go home after a long shift like this. Felicia is usually the one who takes my report and my register drawer." He glanced at the bottles on the wall. "Did you want a drink? I can make you something as a nightcap."

"I have to drive home, so I'm sticking with coffee to fill my travel mug." She leaned closer. "Those last few customers, did you hear what they were talking about?"

Jeorge glanced at the doorway, then leaned on his forearms. "The one guy, he'd gotten laid off or fired or something. The others seemed to be pumping him for information about the client he'd been working with. I guess his replacement hadn't been picked yet, and they all wanted to take over for him. I thought it was a little cold. You invite your buddy out to drinks to support him, but then want to take over his job?"

"Did they get anything from him?" Angie started to stand, thinking this was a dead end.

Jeorge shrugged. "It didn't make any sense. Not to me or to the other guys, but the unemployed guy, he said something like no one would be able to please this client and that they might as well go sniffing around someone else because he wasn't telling them anything."

"That's all?"

"Mostly, but I thought he was going to punch someone when they said something about his wife and how he really should be figuring out why that guy is still in town." He glanced around the shiny bar. "Okay if I head out? I told my girl we'd go grab a bite before heading home."

"Leave your report on the bar. Felicia's grabbing some food. See you tomorrow." Angie waved as she moved toward the kitchen.

When she stepped inside, both Felicia and Estebe were watching her.

"So, what did you find out?" Felicia asked at the same time as Estebe.

"Come sit down and eat. You need the energy." He turned toward Felicia. "You need to let her eat."

"I'm fine, guys. But I am hungry." Angie sat down. "And they were already gone by the time I got out there. Bad timing, I guess."

Estebe stood and took her bowl back to the stove. When he returned, he said, "Or good timing if one of them really did kill his wife."

Chapter 6

Thursday morning there was a thin layer of snow on the ground when Angie went out to feed Precious and Mabel. The hen clucked a little at her, but Precious was almost dancing in her stall. The barn had a door that swung back and forth so she could go outside when she wanted, but it was set up in a kind of foyer area so it didn't let wind or snow inside. Ian had designed it for the goat and built it last summer.

"Are you excited to get out and play in the snow this morning?" Angie filled her food trough and then rubbed the goat's neck.

When a loud bleat came from Precious, Angie laughed, but Mabel moved back to her roosting area in between two straw bales. She probably wouldn't go outside until spring unless the cold disappeared one day.

Angie pulled her coat closer. "I think I agree, Mabel. I'm ready for spring, too."

Back inside the house, Angie made a pot of coffee instead of just a cup at a time. She took what was left of the breakfast casserole and put it in the oven to warm, then she pulled out her mom's journal. She didn't have to be at the restaurant until three. Her "investigation" for Barb was going nowhere. And she couldn't call Maggie and tell her that Bleak was fine until after nine, when Bleak would be at school.

She had time to find out what kind of teenager her mom had been.

By the time she set the journal down, the pot of coffee was gone and so was the breakfast casserole. She glanced up at a picture of Nona and her mother that Angie had hung on the wall when she moved in. "Oh, Nona, how did you live through my rebellious teenager stage?"

The smile on her grandmother's face seemed to say, *It wasn't hard because I loved you both.* At least, that's what Angie heard in her head.

Her mom had been quite the party girl. At least in high school. Angie had thought her parents hadn't met until college, but she'd never guessed how wild her mom had been. Maybe it was the vibe from the yearbooks she had from her mom's high school years, but Angie had always thought of her mom as practical and well prepared. For anything.

Thinking of teenagers, she realized it was almost ten. Maggie needed to know that Bleak was alright and just dealing with the ramifications of the upcoming trial. She picked up the phone and dialed Maggie's number. Instead of getting Maggie, though, Allen Brown picked up the call.

"Should I be concerned that you're getting my wife into one of your schemes to investigate this most recent murder in River Vista?"

"Actually, she should be concerned that you're screening her calls. What's going on with the investigation, anyway? Did you find out who it was?"

He sighed. "Yes. The media already has this, so I guess it's not a problem telling you. She was the wife of a local decorator. They ran a shop together in Boise. He's devastated, from what I could tell. And, strangely enough, he thought his wife was visiting her mother."

Angie took in a breath. "You're thinking the cases are connected?"

"It's too soon to tell, but it is interesting. Keep my wife out of this, okay?"

Maggie's laughter bubbled in the background on the other end of the line, then she must have taken the cell from her husband. "Sorry about that. I was just getting the newspaper off the porch. My husband thinks you're a bad influence on me, which makes me like you even more. What's going on?"

Angie told her the basics of Bleak's visit yesterday without, she hoped, breaking any confidence. "I'd rather you not mention to Bleak that I called. I just didn't want you to keep worrying. I believe she'll figure out what she's going to do on her own."

"No child that age should be put in that predicament. I don't understand what her aunt was thinking." The line went quiet for a minute. "Anyway, I'm glad you called. You and Ian should come over Sunday for dinner."

"I'm in an investigation, dear. I may not be here for dinner," Allen said in the background.

"Well, I wasn't inviting you, now, was I?" She chuckled. "I guess we should play it by ear."

After hanging up with Maggie, she texted Ian the possible Sunday commitment. Then she glanced at the clock again. She had five hours to kill before she left for work. And a lot on her mind. She pulled out a notebook and started writing down everything she knew about the missing Susan Ansley. That didn't take long. She sighed as she reviewed her notes.

She knew her real mother. That she'd been raised by an aunt. And that her husband was a complete jerk. Okay, so that was a personal observation, but it didn't mean it wasn't true. She loved her dog. That was something Jon had told her earlier.

She texted Felicia. They'd had to put off the chat with Susan's friend until today. Maybe Felicia would be open to grabbing some lunch afterward. Felicia hung with this crowd, at least for the yoga classes. Maybe she had some insight she didn't realize was important.

When she read the response, Angie glanced at the clock again. She *didn't* have five hours to kill. She was expected in River Vista in less than an hour. Angie glanced at the paper calendar she kept on the kitchen desk. She hadn't written down the meeting time when Felicia had called her yesterday. She really needed to get better at making a point of reviewing her calendar and adding things when she scheduled them.

She parked behind the restaurant with five minutes to spare. Felicia must have been watching for her because she came out of the back door and hurried to the car. The ski parka she wore should have been warm enough for a trip to Alaska mid-winter, but Felicia still looked chilled.

Rubbing her hands together through the leather gloves, Felicia reached to turn up the heat as soon as she was inside the car. "Don't tell me you forgot about this."

"I did. I can't believe I didn't write it down or something."

Felicia laughed as she put on her seat belt. "My fault. I should have called you this morning. I know how you get when you think you have kitchen time. Head down the highway to Columbia and turn right. The subdivision that Holly and Susan lived in is a couple miles east on the right."

"I wasn't cooking this morning. I found my mom's high school journal and started reading. Man, she gave my grandmother a hard time. I guess I always thought she was perfect, or at least a little calmer than she seemed from her writing. She was part of the cheerleading squad. I would have never tried out."

Felicia looked at her funny.

"What?"

"You have to realize that you're not the person you would have been if your parents had lived. You are you because your grandmother raised you. If your mom had been alive during your high school years, you might have taken another path." Felicia pointed to the crossroad ahead. "That's Columbia. Take a right, and the subdivision's called Mountain View Estates."

"I thought we were meeting at the coffee shop. The name of the subdivision's not very original," Angie said, but she was thinking about

Felicia's words. The path she'd taken had been because of her Nona's love for food, which she'd passed on to Angie during her school years. Who would she have been if she'd been raised by her parents instead?

"You're thinking too hard. I can hear the wheels turning from here." Felicia looked over at her as they made the turn. "Are you okay?"

"I'm just thinking about mothers and daughters. It's been a lot of what's going on lately. I find my mom's journal. Barb's worried about her Sunny. Maggie's worried about Bleak. Of course, she's not her real mom, but she's stepped into the role." Angie slowed down and entered one of many new roundabouts the county highway division had installed on the main country roads, especially those that were closer to city limits.

"Maggie's not just acting as Bleak's mom; she's being the role. Being a mom doesn't always mean you gave birth. You take care of your kitchen staff like a parent would." Felicia giggled. "And you have my boyfriend as your staff's father figure."

"Gross, but accurate. I guess you're the baby mama? Or maybe I am, and you're the new trophy wife." Angie slowed down for a tractor that was taking up more than one lane and seemed to be turning into a field just a few feet in front of them. Of course, a few feet took much longer to travel with the tractor and its attached plow than even the slowest car ever would.

"Don't get tied up in the titles. Just know that people care for others. That's when the relationships really become important." Felicia pressed her lips together. "I've been thinking about Holly. If we can, maybe we shouldn't talk about Barb and her involvement."

Angie did a quick double take. "You don't think that Holly would understand?"

"I don't think that Holly wouldn't use the information against Susan at some point." Felicia's words were blunt.

Angie's jaw dropped as she turned the car onto the entry road for the subdivision. A man sat in a brick gatehouse in the middle of the road, but after he took a peek into the car, he waved them on inside. "I can't believe you said that. Aren't they friends?"

"Friendship has a totally different meaning for these people. I'm so glad I have you and Estebe to keep me grounded. If I thought these people were normal, it would scare me." Felicia glanced at the numbers on the mailboxes.

"They scare me now, and you're just talking about them." Angie pointed to the next house. "Is that where we're going?"

"Okay, eagle eye, you're spot-on." Felicia flipped down her mirror and glanced at her hair. She dug in her purse and found a tube of lipstick. "Let's go see the show."

"Do you think she'll be honest with us?"

"Honest, yes. But if she thinks she knows something that might be worth trading, I don't think she'll tell us. We'll have to play her game." She fluffed her hair, then studied Angie. "I'm glad that I've already explained what a creative soul you are. They won't be expecting much."

"What do you mean about that?" Angie glanced down at the clean pair of jeans and BSU sweatshirt hoodie that she'd put on that morning. She watched Felicia get out of the car and start walking toward the house, ignoring Angie's question. "Felicia? Come back and explain!"

Felicia stopped about halfway to the door and waved at Angie to catch up. Angie turned off the engine and grabbed her tote. "Whatever," she mumbled.

"We'll talk later," Felicia said when Angie caught up. "Let's go play."

"I'm not sure I want to." Angie glanced at the oversized house. "How many kids do these people have?"

"None, why?" Felicia rang the doorbell.

"I can't believe only two people live here."

Felicia laughed. "This is a small house in a neighborhood of big homes.

The door opened, and a tiny older woman with short gray hair dressed in a black suit opened the door. "May I help you?"

"Felicia Williams and Angie Turner to see Holly Otter? She's expecting us." Felicia smiled at the woman who must have been the Otters' version of a butler or a personal assistant.

"Oh my. I'm Hester Smith. I'm so honored to meet you." The woman smiled broadly and held the door open wider. "Of course, Mrs. Otter is excited to meet you, as well. Please come inside. I have to say, I'm a little bit of a fan girl for both of you due to the County Seat. I'd eat there every night if I could."

"We appreciate your business. Next time you're in, let your server know, and I'll step out of the kitchen." Angie followed Felicia inside the large marble foyer. A wide staircase ran the length of the back of the room and ended on a balcony that must have led to the bedrooms. "What a lovely home."

"Mrs. Otter just finished redecorating this year. The furniture is all special-ordered from New York, and the floors were all replaced or refurbished. It really is quite lovely." The woman spun toward the left and the open doorway. "She'll meet you in the parlor. May I get you some refreshments? Some coffee or sparkling water?"

"I'm fine." Angie glanced at Felicia, who shook her head. "This room is beautiful, as well."

"I'm so glad you like it," a woman's voice came from another doorway. "I wasn't quite sure about the color, but it works with the fireplace quite nicely."

Angie watched as a tall blonde strode into the room. Her hair shimmered with highlights, and she wore an all-white pants-and-blouse combo. Something Angie would never even try to pull off. If Dom didn't jump on her, or Precious, she'd drip something on the white canvas. But it looked amazing on this woman. "Holly Otter? I'm Angie Turner, and this is my partner..."

"You don't have to introduce our Felicia. She's the joy of the yoga group. And I hear you are stepping in to help with the Winter Cotillion. Although I hope everything is done. Susan left quite a hole in the planning committee when she left." Holly stepped closer and gave Felicia air-kisses. She reached out a hand to Angie, but her shake was weak and her hand, cold.

Angie tried not to let her first impression show on her face. "So sorry to bother you at this time, Holly, but I'm doing a bit of legwork for our local sheriff. He's so busy with the new murder, he hasn't had time to tie up any loose ends around Susan's disappearance. Do you mind if I ask you a few questions?"

"Of course not. Anything I can do to help find Susan, I'm willing to pitch in. Although I didn't think real police units liked amateurs messing with their investigations."

The look Felicia shot Angie was one of pure *gotcha*. But this wasn't her first dialogue war. She smiled at her friend. "Oh, you'd be surprised at what all they contract out now. I swear, property taxes are being carved out from under our town by the silliest things. It makes any city office hard to run on such a lean budget. And I just like to be helpful. Do you mind if we sit?"

Holly motioned them to the couch while she perched on a full-white accent chair. "This is so exciting. What can I tell you?"

"When was the last time you saw Susan?" Angie got out a small notebook and prepared to take at least a few notes. Holly Otter might be focused on decorating, but Angie didn't think any detail got past her. Not a one.

"Well, aren't you the direct one." Holly smiled at Felicia like they shared a secret. "I know why I know you."

"The County Seat, I'm the head chef."

Holly shook her head. "No, I mean, yes, I know that. But you're the one with the land that's going to be part of the soybean plant project. That's going to be such a boon to the local economy. When you get your payout, you should definitely call me. I'll have Vance's administrative assistant set up a meeting for you. You'll love what he can do for your money."

"I'm not sure I'll need a financial advisor, but I'll keep Vance in mind. Now, when was the last time you saw Susan?" Angie let her face go blank, hoping that Holly wouldn't see the anger that the assumption she'd sell her farm to the soybean people had brought up.

"She came to the November planning meeting. She had all the plans done, and the committee just had to approve them. Of course, we made small tweaks, but mostly, she got the party she wanted. It was a bit juvenile, but that was Susan. She loved nostalgia." Holly took the glass of sparkling water the other woman had brought in and took a sip, setting the glass down on the coffee table. The woman picked it up and put a coaster under it. Holly's eyes narrowed for a moment, then the emotion was gone. "You can leave us, Hester. I'm sure you have some work to attend to."

After Hester had left the room, Holly sighed. "She tries so hard, but she just doesn't have the demeanor to be a true assistant. But my husband adores her, and I don't have to worry about anything happening, if you get my drift."

Felicia nodded, keeping her face serious.

Angie glanced at the two women, who seemed to be talking in code. She wondered how anyone could work for someone like this. Someone this... She couldn't even come up with an appropriate word. All the words running through her head seemed mean and spiteful. And besides, Angie didn't know Holly at all. And she wasn't going to make a snap judgment, no matter how much she wanted to. "Now, about Susan?"

"Oh yes. Anyway, she was at the meeting. Then we all went to lunch. Afterwards, we went to the winery for drinks. I came home about five as we had dinner reservations. I suspect she went home, as well." She leaned toward Felicia. "Are you still dating that amazing Basque chef? You probably already know he's got a ton of money stashed away in both cash and real estate. Vance says his portfolio is being totally mismanaged. You really should come over some night with your man and we'll get him set up with a new advisor."

"I think Estebe manages his own money. Of course, I don't really know because we never talk about the financial side of life. The man is so romantic, I can't get him to stop doing sweet things for me to have even one serious talk." Felicia turned her head away from Holly and winked at Angie.

Yeah, this was going to be an interesting discussion. Angie sat back to watch the games between the two women continue.

Chapter 7

"So that was a complete waste of time," Angie grumbled as she drove back to River Vista to drop off Felicia.

Felicia shook her head. "I'm not sure that's true."

"What did you hear besides Holly wants Estebe to invest with her husband?" Now Angie was curious.

"Well, for one thing, if she knew that much about Estebe, she knew what was going on with Jon and his financial life anyway. And yet she *said* she didn't know anything about Susan and Jon's life," Felicia explained.

"Because she would have looked at the friendship as a way to get her husband a new client. Man, that's cold." Angie shook her head and watched the road. "Are all your yoga friends like that?"

"Not all of them, but it's a common problem. They call it networking. I call it being sleazy." Felicia tapped her fingers on the door frame. "Either Jon wasn't doing so well as a lawyer, or he was doing well but had a bigger financial firm involved in his money. She would have played it softer with Susan if that was the case. You never know when an opportunity would come up that would benefit her husband."

"What if he was still up and coming in the law firm? He made good money, but not great. Not like Holly and her husband," Angie added to the picture.

Felicia nodded. "That would be another reason for Holly to be friendly with Susan. Just in case. But it still doesn't give us anything to help find Susan."

"I know. I wanted her to say, 'Oh, Susan's just avoiding Jon, here's the Mexican resort she's staying at under the name Alicia Sims.'" Angie laughed as she slowed the car down to meet the city limit's new speed limits sign. "One mystery solved."

"You're too much of an optimist at times." Felicia flipped through her phone. "Look, I've got a few more contacts in my phone of the ladies who lunch with us. I can see if I can get any new information. It's only natural since I'm stepping into her place for the cotillion. I've got a meeting tomorrow. You're coming, right?"

"I've already told Ian he's my date next Saturday. How fancy do we need to dress?" She glanced at the restaurant. "With both you and me out, there's no way I can lct Estebe off to escort you."

"No problem. I've got a guy who will take me with no strings attached. He's off the dating market right now, but he doesn't want the others to know. They're big on matchmaking." She put her phone in her purse. "And it's black tie. So, formal. Do you need a dress?"

"I've got that black one I wore to that New Year's Eve party in San Francisco. I'm fine." She took out her phone and texted Ian. "Hopefully Ian has a tux, or we're going to have to rent one and charge the police station for the costs. Undercover work costs money."

"Spies are us." Felicia got out of the car and leaned back inside. "I'll call you if I get anything. You heading home for a while?"

"I was going to see if you wanted to go into town and grab some lunch, but I forgot and now we're here. I guess I'll warm up some soup at home before I come in for the dinner service. Dom will appreciate seeing me for a bit." She waved at her friend and backed out of the parking lot. As she drove by the Red Eye, she felt a pang of sadness. She wasn't doing anything to help find Barb's Sunny. Of course, it wasn't her fault that every lead she followed seemed to be a dead end. Holly knew more than what she was saying. That had been crystal clear when she'd sent Hester out of the room. She'd let Felicia do some digging and let her mind play with what she knew so far.

Her phone rang just before she arrived home. She didn't recognize the number, but she always picked up on days when the restaurant was open. She didn't want to miss a call from a sick employee and not get them replaced. "This is Angie."

"Miss Turner, I need a favor." A familiar male voice came out of the car's speaker. One Angie couldn't quite place.

"I'm sorry, who is this?" She turned the car south onto the highway that would take her home.

"My apologies, it's been a strange week. I assumed, but yes, I guess I overstepped. This is Jon Ansley. I was wondering if you could meet me tonight after you finish your service. There's something in my wife's belongings I'd like to show you."

Angie hesitated. She wanted to talk to him, but… "I'm sorry, Mr. Ansley, I'm working until late tonight, and I don't make a habit of going to a stranger's home in the middle of the night."

"Then maybe you'd feel more comfortable coming tomorrow? And you can bring a friend or two. I really think I need someone else to see this, because it's not making any sense to me." He hesitated. "Please?"

Angie shook her head. It might be a trap. Going to his house would be stupid. But there was something she heard in his voice. A pleading for help. "I'll come by tomorrow. What time?"

"Doesn't matter to me. I don't have a job to go to, remember?" He laughed; the sound hard. "And as I'm finding out, you can have anything delivered. Food, alcohol, dog treats. I might not ever leave the house again."

When he hung up, Angie called Ian. She would have asked Felicia to come along, just to avoid the lecture Angie was going to get, but Felicia had a cotillion meeting tomorrow. Maybe, between the two visits, someone might tell them where they could find Susan.

"Let me get this straight. You want to go talk to the guy who's trying to buy your house out from underneath you and is suspected in killing his wife, just because he asked 'pretty please'?" Ian didn't sound convinced.

"When you put it like that, it does sound a little crazy, right?" Angie tried to make a joke out of the request. "Seriously, Ian, I'm going. But I'd feel a lot better and safer if you'd come with me. I'd take Dom, but Timber will be there and I don't want there to be a fight."

"And you're not expecting one between your boyfriend, who loves you, and this piece of scum, who's messing with your life?"

Angie hadn't thought of it that way. Ian was always the turn-the-other-cheek guy. She softened her tone, wondering if it was too much of an ask. "Okay, I get your point. If you don't think you can be civil, then yeah, you shouldn't come. Maybe I can get Estebe to come with me. At least I'd feel safe with the big guy there."

"Look, I didn't say I wasn't going to go with you. I just want you to understand what you're doing. I know my uncle doesn't think Jon killed his wife, but he likes everyone."

Angie laughed. "Your uncle doesn't like anyone, and he typically makes snap judgments on people until they prove him wrong. So, if he says Jon's not a killer, I feel a lot safer."

"Yeah, you're right. I just want you to be safe." He sighed. "I thought this dance was this weekend?"

"You're just hoping it conflicts. It's next Saturday. And by the way, the dance is formal. Do you have a tux?" Angie glanced at her watch. Almost noon, so she'd have time to eat and play with Dom for a while before she had to drive back into River Vista.

"Yes. You're making a lot of dates for us lately. I think I need to give you access to my online calendar. That way you can fill in wherever you want." He chuckled. "Not that I mind, but what's going on between you and Aunt Maggie? You two seem chummy lately."

"She wanted to talk about Bleak." Angie didn't mention the fact that his aunt hadn't wanted her to tell anyone about the talk. "She's worried, but I think Bleak's just going through some normal teenage things. She's got a lot on her plate. She works, goes to school full-time, has this trial with her aunt coming up. It's a lot for a sixteen-year-old. I couldn't have worked as many hours when I was in school. I had other activities that took up too much time."

"Like hanging out with the bad boys?"

"Close enough. I put my grandmother through hell." She paused, thinking. "Did you know I found my mom's diary from when she was in school? All I can say is my Nona was a saint. She must have earned wings raising my mom and then me, for her entry to heaven."

"I don't believe it works that way, but I'll give you the benefit of your own theology," he said. "We're starting a study session on angels next Sunday if you want to attend my Bible study class."

"I'm not sure I want to know what scripture says about the cute little cherubs that Nona collected. I hear some of the angel corps was a little more fire than love and wish granting."

"You're thinking of a fairy godmother. And yes, your image of angels would be blown away." A bell sounded on his side of the line. "Someone's here. I'll pick you up tomorrow at ten. You're buying me lunch for this favor."

"Sounds great." She paused. "Thanks, Ian."

"No problem. See you tomorrow."

When she got home, Dom was sleeping on his bed. He hadn't even gotten up when the car pulled into the driveway.

She pulled some soup out of the freezer and put it in the microwave to thaw. Then she grabbed Dom's leash. He had two. One they used around the farm. The other one was his walking lead. He glanced up at the walking lead and sniffed, but let her put on the around-the-house lead.

"I have to go to work this afternoon." She rubbed his ears while she explained. "At least you get to go out to visit Precious and Mabel with me."

A snort made her laugh. Dom didn't really like the goat. She moved too fast for him, and it made him jumpy just to watch her. Besides, having Precious around took some of Angie's time. And Dom didn't like sharing.

They refilled the water dishes, and Angie fed the barn crew and made sure their water wasn't frozen over. Then they ambled back to the front porch. The mailman paused at her mailbox out by the road, and Angie waved at him. Then she put Dom back in the house before she went walking out to the street. She didn't want Dom thinking he could go this way. Not at all. When they visited Mrs. Potter across the street, she made sure to put his walking leash on, and they took a walk after the visit to solidify the idea. Dom wasn't allowed to go off the property without Angie by his side. Or at least she hoped it was set in his brain that way.

She was surprised to see he'd pulled his van into her driveway and was walking toward her with her mail. "Good afternoon."

"I didn't think I'd see you today since the restaurant is open, so I was starting to make a call slip." He handed her a clipboard and a pen. "Looks like the county is taking evidence on rezoning for the new soybean plant. I'm sure going to miss you all out here. I love this part of my route."

"I haven't agreed to sell yet." She signed the form and handed the clipboard back. "I just can't see letting Nona's place go. Even for a lot of money."

"Money comes and goes, but family? That's forever." He glanced up at the house. "Your grandmother and Mrs. Potter, they were here when I first started this route almost twenty years ago. I was hoping you all would still be here for my retirement. I was going to wear one of those top hats and hand out cupcakes or something on my last day."

Angie smiled as she took the mail. "You may still get your wish, Frank. I've got to go call my lawyer and see what we're doing about this. I think they're charging me every time they see my phone number come up on their phone display."

"Lawyers. They have to make their money somewhere, I guess." Frank climbed back into his van. "See you next week. The wife and I are celebrating our anniversary at your place. Looking forward to seeing what all the hype is about. But if you cook half as good as your grandmother, I know I'll enjoy it."

Angie watched him go, standing in the cold, taking in Nona's, no, her home. You didn't give up on home, no matter what was going on. She decided to do some research on the old meat packing plant. Maybe if she found something that made it more attractive to the soybean plant owners, she could sway their minds. Otherwise, she was going to be rezoned out of her house.

She worked on her computer, taking notes about the land around her property and looking for any historical significance of the area. Was there something here that would keep developers from being able to dig? There were Indian petroglyphs in Celebration Park in the Snake River Canyon, but that was miles away.

She made another note. What kind of water drain off did these kinds of plants need? Was there any problem with the plant polluting the area? And just because she was desperate, she wrote down, were the coyotes that had been seen in the area protected? She had worried about Precious's safety when she was little because a coyote band had killed the goat's mother down in the river canyon, but Ian had told her that they didn't come this far into civilization.

She sighed. Everything she'd written down was a long shot. But at this point, that might be all she had. She closed the laptop and put that and her notebook away in the kitchen desk. Then she went to get ready for work.

Since she was already in a bad mood, when she got to the restaurant, she shut herself in her office and worked on the accounting. Doing math just wasn't her thing. She was glad she trusted their accountant, because if she had to do all of this, having the County Seat wouldn't be worth the hassle. *Trust but verify* was her motto, so she spent a few hours a week going over the books and making sure everything seemed correct. Then Felicia did the same. It was their name on the door, and if they made a mistake and didn't pay the right amount of taxes, saying the bookkeeper did it didn't hold much weight with the tax man.

But she kept the pain point down to a minimum and always rewarded her financial stewardship with some recipe-building time the next day. Except tomorrow she was going to go talk to the enemy. Maybe he'd be able to give her some insight she could use against the new lawyer assigned to the land development project. A girl could only hope.

She closed her computer and moved to grab her chef coat. The door to her office flew open, and Bleak stormed in.

"You said you wouldn't tell Maggie."

Angie studied her. The girl was red-faced, like she'd run there from the Brown home. "Calm down. I didn't tell her what was going on, just that you were worried about the trial and your aunt."

Bleak's anger faded for a second. She took in a deep breath. "Then why is she asking me if I want to see a shrink? I'm not crazy."

"No, you're not crazy, but you are under a lot of stress. Hell, just being a teenager is hard enough. But you're getting straight As, taking college-level AP classes, and working almost a full schedule. Then you add in the trial. Talking to a counselor about what's going on might not be a bad idea." Angie could see the girl calming down as she spoke.

"So, she doesn't think I'm crazy?"

"Maggie? Why would she? A lot of people go to counseling. Sometimes they use their support groups, like their church, or people who are going through the same type of things. Some people go to counselors to talk about their situation and their futures. Maggie probably just wants you to have someone you can talk to who won't judge anything you say." Angie took a breath and decided to share. "My Nona sent me to counseling after my folks died. I was having some issues fitting in at school. I was mad that everything was still the same, even though my world had blown up when my folks died. It didn't seem fair."

"I didn't know you lost your parents." Bleak picked up a cookbook that Angie had bought over Christmas and thumbed through it.

"Just before my freshman year. Then I moved here to live with my grandmother. All my friends. My parents. My life. It was all gone." Angie leaned against the wall. "You must feel the same way, moving up here from Utah."

"It's nice here. I mean, I loved my family, but I was responsible for a lot. I feel bad that now Karen is probably having to do everything. She's my younger sister." Bleak closed the book. "Maggie said something that made me think. She said that you have to put your own oxygen mask on in an airplane incident before you help others. I think it means I have to take care of myself first, then I can help my sister."

"I think that's exactly what she meant." Angie nodded to the book. "Do you want to borrow that and try out some of the recipes? I brought it in for staff to look it over."

"Can I?" Bleak touched the book's cover in awe. "I mean, I'm not really kitchen staff."

"You're part of the family. And for some reason, I think there might be a chef hiding inside you. And Maggie would love working with you on a project. I think she's a little lonely since Allen works a lot."

Bleak nodded. "She and I have been baking cookies all month. This would be something more substantial. I'm beginning to like soups."

Bleak had announced to the family table when she'd just joined the team that soups weren't her favorite food. Maybe now that she saw how lovely a soup could be when done right, she'd changed her mind. "No food deserves to be banished from our table forever. You just haven't found a way that met your taste buds."

Bleak stared at her. "Even liver?"

Angie laughed. Bleak would have to pick the one thing Angie didn't like at all. "I have to admit, I haven't found a way to like liver. Yet."

"Good, because I was beginning to think you were crazy or one of those people who always says they like everything, but really, they don't. That's being false, right?" Bleak picked up the book and put it in her backpack.

"Yes, it is." Angie watched as the girl made her way to the employee area to hang up her backpack and get ready for the day. She was really glad Bleak had come to be part of their River Vista family. And she sent up a quick prayer that she wouldn't leave too soon. Not until she had on her own oxygen mask.

Chapter 8

Ian was in the kitchen, talking to Dom and cooking bacon, when Angie woke up that Friday morning. She could hear the tone but not the words and Dom's responses every once in a while. Dom liked it when Ian talked to him like he was a person or something. Angie wondered exactly how much of the conversation her dog really understood. If she'd been a character in a novel, her dog might just be able to talk back. But as it was, she was just a regular human. Yet she, too, had long conversations with the Saint Bernard.

She showered and dressed, then headed downstairs to join the conversation. Today they were going to go talk to Jon and hopefully find a clue to where Susan was. Angie just hoped she was still alive by the time they found her.

When she got downstairs, she realized Ian and Dom weren't alone. Sheriff Allen Brown sat at her table drinking coffee and eating eggs and bacon. Ian stood at the stove and didn't see her come into the room, but Allen did. And he laughed.

"Ian, your girlfriend's awake." He set his fork down and nodded to Angie. "Good morning. I was beginning to think I was going to have to set off my sirens to get you out of bed."

"It was a long night at the restaurant." Angie took the cup of coffee Ian handed her and gave him a quick kiss before she sat down. "Since the law is sitting at my kitchen table, I suspect something bad happened?"

"No one died, if that's what you're thinking." Allen wiped his mouth and handed the empty plate to Ian. "Thanks for the breakfast, son."

Angie watched as he pulled out his notebook.

"Do you want something to eat? I have bacon going, and I can make you eggs." Ian smiled at her as he walked past with the plate in hand. "And besides heating up food you send home with me, that's the extent of my cooking skills."

"I'm fine with coffee right now." Angie nodded toward Allen, who was studying his notes. "I'll tell you if I'm hungry in a couple of minutes."

"Like I said, no one is dead." He picked up his pen. "Your cook, Nancy Gowan, her house was broken into last night while she was at work. She says her ex-husband must have done it."

"So, why are you talking to me and not him?" Angie eyed him to watch for a reaction but got nothing. "You're sure Nancy's okay?"

"She's fine. Nothing she can see was taken. She thinks Mr. Gowan did it to mess with her. He likes playing the 'I'm watching you' game. At least according to Mrs. Gowan." He looked up from his notebook. "What do you know about her ex?"

Angie leaned back into the chair and blew out a breath that made her bangs flip on her forehead. "I know he left her in a lot of debt. And now, knowing that he actually has money, I think less of him."

"How do you know he has money?" Allen studied her.

Angie sipped her coffee before answering. "He came into the restaurant a few days ago. He asked if Nancy could come out of the kitchen to talk to him. Since that's an odd request, I assumed it was an old friend. I watched with Felicia, well, because Nancy hasn't dated anyone since the divorce and she's a really great person. She deserves a great guy."

"And her ex wasn't a great guy?"

Angie shook her head. "He basically threatened her. She told him to leave her and the kids alone. But I could see it in his eyes. He wasn't hurt by her words. He was enjoying the fight. Like he knew he was going to win, no matter what."

"That's the impression I got, too, when I pulled him out of his hotel bed at two this morning. He seemed to be challenging me to find something that proved it was him." Allen sipped his coffee. "I know it's not Christian to judge, but I got a bad feeling about the guy. Your assistant is helping her change the locks this morning."

"Felicia's not my assistant. She's a co-owner." Angie was surprised that Felicia hadn't called her, but then again, she kept the phone downstairs, since she didn't sleep well anyway. She didn't need the phone's bells and whistles keeping her awake.

"Honey, he's talking about Estebe, not Felicia. Nancy called Estebe, who came over and slept at the house last night. I'm not sure how Felicia's going to take that, so you may want to wait for him to tell her."

"Felicia trusts him." Angie considered the steps they'd taken to keep Nancy safe. "Did you arrest him?"

"Charles Gowan has an alibi for the time in question. His new wife said they were together all night. Either she's a few marbles short, or he's got her kowtowed, as well." He stood and finished his coffee. "I didn't think you'd know much, but I was hoping. Sometimes these guys mess up and say stupid stuff, thinking they're going to get away with it. If you talk to him, let him hang himself, okay?"

"Sounds lovely, but I'm pretty sure he won't be talking to me anytime soon. I told him he was a jerk." Angie stood and refilled her coffee cup from the pot. "He's this huge developer, and Nancy's working three jobs just to keep the lights on and pay off his debts? What kind of a man does that?"

"He's a developer?" Allen paused at the doorway.

"That's what he said. He told Nancy he was in town to seal the deal on something." Angie looked at Allen and Ian, who were both looking at her. "What?"

"Weirder things have happened," Allen muttered. "I've got to go to work. Explain what we're thinking to her, will you, Ian?"

"Let me walk you out first." Ian followed Allen out to the police cruiser, and Angie watched through the kitchen window as they chatted for a few minutes. When Ian came back inside, she turned away from the window and leaned against the counter.

"What don't I get? And what were you talking to your uncle about?"

"Do you want some eggs? I do a mean scramble." He went to the fridge and got out the eggs and bacon.

"If I say yes, are you going to talk to me?" Angie watched as he got down a bowl and started cracking eggs.

Ian set the bowl aside. Then, wiping his hands on a towel, he walked over and took the cup out of her hands. Setting it down on the counter, he put his arms around her. "What Uncle Allen and I were thinking is maybe this Gowan dude is the developer behind the soybean plant. And he's wondering if this guy is somehow attached to the other murder too. The girl was from the same town in California where Nancy said Charles and Jane lived. It might be a coincidence, but we're just going to keep a close eye on you for a few days."

"Me? Why?" Angie started to move away, but Ian tightened his grip. Fear flowed through her as she studied his too-serious face. "Ian, you're scaring me."

"I'm glad. You need to take this seriously, Angie. If this woman is connected to the development somehow, like Susan was by her husband, maybe you're the only thing standing in this guy's way." He watched her face as the realization hit her. "Yeah."

"You think he might go after me to get the house." Angie lifted a hand to her chest, feeling her heartbeat speed up. "I think I need to sit down."

"It's probably not an issue, but if you don't mind, I'm going to be spending some time with you for the foreseeable future." He took her arm and walked her to the table, where she sank into a chair.

Dom, sensing something was wrong, came over and laid his massive head on her lap and stared up at her. His big brown eyes were questioning. She stroked his back, trying to think this through. "Tell me more about the break-in at Nancy's. Nothing was taken?"

"The neighbor saw the lights on and thought one of Nancy's kids had come home from their sitters early. Nancy's sister watches the kids while she works. I guess the oldest had been sneaking out and meeting up with her friends, so the neighbor went over to see what was going on. She's friends with Nancy." Ian set a glass of water in front of her, then went back to the stove to cook.

"Of course, she is. Nancy is one of the nicest people you'd ever meet. She's active in her women's group at church, volunteers at the kids' schools, and she cooks at the women's shelter once a week. The woman is a saint." Angie took a sip of her water, her mind reeling with the information. "So she went over and found the intruder? Can't she identify him?"

"He pushed his way past her when she called out at the front door. I guess she has a key." Ian put bread in the toaster. "The guy wore all black and a ski mask, so Christy, that's the neighbor's name, couldn't identify him."

"But Nancy thinks it's her ex." Angie stood and took the toast out of the toaster and put more bread in. Then she grabbed a plate and buttered the two slices that came out. She brought a second plate out and looked at him. "You are eating with me, right?"

"I am. I told Uncle Allen that I'd wait for you." Ian stirred the eggs. "Do you want bacon? I feel like I haven't timed this meal right. And yes, Nancy swore it was him. A 'gut feeling' was how she put it."

"I think she's right, but I can't tell you why." Angie took the bacon packet and put it back into the fridge. Then she paused. "Unless you wanted more?"

"Bacon? No, I'm good." He dished out eggs, half on each plate, as Angie grabbed the last two slices of toast and buttered them. "Have you thought about not going to visit Jon Ansley?"

"No. I'm going. No one's going to scare me into hiding away in my house. I'll let you follow me around because I like being with you. But I'm not changing anything else. It's not fair. And besides, I'm curious what he wants to show me. Aren't you?"

"Curiosity killed the cat, you know." He brought the dishes over to the table.

"Good thing I don't have a cat." She smiled over at Dom, who'd moved back to his bed, convinced that his owner was just fine.

"Let's get breakfast done, and then we need to take off to go talk to your friendly neighborhood killer lawyer." He glanced at her water. "Do you need some milk to drink?"

"I'm fine." Angie started eating her breakfast. "The only word out of those we don't know that accurately describes Jon is killer. He could just be a jerk and have a wife who gave up on the marriage and left him."

"If you ever get that mad at me, I hope you at least tell me you're leaving. I'd hate to be in that guy's shoes if he's on the up-and-up."

"You question everything."

"And everyone. Paranoid and proud of it."

After putting the dishes in the dishwasher, they told Dom goodbye and got into Ian's truck. Angie watched out the window as they drove away. "I may not be able to get back here before service. If I don't, can you come out and feed the zoo?"

"Of course. Then I'll stop by the restaurant and eat. Just stay in the kitchen until I get there, okay?"

Angie shook her head. "This guy isn't getting me to adjust my life, just for him. But"—she put a hand out to stop Ian's response—"I will let you hang around for the next few days. I think it's overkill, but I'm not stupid, either."

"And I'll drive you back home and sleep in the guest room." He winked at her. "At least that's our cover story."

"Are you sure you're not just campaigning for more time together?" She leaned back in the seat, trying to relax.

"Would you mind if I was?" Ian turned on the stereo, and the rest of the trip was filled with music and a little car karaoke.

When they got to the Ansley home, Ian parked on the street. They stared at the house. The snow from the last big storm still covered the yard, but the driveway and sidewalks were cleared. The blinds were closed, and the house looked dark.

"You ready for this?" Ian took the keys out of his truck and jangled them. "We could just go home, or maybe out to lunch."

"He might tell us something important." Angie reached out to squeeze Ian's hand. "Let's go talk to the guy. If he's crazy, we'll leave. If he gives us anything, you can call your uncle on the way back to River Vista."

"Sounds like a plan. But I didn't hear any lunch stops added in there." Ian grinned at her. "Promising me a meal will make sure I protect you as we go inside the fun house."

"Dude, you've already shown your hand. You've set yourself up as my protector this morning. You should have negotiated better." Angie opened the door to the truck and slid out until her feet touched the sidewalk.

"You know the fire and frying pan saying, right?" Ian got out on his side and walked around the truck. "Let's do this thing."

"Okay, Rambo." Angie laughed as Ian took her arm in his and they made their way up the driveway.

When Angie rang the bell, she heard a rustle inside. She rang again, and a dog started barking. "Hey, Timber, is your dad home?"

The barking was closer now, but Angie also heard some footsteps. The door opened, and a sleepy-looking Jon poked his head out, squinting at the sun. "Is it already that late? Damn, I was hoping to get a shower first to make it appear like I'm not some unemployed bum."

"You look fine." Angie glanced around him to see Timber standing in the hallway. "Can we come in, so Timber doesn't escape?"

"What? Oh yeah, sorry, please come inside." He opened the door wider and reached back for Timber's collar. "The maid didn't come this week, so the place is a mess. I think I was supposed to pay her or something last time. How was I supposed to know? Susan took care of all of these things."

They walked inside and stood in the foyer. Angie decided to take some control over the situation. "We can't stay long, Jon. What did you want to show us?"

"First, I wanted to tell you that she's not at the cabin. Timber and I went up a few days ago. It's empty. And second, you need to tell me if that dress is something she would have ordered for the cotillion. I don't know much about dresses, but it's all sparkly and crap. She had to have bought it for that stupid dance." He stared at her for a long time, then nodded to the stairs. "Go look in her closet. The gown was delivered yesterday. She ordered a freaking dress for this dance she was working on. She wouldn't have just left if she ordered a dress, would she?"

Angie and Ian moved up the stairs and looked down at Jon for directions. He pointed and they turned left. Ian pulled her closer. "I think the guy is over the edge. A long way over the edge."

"If there's a dress in the closet, he's right. Those things cost a lot of money, and no one is going to just pack up and leave a few months before an event like this. She wouldn't have even ordered a dress. She was planning on being at the cotillion." She swung open two double doors and stepped inside what could only be the master bedroom. "I wonder if any of her suitcases are gone."

"The point is, she's gone. And no one knows where she went off to." Ian pointed to the full set of matching luggage in the closet.

Angie pointed to the dress. "It's here too. If she was running away with a lover, wouldn't she at least have packed some clothes?"

Chapter 9

Angie and Ian were sitting in the office of Sheriff Allen Brown. He'd been out on a call when they'd arrived, but Ian talked the receptionist into letting them wait there until his uncle returned.

Angie glanced back at the open door and at the officer who had turned his chair sideways so he could watch them as they sat waiting. "He's not happy you talked him into letting us sit here."

"Blake's a tool at times, but he means well. And he's devoted to my uncle." Ian picked up a magazine from the coffee table in the large office. He pointed to the cover. "Look, according to *Law Enforcement Quarterly* cybercrime is up ten percent over last year."

"Soon you're going to have to be a computer geek with a master's degree to even apply for the police force." Angie raised her voice a little, hoping that Blake, the tool, might hear her. She was pretty sure the guy hadn't finished college, since he looked like he should be in high school.

"Be nice." Ian spoke in a low voice and didn't look at her. "And you wonder why you run into roadblocks at times. Sometimes I think you like twisting people by their chain."

"He started it," Angie murmured.

Ian chuckled and set the magazine down. "I don't doubt it."

Sheriff Allen Brown came through the door and slipped off his gun belt. He closed the door and hung the belt on a hook, taking the gun out. Sitting at his desk, he unlocked a drawer, slipped the gun inside, and then keyed in a code. Finally, he looked at both of them. "Before I yell at Blake for letting you in my office, tell me why you're here."

They went through the morning's visit to Jon Ansley. Angie finished up with a question. "Since her luggage is still there, doesn't that prove that she's missing, not just a runaway wife?"

He picked up a pen and tapped it on the desk. "Tell me, Angie, what would you do if your house was on fire?"

Fear gripped her. "Oh no. Is that where you were? Is Dom okay? Did the barn get damaged? Where's Dom?"

He shook his head. "No, there's nothing wrong. Sorry, I used a bad example. I guess you and Ian talked about our concerns for your safety?"

Angie nodded, rubbing her suddenly sweaty hands on her jeans. "So, Dom's okay? There wasn't a real fire?"

"Merely a what-if. Tell me what you would do if you were in the building and your home was on fire."

"I'd take Dom outside and put him in my car and I'd grab his bag and mine as we're going. And if there was time, I'd move the car near the barn and then go back in to get my Nona's recipe books, my jewelry box, and my knives. Then…"

"You'd take your knives?" Both Allen and Ian were staring at her.

"Yeah. My chef knives. I paid a lot for them, and I'd hate to have to replace them. You know how things start to just mold to your hand? That's the way these are now." She rolled her shoulders. "So why are we playing a sad game of what-if?"

"Let me change the question. What if you were an abused wife and saw a chance to escape, what would be so important that you'd risk being caught to take?" His brown eyes stared into her.

"My dog. I'd take my dog if I loved him as much as Susan is supposed to have loved Timber."

Allen leaned back in his chair, now tapping the pen on the arm of the chair. "You're right. I should have realized that." He opened a file and started writing.

Ian leaned toward the desk. "So, you agree with us. You think she's been kidnapped?"

"I think she was taken unwillingly from her home, yes. Now, was it her husband or someone else? That I don't know yet. But I suspect she was kidnapped." He set the pen down and rubbed at his face. "I really don't like having two open cases involving missing or murdered women on my desk."

"I don't blame you." Angie stood. "I guess I need to go and get the County Seat ready for service. Have you found out anything about the woman you found in the park?"

"She went missing about three months ago while walking home from a yoga class in California. Then she shows up here. That's all I've got so far." He shook his head, and Ian stood to go with Angie.

"Thanks for seeing us." Ian held out his hand, and the two men shook. "I guess we're coming over for dinner on Sunday?"

"Maybe, depends on where this case goes in the next two days. I'll have Maggie call you." Allen stood behind the desk. He nodded at Angie, then sat back down.

Angie looked at Ian. They had been dismissed. He didn't say anything until they got outside the station. "Look, he means well. He's just got a lot on his plate."

"Believe me, that's one of the best conversations I've had with your uncle. Don't worry about it." Angie tucked her arm into Ian's, and they crossed the road. "Sorry to have you run back out to the house."

"Animals need fed. It's a fact of life. You can't have animals if you're not going to adjust your lifestyle to take care of them." He glanced up at her face, then quickly added, "I didn't mean you. You have adjusted your life. You let me in."

"And you get stuck taking care of my zoo." They paused outside the front door of the restaurant. She tried to open the door and then let it go when she found it wasn't locked. "We might have to change the way we work here. Maybe we should be more careful."

"In your favor, you tried to give Precious back when we realized she was from the Moss Dairy farm. It just didn't happen before you fell madly in love with the silly girl." He brushed back a lock of hair from her eyes. "Besides, I'm one of the zoo. They like me."

"They like anyone who feeds them." Angie smiled up at him. "Are you coming back for dinner?"

"Yes, but probably pretty late. I've got some work I needed to finish today, and since we've been out playing, I haven't gotten it done." He squeezed her hand. "Stay safe, okay?"

"You too."

He laughed. "I don't have a crazed developer out there wanting to kill me for not selling the linchpin for his new development." He held the door open for her.

"And for me, that's just a rumor." She patted his chest. "That being said, I loved our time together today. We're going to have fun when we retire."

"I like the sound of that." He leaned in for a sweet, slow kiss. Taking a step back, he looked at her.

Angie felt a heat wave run down her body. So not fair. "I've got to go."

"Your carriage will be here when you're ready to return to the castle, my lady." He grinned.

"Great. Maybe you can upgrade the truck before we're seen inside it and rumors start to fly."

He motioned her inside. "Small town, big rumors. Get inside before you freeze."

Nancy was waiting for her outside her office. Angie gave her a quick hug. Holding her at arm's length gave her the ability to study her drawn face and sunken eyes. "Nancy, how are you?"

"I'm fine. It's been a long night, though." Nancy rubbed a hand over her face. "Anyway, I need a favor. Just for tonight. I couldn't find a sitter, and my mom's out of town."

"Do you need to take off? I can call in a temp." She unlocked the office door and motioned Nancy inside. "Sit down. You look terrible."

"Gee, thanks." But Nancy sat. "Actually, I'd rather work if possible. I don't want to get behind on my budget, but in order to do that, I have to bring the kids with me."

"Sure." Angie powered up her computer. "You can put them in the banquet room. Will they be okay alone, or should we have one of the servers watch them?"

"My oldest is thirteen. She's already babysitting for other families. She'll keep the younger two in check. I'll have to feed them, though."

"Take a break when you need to and make them something to eat. We have plenty of food here. Of course, they might not like some of our more upscale items." Angie smiled at an unbidden memory. "I don't think I ate mushrooms until I was in culinary school."

"Felicia told me the same thing when I asked her about the kids." Nancy sank back into the chair. "But I wanted to make sure it was okay with you. Kids don't belong in the workplace."

"Families do belong." Angie ignored the unread email that was calling to her and focused on Nancy. "You had a break-in yesterday. It's only normal for you to want to keep your kids close by. I think you'll be a better chef if you're not worried about what is happening at your house."

"They can burn the house to the ground, as long as they let the dogs out first," Nancy admitted. "But my kids, I need to know they are safe."

"Then they'll be in the banquet room. We'll set up the TV and DVD player we use for trainings if you want to bring in some movies. If not, Felicia has a large collection. I'm sure you'll find a few the kids will like."

"I love working here. For you." Nancy stood to leave. "I'll make it up to you somehow."

"Just get them settled, then go to work. This isn't a favor, it's an accommodation for a team member." Angie watched her leave the office and opened a new window on her computer. Then she spent the next hour trying to track down any information on Celcat Developing. She needed to know if there was a connection between Nancy's ex-husband and Taylor Farms.

By the time she had to go to the kitchen, she hadn't found one. Yet, she told herself. Not yet.

As service progressed, Angie focused on the food. Cooking eased her mind. Feeding people made her happy. And those two things, ease and happiness, had been in short supply lately. When Felicia came in to let her know that Ian had arrived, she let her shoulders relax.

"Is something wrong?" Nancy stepped close to her and asked, her voice low.

"No, I'm just a little on edge." Angie wiped the edge of a plate before giving it to a server.

"I know what that looks like. I had just stopped looking over my shoulder when I went outside, and now Charles is back in town." She picked up a towel and refolded it. "He's the one who was in my house. I don't care what anyone says, it was him."

"Are the kids doing okay?" Angie asked. "You know you can leave if you need to."

"I'm not staying inside and hiding. He's not controlling my life again." Nancy took a big breath. "I want you to know that I'm going to be here, doing my job."

"Nancy, I totally believe in you. And if you need to be here, you're more than welcome. But if you need to leave or take some time for yourself, I'll understand." Angie put a hand on Nancy's arm. "We're family. We take care of each other."

Nancy's eyes filled with tears. "Now you've done it. You've made me cry."

"Tears are a sign of hope and joy," Estebe said from his spot on the line. "You tell me if you need a new house. I have several rentals empty right now. We can get you to a different place where he won't know where you are."

"You are a good friend." Nancy nodded and wiped her eyes. "And now I'm going to go back to cooking and forget we ever had this conversation."

"Except for my offer," Estebe called after her. "I can hire movers and have you moved in twenty-four hours or less."

The others were quiet for a while, but soon, the chatter of the kitchen started up, but on a happier tone than the night had started. The ice had been broken and the problem addressed. They'd all be okay.

When service ended, Angie walked out to the almost-empty dining room and joined Ian at the bar. He was just finishing his dinner. He grinned up at her. "This home-fried chicken is the best thing I've ever tasted."

"Thanks. It's one of Nancy's recipes we brought in from last month's family meal." She took a spoon and ate a bite of his potatoes. "I've got Estebe making me something to eat before he leaves, if you don't want to leave quickly."

"Eat. You probably need fuel. You had a full house out here." He glanced around the dining room.

"Anyone look off?"

He shook his head. "A lot of couples from my church, but not a suspicious character in the lot."

"If you are the one vouching for people, we may have a problem." Estebe set a French dip in front of Angie, then reached out to shake Ian's hand.

"Hey now, I'm a good person. I know good people." He slapped Estebe on the back. "How have things been? Angie's not working you too hard, is she?"

"Your sweet girlfriend is a slave driver here in the kitchen. You should marry her and take her away from all this before she runs us into the ground."

"You two are cute, you know that, right?" Angie picked up the sandwich and dipped it into the au jus. She almost groaned, it tasted that good. "You are a food god, Estebe."

"That I know." He nodded to Ian. "I have to go clean the kitchen. No rest for the wicked."

Nancy came up behind him with a sleeping five-year-old in her arms. The girl's curly blond hair covered her face as she turned into her mom's shoulder. An older girl stood holding hands with a boy who must have been about eight. "We're out of here. I'd have them say thanks, but I think this one is out for the count."

"Celena can't stay up past eight, especially when you put her in front of a princess movie." The older girl smiled. "My name's Elna. Thank you for letting us hang out here. I didn't want to stay home alone with these guys."

"I would have been fine." The boy held out his hand. "I'm Rider, and I'm nine. I don't need a babysitter."

His confidence told Angie that they'd had this conversation several times before. She shook his hand. "I'm just glad you all could come and visit with us."

"I'm going to be a chef when I grow up. And then I'm going around the world to cook in every country there is," Rider explained.

Nancy rubbed her son's head. "My son is a big dreamer. I like it that way."

"Could be worse." Angie smiled at the little boy. "He could want to play video games."

"Oh, he does enough of that too." Nancy pointed to the back. "Come on, kids, let's get you home so I can crash on my bed."

"Tomorrow you have to help me with my homework," Elna said as they were walking out. "You promised."

"First thing after we take Rider to basketball," Nancy responded.

Angie watched them leave, then returned to her sandwich.

Ian laid his hand on hers. "Gets you thinking, right?"

"Yep, that my zoo is more than enough responsibility right now. Nancy looks beat." Angie polished off her French fries. "And when would I create new recipes?"

"Don't tell me you don't want kids." Ian leaned back away from her. "Seriously?"

"Man, you should see your face." Angie grinned at him. "Let's just say I don't want three kids right now."

"I can work with that. Typically, they come one at a time." He leaned over and grabbed the last fry on her plate. It had been hiding behind the au jus cup.

"You have to remember, I'm an overachiever. Triplets do run in my Nona's family." She took a big bite of the sandwich, feeling her energy level rise. She might just stay awake for the entire drive home.

"Heaven help us." Ian sipped his coffee, watching her.

Chapter 10

As promised, Ian had stayed with her at the farmhouse. He'd brought in a suitcase when he'd fed the zoo Friday and set himself up in the guest room. Angie found him in the kitchen Saturday morning working on his laptop when she finally came downstairs. He stood and pointed to a chair. "Sit and I'll get you coffee."

Angie grunted in response. She really wasn't much of a morning person. Which meant typically all she had to do was deal with Dom's over-the-top energy when she got up. But even her dog had started leaving her alone until she'd gotten a couple of cups in. "Thanks. What are you working on?"

"Exciting stuff. Projections for this year's farmers' market budget. I've heard from ten new farmers who want to commit, which will ease the pain of the four I lost last year." He grinned at her. "Too much rah-rah for nine in the morning?"

"A little. But I love your passion for your work. And I'm excited to meet your new farmers. I've been working on Nona's recipes to try to pull several together for a cookbook with Felicia. We're calling it *From the County Seat's Kitchen to Yours*. All the kitchen staff who wants a spot will have a recipe and an essay in the book. We're thinking about doing one a year. Or maybe doing themes. I think this first one will be just recipes we've used since the restaurant opened." She smiled at Ian, who was staring at her with wide eyes. "I know, too much passion."

He shook his head. "I've just never heard you string so many words together before noon. You must really be excited about this book."

She sipped her coffee, letting the warmth ease into her. "I am excited about the book. One of the best things about living here has been having immediate access to all of Nona's recipe books. I remodeled this kitchen just to be my test kitchen. If I have to move, I'll have to do it all over again. I know, I'll have money, but I love this place."

Dom yipped in his sleep.

"I think Dom's agreeing with you." Ian reached for her hand. "The deal's not done yet. Have some faith. I've put you and the farm on the church prayer list, although I think some of them are confused on what they're praying for. I kind of made it vague so even if they supported the plant being built, they could still pray for you to find peace. Peace to you is that the plant builds elsewhere."

"Well, let's hope your church has a direct connection with the higher power. I could use all the help I can get." She glanced at the window at the top of the barn. "I'm assuming you already fed Precious and Mabel?"

"About two hours ago." He returned to staring at the laptop. "That way we can feed again right before I take you in to work."

"You're so good at the planning." She pulled her calendar off the credenza behind her and glanced at her notes. "I am supposed to be working on the book this morning. I've got a couple recipes I want to make sure to translate for the home cook. Do you mind if I cook a bit today?"

"What else would we do?" He looked over at her, confusion showing in his face.

She made some notes into the next week. "One, I'm supposed to be finding Barb's daughter. All I've done on that is get your uncle to reexamine the case using the lens of her being kidnapped."

"Having him look into her whereabouts again is doing something. He has the tools, not you." He glanced at the calendar. "Did you put dinner with Allen and Maggie on the list?"

"And Bleak. They're a family now. You should call out all of them." She wrote a word into the calendar. "Did they say what time?"

"I'm thinking about two. Maggie's old-fashioned country. Sunday dinner is an afternoon meal where supper is the evening meal."

Angie frowned. "Nona used to do that, but then she'd call Monday's midday meal 'lunch.'"

"The weekends are different. We don't really do brunches on Monday, either." He stared distractedly at the screen.

Angie filled out next week's schedule. She needed to talk to Barb again and tell her that she wasn't helping her one bit. Maybe she should suggest that Barb hire a private investigator. Although she did know one thing. At least in her heart. Jon didn't kill his wife. Not unless he was totally bonkers and able to hide any trace of wrongdoing from his facial features or his body language. It wasn't much, but it might give Barb hope. And that's really all she needed right now was hope.

She took out the notebook and started figuring out which recipes she wanted to play with today. The results of her testings would make a nice breakfast and lunch before they went into town, if she timed it right.

She made a list of ingredients and went to set up her mise en place for the first round of food. Then she started cooking. She could run the other problems she had through her head while she was cooking. It made it easier.

They were eating three different types of quick bread along with an assortment of deviled eggs when she had an idea. "Susan had to have more friends than just Holly. Especially since Holly was such a witch. Maybe she told Jon whom she was hanging around with. Or if she had a calendar."

She grabbed her phone and went into the living room to make the call. When she came back, she grinned at Ian. "Jon's sending over a link to her calendar and her contact list. She kept everything digital so I can flip through that. Of course, he had no idea who her friends were besides that yoga group she talked about."

"Okay, but I'm betting he does know more. We're not even married, and I bet I could name off your friends, acquaintances, and the people you hate with a passion right now."

"I don't hate anyone," Angie countered.

"You hate Jon Ansley, or you did before this whole 'poor me' routine he's playing with you." Ian held out his hand before she could speak. "Hold on, let me continue. You hate this guy who took advantage of you and Felicia at your previous restaurant."

"Hate's a strong word. I just want Todd sent to live on the surface of the sun so I don't have to think about him ever again."

"He couldn't take a step outside without burning to death," Ian pointed out.

"And that's my problem how?" Angie lifted her eyebrows. "And no, I don't sympathize with Jon. I'm just doing this for Barb. She deserves to know where her child is. You should have seen her talk about the picture. She loves that little girl. And even though Susan isn't the child she remembers, there's a bond there."

"I know. I see the same attachment in Maggie's eyes when she looks at Bleak. She's accepted the role of mom and all the emotions that go with it." Ian nodded at the dishes. "I'll stop giving you crap about Jon. Are you done creating for now? Are we back in research mode?"

Angie shook her head. "I can look through her calendar tonight after work. I'd like to try these soups out so I know which one I'm taking to the family meal at the end of the month. I'll need to do at least one more narrowing before I'm ready."

"I'll clean up dishes from round one before I go back to working on my budget. I'm really liking working here with you. At the office I usually eat cheese and crackers for my morning break." He grinned. "Maybe my winter hours should be remote and away from the office."

"I might have to charge you rent." She opened her notebook and started making notes. "Out of the three quick breads, which was your favorite? And why?"

By three, Angie and Ian were ready to go back to River Vista. Ian, as promised, had fed the zoo while Angie showered and got into her work clothes. In the truck, she checked her phone. "The email from Jon is here. I guess we have homework tonight. What are you doing while I'm working?"

"I'm heading to the office, grabbing stuff to work on tomorrow and checking the mail. Then I'm going to check in with Allen and Maggie and see if everything's all right there. Maggie gets a little freaked out about having you over for dinner." He turned right off the north-and-south highway to the road that would take them directly into River Vista.

Unless there was a railroad or irrigation canal to work around, most of the rural roads ran north-south or east-west directly and intersected to make perfect mile squares. Angie had never seen an aerial view of the valley's farmland, but she suspected it would look like a crossword puzzle with some blocks empty of houses or buildings and others with a scattering of life among the large patches of farmland.

Unfortunately, if Susan was missing and had been hidden nearby, there were all kinds of abandoned buildings and farmhouses that might fit the bill. Some were so remote that no one would even notice if a vehicle showed up now and then. And some, the neighbors might think the old Robinson house had finally been rented or was getting ready to be sold. Eventually, someone would question the cars, but if he kept moving her, no one would ever see a pattern.

Angie sighed, staring out the window at a pole barn that held the land owner's machinery out near the fields. "Look at that barn. With all the work done until spring, the farmer might not even go into a building like that for months. A perfect place to hide a woman. Or a body."

"You think she's already gone?" Ian's voice was quiet.

Angie shook her head to get the image out of her mind. "No. I'm not going there. At this point, I'm focusing on the hope that Susan is just missing. Funny how saying that aloud makes it seem totally strange. I'm hoping that a woman has been taken from her home and held against her will for months. And that's the most positive outcome."

"She could have gotten tired of Jon and just left."

Angie turned the heat up higher in the truck. She was chilled to the bone and didn't know if it was the cold winter day or the topic of conversation. "We both know if she'd left on her own, she would have made arrangements for Timber, her dog. Put him in a kennel for a few weeks while she found a place. Or with a friend. No, voluntarily leaving the jerk is probably off the table."

They didn't speak again until Ian pulled the truck into Angie's regular spot in the back parking lot of the restaurant. Estebe's Hummer was already there, as well as Hope's compact beater. The car looked like crap, but it ran well and had new tires all the way around to help her on snowy days.

"You've got people here early." Ian glanced at the clock on his dash. "I thought prep started at three."

"It does, but they like to use the kitchen to try new recipes. Estebe's teaching Hope some Basque family favorites. That girl is going to be a beast in the kitchen once she gets her own place." Angie grabbed her bag. "You can leave the truck here if you want."

He shook his head. "I'm going to talk to Maggie first. Get that over with, then I'll be at my office or apartment if you need me. I'll be at the restaurant for dinner about six or seven and wait for you to get off work."

"You could stay at the apartment. Watch television. I could come get you when I'm done," Angie countered.

"You don't get the part of me being the boyfriend protector from the unknown fear. Or you haven't watched enough horror movies. The vampire always gets the girl when the guy goes to the shower building at the campsite." He reached out and stroked her cheek. "I know, we're just reacting on a hunch, but I'd rather be safe than sorry. And if the zombie hoard is coming, I'd rather be at your side."

Angie laughed and squeezed his hand. "You make being stalked by a murderer and-or a kidnapper tame against your zombies and spooks."

"Just trying to keep it real, love." He winked at her. "I'll see you at seven. Do you want me to pop in the kitchen?"

"Just tell Felicia to let me know you're here." Angie smiled. "The kitchen can get a little crazy during service."

She walked to the back door and unlocked it with her key. There was a buzzer on the door that she could have used that sounded in the kitchen and the upstairs apartment, but she didn't want to disturb anyone. She watched as Ian pulled the truck out of the parking lot and onto the road.

She didn't like the fact he had to be inconvenienced to watch out for some unknown threat, but it felt good knowing he was there. She didn't want to be the stupid one in the movie who always went home alone through the dark alleys and got herself killed.

"Now he has me talking in movie scenarios." She bypassed the kitchen entrance and went straight through the hallway to her office to dump her tote and check the emails for the day. When she got there, the door was open.

Sheriff Brown sat at her desk, and a clearly upset Nancy sat on one of the visitor chairs with Felicia next to her. He waved her inside. "You might as well hear this too."

"What happened?" She dumped her purse and coat on a table and knelt next to Nancy.

Nancy shook her head. "Nothing, really. I'm probably overreacting."

"I'm not sure about that, Ms. Gowan, but tell Angie why you want to bring the kids to work with you again." He spoke in a gentle voice, like the one Ian used on spooked horses. "Please?"

Nancy nodded. "As soon as we got home last night, the landline started ringing. I have one because I don't want the kids to have a cell phone and they are there alone a lot." She shot a glance at Sheriff Brown. "Elna's taken a babysitting course with the Red Cross, and she's very responsible."

"No one's questioning your judgment here," Felicia assured her as she shot a glance at Sheriff Brown.

"Okay, sorry, I'm jumpy. Anyway, I'd pick up the phone to say hello and they'd hang up. This happened five times. When Elna picked up, a man asked her name. I took the phone out of her hand, and they hung up again. I wouldn't let anyone pick up again. I unplugged the phone." She shook her head. "I figured it was one of the guys at school, messing with her, but then this morning when I re-plugged it in again, the calls started again. It's my ex-husband. I know it is. He's just that petty."

"I've got someone over at Ms. Gowan's house putting a tracker on the phone. I don't have manpower to keep him there twenty-four-seven, so if it's okay, the kids are going to be here tonight, then my guy will go home with the family and stay until the morning." His tone made it seem like this was the most normal thing in the world. And Angie knew it was to help Nancy calm down.

"I told you yesterday it's no problem at all." Angie squeezed Nancy's hand. She looked up at Felicia. "Do you have more age-appropriate movies?"

Her partner laughed. "You're kidding, right? I buy every fun movie out there, just so I have them on hand. I've already brought down a good collection, but Rider's campaigning for some more boy movies. I think he's tired of princess movies."

"Don't let him fool you. He loves the fairy tales." Nancy smiled, thinking of her son, and for the first time in a few days, Angie saw her face soften. "I'm so lucky to work with you all."

"I'm glad you put up with us." Angie nodded. "Especially the guys. They can be a little over the top at times."

"Boys will be boys." She glanced at her watch. "Service prep started ten minutes ago. Can I go clean up and go to work now?"

Sheriff Brown stood. "Of course. I'll have a man here waiting for you at ten, ten thirty?"

"Better make it eleven. We're fully booked on reservations tonight." Felicia glanced at Angie. "Do you think you could spare her then?"

"Yes. As long as the kids can stay out that late." Angie turned to Nancy. "When do you need to leave?"

"Eleven would be great. It's a weekend, so we can sleep in tomorrow." She rubbed her fingers under her eyes. "And maybe I can get some sleep and get rid of these circles."

Angie knew Nancy didn't care about how she looked. It was just a way to defuse the tension in the room. The woman always thought about others. She watched Nancy and Sheriff Brown leave the office, talking about next steps.

"I hate that this is happening to her. She's too nice a person." Felicia stood, watching them leave.

"Worse, if Allen can't figure out who's doing this and get him to stop, Nancy will quit and go into hiding. She'll protect those kids no matter what." Angie's eyes flashed with anger. "She shouldn't have to uproot her home just because someone likes playing games with her."

"She and the kids need to be safe. No matter what." Felicia glanced at her watch. "I've got a couple new servers trying out tonight. I hope everything goes well."

"Me too." Angie pulled her hair back into a high pony, then slipped on her chef jacket. It was time to go to work and let the rest of this fall around her. To a place where it wouldn't hurt anyone anymore.

Chapter 11

They were all seated around Maggie's oak dining table in the formal dining room the next afternoon. Dinner had been served, and Bleak had eaten, then asked to be excused. Maggie watched her go.

"She's meeting a study group over at the drive-in to talk about their debate project. I can't believe how well she's already fitting into the school. She's even taking a cooking class this semester. She brings home recipes, and we try them here, as well. She's a really good cook." Maggie prattled on about Bleak's adjustment.

Angie waited for the door to shut. "I think she's getting more interested in the hospitality side of the industry. She's already making positive changes to the hostess position. And Felicia says she's amazing with customers."

Maggie beamed at the praise. "She's such a good girl. I can't believe how lucky we are that she's in our lives."

This was a complete one-eighty from the frantically worried Maggie she'd met with a few days ago. Angie pointedly glanced at Allen and Ian before she asked her question. "I don't want to bring up a sore subject, but everything's okay now?"

"Oh yes. I appreciate your advice. I was just overthinking things. I know she's a little concerned about testifying against her aunt, but really, how many times do those things actually go to trial? We might get out of this with the woman confessing for a lower charge. Then all our worry would have been for naught." Maggie took some of the salad in the bowl next to her and refilled her small plate.

"I'm glad things are going better. But if you ever need to talk…" Angie left the statement open-ended so that Maggie wouldn't have to say more about the issue she'd tried to keep from her husband and nephew.

"Actually, I am talking to someone about how to raise a child. It's been very helpful." Maggie held out the salad bowl. "Anyone else want seconds?" The three of them shook their heads, almost in unison. The salad wasn't bad. It just wasn't good. From what Angie could tell, it had been a mixed greens bag with a tomato chopped up and sprinkled on top. Finding salad ingredients, especially locally in midwinter wasn't an easy task, but Angie knew a greenhouse that grew greens and herbs for the local restaurants all season. At least the ones who wanted to keep their customers in fresh produce. Others used the same bagged salad as Maggie had served for dinner.

"That's wonderful. Is it another parent from one of the high school groups? I always thought each subsection should have a parent advisory group. Like the band kids. Or the math kids. People who have common problems." Angie took another bite of the baked chicken Maggie had made for dinner. Dry, but not bad. She'd even used some seasoning.

"Actually, no, but that's a great idea." Maggie smiled. "Although I'm not sure which parent group I'd join for Bleak. She has so many interests."

Angie glanced up at Ian, who grinned at her. Maggie was one hundred percent in love with her new foster daughter. She didn't think Bleak would get away when she turned eighteen. Maggie was going to be in her life for the rest of time. Angie smiled back, then realized Maggie had avoided the question. "Who are you meeting with?"

Maggie blushed and dropped her gaze to the floor. She hesitated a bit too long, and Allen looked over at her, concerned.

"Maggie? Who are you talking to, dear?" His voice was calm, but even Angie could feel the concern in the tone.

"Now, don't get upset, Allen. She's a lovely woman, and she knows a lot about unconventional family structure."

Angie blinked her eyes. It couldn't be! These two women had nothing in common with each other. But just before Maggie said the name, she'd already guessed. She wondered how Allen was going to take the news.

"Maggie?" Allen prodded.

She set her fork down and wiped her mouth on her cloth napkin, identical to the ones she'd set out for every plate. "If you insist on knowing, it's Barb Travis from the Red Eye."

Ian had just taken a drink of his water and almost spit it out all over the table, then he started choking. His uncle came over and patted him hard on the back. "Easy now, son. No use overreacting."

"What do you mean, overreacting? Barb Travis is the nicest woman I've ever had the pleasure to meet." Maggie stood and stared at Angie. "Do you see why I wanted to keep the Bleak issues just between us? These men have no ability to see compassion in another human being. None at all."

They watched as Maggie stood, picked up her plate and salad, and left for the kitchen. The three looked at each other, stunned.

"I don't think I'd heard more than ten words out of Maggie before Bleak came to River Vista." Angie smiled as she took her napkin off her lap. "She's totally amazing."

"She's getting advice from a bartender. We have friends at church. She could have talked to one of them. They would have kept her confidence." Allen rubbed his face. "I guess I'm going to have to put a stop to this."

"Why?" Angie asked, staring at him.

"Are you kidding? Barb Travis is a really nice woman, but she has no business telling anyone how to raise a child. Especially since she knew Bleak's background. We need a normal voice helping make decisions, not a crazy one in my wife's head." He studied his empty plate. "Sorry dinner was interrupted by this."

"No worries." Ian walked over and patted his uncle on the back. "Everything is going to be all right. We have to have faith."

Angie squirmed a bit. She'd grown fond of Barb after she'd returned. And Allen's concern wasn't justified. Finally, she couldn't just let it sit. She stood and left the table, pausing at the doorway. "Faith won't help here. You're being judgmental. I'm shocked that you of all people can't see that hope and comfort come from a lot of different places. Like Maggie said, Barb's good people. What she does for a living doesn't matter. Or if it does, it's given her even more compassion for people than you could even know."

Allen looked shocked at her outburst. "I didn't mean…"

"Yeah, you did." Angie looked at Ian. "I'm going to say goodbye to Maggie, then I'd like to go home please."

She made her way to the kitchen, where Maggie sat, a book open in front of her and a journal and a pen on the other side. She sat across from her. "Ian and I are taking off. Thank you so much for dinner. Can I help with cleanup before I leave?"

Maggie shook her head. "No, I think cleaning the kitchen will give me something to do so I don't yell at my husband. He's a good man, but sometimes he can be a little narrow-minded."

Angie reached out and touched the top of Maggie's hand. "I'm glad you found someone to talk to about Bleak. Raising a child isn't easy, and it's not like you can take her to Mommy and Me classes."

Maggie snorted. "You're right there. Although we are going for a spa day next Saturday. Don't worry, she'll be at work on time. I just think we need some girl time to chat."

"That's a great idea. Bleak's at that in-between stage. I forget she's not an adult already." Angie thought a moment. "You know, she's really into reading fantasy. You might want to check out the bookstore and see who's coming to the area to speak soon. I bet she'd love to share that with you."

"I'm so glad I have angels to talk to. Barb suggested the spa day, and now you give me the book idea. I've been looking for something for us to do besides cooking together, and both of those ideas are perfect. And they give her a break from all the work she already does. The girl's a hard worker." Maggie made a note in her journal.

"I know she is. And she's lucky to have someone in her life who cares about all sides of her development."

Maggie laughed. "Being an insta-mom to a sixteen-year-old isn't easy. But I'm hoping my enthusiasm makes up for my lack of experience."

"Just do your best, that's all she needs."

When they got into the car and started driving home, no one talked. Finally, Angie broke the ice. "Look, I know you're mad, but Allen was totally out of line."

"I agree." Ian turned down the stereo.

Shocked, Angie turned to him. "You agree?"

He nodded. "You were right. Barb Travis is a good person. God works through all people. You don't have to be in our church to have good influences on others. Allen just worries about Maggie. It's only been the two of them for so long, and now he has to share her with Bleak. He's having some adjustment issues."

"I figured you were going to be mad at me for yelling at him." Angie relaxed into the seat, watching the farmland as they drove past.

"I should have said something, but I failed both of you. You said what needed to be said. I'll speak up next time. We can tag-team these things, although you're better at getting to the bottom of stuff than I am." Ian glanced over at Angie and took her hand. "I know we just ate, but do you want to make some brownies tonight and watch a movie?"

"You're staying over again?"

"You're not getting rid of me until Uncle Allen has this murderer under wraps. I have a feeling somehow this thing is connected to the whole soybean plant development. I can't prove it's your new friend, Jon, but I think he knows more than he's saying."

This time it was Angie who nodded. "I agree. But let's take the night off from our Scooby-Doo roles and just relax. I don't want to think about murder or missing wives or losing the farmhouse. At least for just one night. Let's veg. And make brownies."

He pulled the truck into her driveway and shut off the engine. "Sounds like a perfect evening to me. I'll go feed the zoo, and you can go inside."

Angie unlocked the door to the house and greeted Dom. No broken furniture or chewed-up boxes greeted her. Dom liked to spend his alone time in the kitchen in his bed, so if he had found anything that he'd decided was his, the remains of it would be there. She pointed to the mudroom where there was a dog door. "Ian's outside in the barn. Do you want to go outside and watch for him?"

Dom woofed and headed to the mudroom. Angie wasn't sure if he really understood her or had just picked out several words he did know. Like "Ian." And "outside." Either way, it gave her a few minutes of peace to flip through the pile of mail Ian had grabbed out of the box yesterday. She'd seen it sitting on the kitchen desk this morning but hadn't wanted to deal with paying bills.

Now seemed like as good of a time to do it as any. Angie had a system. Bills came in, she paid them and sent them back out. That way she never had to think of whether it was the fifteenth and she hadn't paid the internet. She didn't get a lot of bills at the house. Tax bills and insurance bills came once a year. Utility bills came monthly. And, thanks to the restaurant being a solid moneymaker, she was able to pay herself a good salary as well as an annual dividend.

If she had to buy a new place, she might owe money on the new house. Especially if she bought somewhere that she could still have Precious and Mabel. Mabel might not be with them for much longer since Nona had brought her onto the farm, but Precious was young. Goats had to live ten, fifteen years, right? She needed to ask Ian.

She opened an envelope, paid a bill, then repeated the process until she was down to two items. A community newsletter that was delivered free every Saturday and a white envelope with her name typed on the front. She opened the newsletter and saw a picture of the large soybean field near her house on the front page. She read the headline aloud. "'New industry comes to the area.' Great."

She tossed the paper farther onto her desk and opened the envelope. It was from the new attorney representing the soybean factory. She leaned back and read the letter.

"Dom's outside running around the fence line like he's in a racetrack." Ian said as he came into the house. He pointed to the letter. "What's that?"

Angie finished scanning the letter. "Just an announcement that Jon is no longer the attorney of record for the soybean people. I have been reassigned."

"That was quick. I wonder if his company really thinks he went over the deep end and did in his wife? I think some of the yoga women have husbands in that firm. Would they have pushed for something like that to happen?" Ian came over and took the letter she handed him.

"In a heartbeat. Especially if it would work in their husbands' favor. It's a dog-eat-dog kind of group." Angie greeted Dom, who had gotten tired of his racing and had come back inside, where his people were hanging out. "I don't know how they pretend to like each other."

"You're sure it's all pretend?" Ian gave her the letter back.

She shook her head. "I wouldn't treat anyone as bad as these women are treating each other. I hate to say it, but Susan might be in a bunch of mean girls. Which means she might be one of the crowd instead of a victim here."

"Are you going to tell Barb that, because there is no way on God's green earth it's going to come from these lips." He went over to the fridge and pulled out a soda. "Want one?"

"Of course." She was still thinking about Susan and her final days at the house. What had she been working on, and why was their fitting in more important than finding friends she could trust? "I don't think I'm helping Barb at all in this. She must be worried sick."

"Sweetheart, I don't mean to be disrespectful, but you're a chef with a good eye for these things, not a police investigator." He stared at her, watching for a reaction.

"I know it. I've been pushing Allen too far in some of these investigations. I'm going to try not to get involved, but Barb's counting on me."

"You should tell her you aren't making any progress and you're bowing out of the agreement." He handed her his phone. "Go ahead and give her a call. You know you'll feel so much better when it's done."

Angie took the phone. "She's going to hate me."

"No, she won't."

Angie stared him down with the next look. "Want to bet?"

She called Barb and let her know she wasn't going to be investigating anymore. Barb didn't say anything through the entire conversation until the end. "Thanks for your help anyway."

Angie hung up the phone and stared at it. It was like snowstorm clouds had overtaken the valley. "I'm a heel."

"You're human. You can't find someone who doesn't want to be found." Ian pulled her into his arms, and for the first time in a while, Angie let the tears flow.

Chapter 12

The next morning, Ian fed the animals, and after he and Angie had breakfast, he needed to leave to meet with some of his board. He held her close at the door. "I can cancel this. I don't like leaving you here alone. Not with all that's going on."

"You're going to be at a two-hour meeting." She glanced at the clock. "I think I can hold down the fort until you get back."

"Are you sure you don't want to come with me?" Ian glanced at his watch. "You could go visit with Felicia or work in your office."

"Felicia isn't up yet, and being alone in my office is just the same as being alone here. But here I can be working on fun things. Like my cookbook." She kissed him, then turned back to the sink. "Go do your job. I'll be fine."

"Okay, but stay inside and don't go anywhere." He reached around and locked the door before he shut it.

"Yes, sir!" Angie gave the closed door a salute. This being on a twenty-four-hour watch was getting annoying. She needed to call Allen and tell him to take Ian off the case. Before she said something to her boyfriend she couldn't take back. Like "get away from me." Or "you're not the boss of me." Which had been one of the choice responses she'd had ready this morning. "Dom, Ian's going a little bit crazy with the protection thing."

Dom woofed his agreement from his bed.

Angie picked up her mom's journal and set it on the table. Then she grabbed a cup of coffee and a plate of cookies and with her feet tucked up underneath her, started to read.

Her phone rang after the first cup, and she assumed it was Ian checking in with her. "Hey, I'm fine. I'm reading, though, can I call you back?"

"Angie? Is that you?" a whispered voice asked.

Angie looked at her phone display. The call wasn't from Ian. "Sorry, Barb, I thought Ian…"

"Never mind, I just need you to come and rescue me."

Angie swallowed hard. "You need me to what?"

"Don't judge. I'm stuck in a closet in Sunny's house. I thought her husband was going to work, but he just left for a bit. Now he's downstairs, and I can't make sure he won't see me," Barb's whisper rasped on the phone.

"What in the world? Never mind. Look, I'll go knock on his door and see if I can distract him and you go out the back door. I won't be able to hold him long, so as soon as you hear me knock on the door, you'd better get going. And then meet me at the Red Eye. We need to talk." Angie pulled on her boots as she talked. When she got to the door, Dom stood between it and her. She sighed, then focused on the call. "Barb, I'll be there in twenty minutes. Stay hidden."

"I will." She paused. "Angie, thanks for your help."

Angie hung up the phone, then slipped on her coat and put the phone in her tote. "I'm an idiot." She looked down at Dom. "I suppose you're saying you're going if I'm going?"

A woof was all the response she got.

"Okay then. Let me grab your lead." She went to the fridge to grab two bottles of water, just in case, and then glanced over at the desk. She grabbed the letter and tucked it into her tote and the water bottles in Dom's backpack. They might not need them, but it was better to be prepared. She got everything and everyone into the SUV, then hooked up her phone. If she was lucky, she'd get voice mail.

As she pulled out of the driveway, she dialed Ian's cell. And her luck held. It rang her into voice mail directly. He must have put it on *do not disturb* for the meeting. "Hey, don't get mad, but I'm heading over to Jon's house for a few minutes, then I'll be at the Red Eye talking to Barb. You can probably catch me there. And I've got Dom for protection."

When he heard his name, Dom barked from the back seat.

"He's on the job." Angie hung up and headed to the subdivision outside of River Vista.

When they got there, Angie parked in the driveway. She saw Barb's Mustang parked up the road a few houses down on the corner. At least she'd been smart about that. She got out of the car and stopped by the window where Dom had his nose out of the car, sniffing. "We won't be long, and I'm not going in. If I disappear, you start raising Cain, okay?"

His tongue reached out, and he licked her hand. Message delivered. Or at least she hoped. Her ability to talk to animals was severely limited by her not speaking Dog.

She pulled the letter out of her purse and glanced at one of the upstairs windows. Barb's face popped into view, and Angie nodded. Then she went to play distraction.

She rapped hard on the door.

When Jon answered, he frowned down at her. His hair was mussed, and he looked like he hadn't showered in days. Working must have been the only thing keeping him on some type of routine since Susan's disappearance. Now he didn't even have that. He stared at her with bloodshot eyes. "What do you want?"

Angie could smell the alcohol rolling off of him—"coming out of his pores" was what Nona had said about a friend who'd get lost in drinking. She dug in her purse and pulled out a letter. "I got this Saturday."

He peered at it, and as he did, she saw Barb sneaking down the staircase. If Jon turned around for any reason, they'd be almost face-to-face.

He waved his hand. "I can't read that. I can barely see the paper."

"How long have you been drinking?" She lowered the hand that held the paper. "You know you need to be alert, just in case."

He snorted and almost turned away, but Angie caught his arm. He stared at her hand, then up at her. "Why are you here? You're ruining a perfectly planned pity party."

"Is that what Susan would have wanted? You to get lost in the bottle?" She juggled the paper in front of him. "What's going on with this company? You said there was something you needed to tell me."

"Oh yeah." He leaned against the door frame, trying to focus on her. "There's a history of this place sweeping up property for cheap prices when the true value is a lot higher. I think there's some strong-arming going on. I can't prove it, but you've been okay about the whole thing and I thought you should know."

She studied him. "You're saying they're putting pressure on people to sell?"

He shook his head. "No, I'm not saying that. That would be leaking my client's proprietary information or his secrets or something. I would never do that—attorney-client privilege."

Angie watched as Barb disappeared out the back door. She saw Jon turn toward the sound, but then Timber came running to the door from the back. Barb's leaving must have woken the dog. Jon leaned down to scratch Timber's ears. "Who's a good boy?"

With Barb safely out of the house, Angie could leave, but she wanted one more try at getting Jon to say something that might help her save the farmhouse. "Then what are you saying to me?"

He looked up from scratching Timber and for a second, his eyes focused on her own and he held the gaze. "If I were you, I'd watch my back. Especially if you're going to continue fighting the land sale. People have gotten hurt before. And even though I don't like you, I don't want to see you wind up dead. Like Susan."

Shock must have shown on her face, because with that, he tried to close the front door on her. Then he paused. "Look, just because my wife's missing after I tried to talk them into buying a different property, that could all be a coincidence. Maybe your life isn't in danger. But even a broken watch is right twice a day."

Angie watched as he shut the door on her. When she thought her legs would move, she sprinted toward the SUV. Dom watched her from his view at the window. He watched her closely, then gave her wet kisses when she climbed into the driver's seat. "Hey, boy, thanks for the assist."

A small growl came from the back, and Angie glanced around, pushing the door lock button as she started the car. She didn't see anything in the direction the dog was watching, but that didn't mean they weren't being watched. And she'd just put herself in the enemy's crosshairs.

A chill went over her as she drove toward River Vista to talk to Barb. She turned up the heat, but she didn't think it was the chill outside that was bothering her. It was the knowledge that Jon was being watched. Or at least his house was. Had the watcher seen Barb break in? Was she in trouble now, too? She glanced in her rearview to see if she was being followed. She'd never felt this vulnerable during an investigation before. It was like the killer had labeled her as victim number two.

As she drove past the park with the construction in the back, she shivered. Maybe victim number three.

She parked in the back parking lot for the County Seat and got Dom out of the car. Then instead of heading to the restaurant, she walked through the alley to the Red Eye. Dom had her pause at his favorite tree for a bit of watering. She saw Ian standing outside the door at the Red Eye, waiting. The man did not look happy.

When they reached the steps into the business, she held up a hand. "Hold the lecture, I need to give one of my own."

He nodded, then opened the door. They walked through the narrow hallway with Dom's nose in full smell mode. He paused at the edge of the entrance to the main saloon and woofed quietly.

"Hey, buddy, I didn't know your mom was going to bring you," Barb addressed Dom first.

His tail went crazy.

"I hope it's okay I brought him in. He's kind of my bodyguard right now." Angie gave a quick glance at Ian. "And he did his business before we came in."

"I hope you're talking about Dom and not Ian." Barb's cackle ended in a spasm of racking coughing. She waved them closer. When she stopped coughing, she reached down to give Dom a rub on his head. "He's always welcome. He's probably got more manners than some of the lot that come in here at times."

Dom sat in front of Barb and stared up at her.

Angie pulled up a chair to the table Barb had chosen rather than her normal perch at the bar. "Tell me what you were doing at Jon's?"

Ian sat across from her and on the other side of Barb. He leaned his elbows on the table, but didn't say anything.

"Okay, so after you called last night to tell me you hadn't found anything, I was worked up. Mad at you. Mad at the sheriff. Mad at Jon. And finally, mad at myself for not believing that we could have been a family. I gave up on her and me too soon. I let my sister talk me into giving Sunny up because it was better for her. I'm not sure that was true." Barb paused to light a cigarette. "Anyway, we don't need to rehash my life and my bad choices."

"Except for the one this morning when you went over to Jon and Susan's house," Ian reminded her.

"You're right. I probably should have just let Sheriff Brown deal with finding her, but I thought if I could just see where she lived, maybe my Spidey sense as a mom would kick in and I'd find the one thing that everyone else had overlooked." She took a drag on the cigarette.

"Did you?"

Barb pulled out a leather-bound book. "Maybe. It looks like Sunny kept a journal. I didn't get to read it much, but the last few entries talk about her meeting someone who could get Jon out of the trouble he was in. Apparently, Sunny didn't trust the firm he worked for and thought something bad was about to happen."

"Then she gets kidnapped."

Ian shook his head. "She could have just left."

Angie glanced at him, and she could see even he didn't believe that line of possibility anymore. It had just been a reaction to the kidnapping word.

"Fine. She was taken." He blew out some air. "Even I can't see this as anything except a kidnapping, and I haven't read the diary yet."

"You'll see when you read this." Barb pushed the book toward him. Then she turned to Angie. "I'm sorry I got you involved, but when Jon came home, I needed some backup. And you're the only one I trust."

Angie squeezed the older woman's hand. "No problem. I found out some information on the development case too. Apparently, the company has issues with other people who stand against them. Like maybe they just disappear. I'm going to pull out any information I can find on Taylor Farms and CelCat Developing and see what I can find."

"Sounds like a plan." Barb put out the cigarette when it was only half done and put it back into the pack. "Look, I know you said you were done, but I need your help. I have to know what happened to Sunny soon. I go into surgery the first of next month, and I need to know if I should change my will."

"You're having surgery, not dying," Angie said, but then something in Barb's face made her wish she could take the words back. "Right? You're not dying, right?"

Barb took a minute before responding. "Look, I have lung cancer. Nothing crazy. The doctor's going to cut it out, and I'll be done with it." She held up the packet of cigarettes. "And I'm done with these too. As soon as I leave the hospital. It might be a little too late, but I'm willing to do my part to keep the rest of my lungs healthy."

"You want to talk to Susan before you have surgery." Angie filled in what Barb hadn't said.

"This might sound heartless, but if she's dead, I need to change my will. There's no way I'm going to let that jerk have my money." She smiled sadly. "Even if he didn't kill her."

As Ian and Angie walked to her car, he held her hand. "I should be mad at you for leaving the house without me, but I get it. Barb needs our help."

"Now more than ever. I can't believe I told her she was on her own." Angie opened the back door for Dom to climb inside, then leaned against the car, watching the back door of the Red Eye. "Sometimes life just isn't fair."

Ian leaned down and kissed her. Then he opened her door, handing her the diary Barb had given him. "Let's get you home. We've got some research to do."

After making plans for Ian to follow her in his truck, Angie pulled out of the parking lot and headed home. Her phone rang soon after crossing the railroad tracks that outlined River Vista's city limits. "Hello?"

"Hey, stranger. I thought you might come in and say hi, but you just got in your car and left." Felicia's voice flowed through the car speakers, and Dom barked at her from the back seat. "Hey, big boy, I saw you too."

"We had to go save Barb, and then Ian and I spent some time with her. She found Susan's diary. If there are names in there we don't know, can I call you later?" Angie glanced in the rearview mirror and saw Ian's truck following her. "Ian's planted himself at the farmhouse and won't leave until this thing with the developer is over. Allen is worried that they may try to do something to force me to sell."

"Well, I'm the heir of your estate, so if they do get through Ian and knock you off, rest assured, I'll continue the good fight."

Angie laughed. "I'm not sure that makes me feel any better. But thanks. Hey, can you deliver a couple of quarts of soup over to Barb before she heads home? And put a note on the calendar that we'll send her a dinner as soon as the restaurant opens each night?"

"Sure, that's sweet. But why?"

Angie filled Felicia in on Barb's upcoming surgery. "I just want her to have food available that she doesn't have to make. Take at least one worry off her list for the day."

"You are amazing." Felicia sniffed. "Let's make sure we do it after she gets home from the hospital too. I'm not sure who she'll have managing the bar while she's gone, but I'll see if Jeorge might be willing to go over to work on the nights we're not open."

"Talk to her. If we have to hire a temp for him so he could work full-time at the Red Eye, we'll do that too. She needs someone she can depend on." Angie hadn't thought about what Barb would do with the bar while she was in the hospital. Of course, she'd work as long as possible at the bar before she went in and probably just close it for the days she was off. But with Jeorge, maybe she could keep it open. Keeping a business open all by yourself was hard work. Thank God she had Felicia to share the burden. She pulled into the driveway and turned off the engine. "I'm at the house. Call me after you talk to Barb."

"Sounds good. I'm going to call Estebe and see if he wants to come over and make up some meals we can freeze for her so she has something later."

Angie got out of the car and took Dom straight to the house. Ian pulled into the driveway as she was opening the door, and the dog woofed at the new visitor. "It's just Ian," Angie told him as she put him inside. Then she waited for Ian on the porch. He walked over, carrying a small duffel bag. Angie pointed to the bag. "What's in that?"

"Provisions, just in case I'm here for a while longer. I've got some books I've been meaning to read, and I brought some more clothes." He smiled at her. "Can I use your washer and dryer today?"

"Of course. I could do it for you." She followed him into the house.

He shook his head. "I can do my own laundry. I'm a big boy."

She laughed and set the book down on the table. "Fine, be that way. I've got some reading to do anyway."

She put water on to boil so she could make some tea and then sat at the table, reading Susan's diary. She probably didn't need to start at the beginning, but she did, hoping it would give her a better sense of the woman.

When the teakettle screamed, Ian stood from where he'd been reading, too, and poured them water for tea. Angie grabbed a packet of oolong and went back to reading while it steeped. When the tea was finished, she stood and stretched. Then she put the kettle on again.

"Did you find anything?" Ian slipped a bookmark into the book he'd been reading.

Angie shook her head. "Nothing about the soybean factory or why she'd go missing. She mentions the women in the yoga group. Most she didn't like, not at all. But she did say nice things about Felicia. She said she hoped Holly didn't eat her alive before Felicia figured out that the woman was a snake. If these two were best friends, Susan didn't trust her much."

"Or at all." Ian threw away his empty tea bag and set up the cup for a new one. "Tell me again what Holly does for a living?"

"Mostly takes care of her husband's networking. He's a financial consultant." Angie rolled her shoulders. "She was trying to get Felicia to have Estebe work with him."

"Maybe Holly has a reason to want Susan out of the picture. Could she have driven her away?" Ian refilled the cups with the teakettle that had just started to scream. "People like that don't have boundaries on what they won't do to advance a career."

Despite the warmth coming from the oil heater, Angie felt chilled to the bone.

Chapter 13

By the time she finished reading the diary, Angie had a headache and a need to cook. Cooking made her feel in control of things, and right now, she needed some control in her life. Ian came inside from feeding and took off his coat, putting on the teakettle after washing his hands in the mudroom. "It's cold outside."

"You were out awhile. Did something happen?" She laid out plastic for the chicken breasts she planned on rolling into a divan with a mixture of broccoli, cheese, and a little pancetta. She turned toward Ian before starting to pound the meat into a thin patty.

"Actually, Precious and I went and walked her fence. I haven't done it since she got out around Halloween. She's an inventive one, so I wanted to make sure she wasn't planning her next escape." He rubbed his hands together. "And it got me outside for a bit. Typically, I walk around town around lunch just to get the blood moving. I enjoy it much more in the summer than I do this time of year."

"The fence is good?" Angie returned to beating the chicken.

"Solid." He took the mallet out of her hands. "That chicken is flat. Hold on a second. What did you find in the diary?"

"Not much. She had a few people she seemed to like. I sent that over to Felicia to see if they are in the yoga group, so tomorrow morning we may go make some visits. And she had a meeting the day after her last entry. She said she'd write more later, that it was too much to try to think about now. And Jon was having an affair. Or at least Susan thought he was." Angie took the mallet back. "I felt like I was violating her privacy and her marriage as I read the entries. Susan seemed to be a sensitive person. One whom I might just like if I ever met her."

"Nature versus nurture. She's Barb's daughter. Probably determined, smart, and a bit calculating, but in a good way." He nodded to the chicken. "Anything I can do to help?"

She shook her head. "No, let me cook tonight. I need to feel useful. Why don't you and Dom go into the living room and watch some television."

"I'll take up your couch offer, but I'm going to read instead. I'm right at the good part of the book, and I'd love to finish tonight. Of course, I brought the next book in the series with me today, just in case." He kissed her on the cheek. "Let me know if you need help or want company."

"You're the best." She watched as he made his tea, then heard his steps as he went around to all the downstairs doors, checking locks. He ran upstairs too. She glanced at Dom, who was watching her cook and waiting for her to drop something. "He's also thorough."

Dom smiled a doggie grin, sticking his tongue out at her.

After dinner, Ian helped her with the dishes. He was drying the last plate when his phone rang. "Hey, Uncle Allen."

Angie took the plate from him and put it away, then took a washrag to the table. She listened to Ian's part of the conversation, then looked at him expectantly when he hung up.

He shook his head, putting the phone back on his charger. "Nothing important. He just wanted to let me know he was on his way out to the caves. A bunch of kids were out there partying today, and some guy ran them off. Their parents are afraid that the guy is living out there."

"Shouldn't they be more concerned that their underaged kids were probably drinking out there?" Angie glanced at the freezer. "I think I have some ice cream in there if you want dessert."

"Are you kidding? After that meal, I'm good for now. Maybe some popcorn later?" He glanced around the kitchen, but it was shiny clean. "You up for a movie, or do you just want to read with me?"

Angie glanced at her mother's diary. Susan's had been so sad. She needed an influx of positive life into her brain. And her mom's high school years seemed full of fun and crazy activities. "I'll read if you are."

"Sounds like a plan. A cup of tea?" He nodded to the pot.

Angie went to the fridge instead. "I'm thinking some hot chocolate with the popcorn. Salty and sweet."

"You're amazing."

They went arm in arm into the living room to settle in for the night.

Angie heard the book snap together with a satisfied sigh from Ian when he finished. She handed him the diary and pointed to a section she'd marked with a piece of paper about an hour ago when she'd found it. She hadn't wanted to pull him out of his book. "Read that page."

When he was done, he frowned. "Is this the same cave where Uncle Allen is tonight?"

"There's only one River Vista Cave. It's been a teenage hangout for years. But I never heard the story about a young woman getting lost in the caves, until I read it in Mom's diary." She stood and rolled her shoulders. "Ready for a movie and popcorn? I know you typically go to bed early, but there's no way I can sleep for a while."

"Not a problem. You make the popcorn. I'll pick the movie." He stood behind her and rubbed her shoulders. "How do you feel reading your mom's diary? Is it hard, knowing she's gone?"

Angie sighed. The man had magic fingers, especially since she held on to all her tension in her shoulders. "Just the opposite, actually. I feel closer to her and Nona than I have for several years. Since I lost Nona, really. It's like time-traveling back in their lives and listening to them squabble. I love it."

He kissed the back of her neck and pulled her into a hug. "I'm glad, then. I like to see you happy."

Angie and Dom went into the kitchen as Ian chose a movie. It was funny that the cave had come up twice today. She hadn't thought of that place since she was a teenager out on a Friday night after a September football game. She'd been interested in one of the football players that fall, but he'd quickly hooked up with one of the cheerleading squad. Angie hadn't been back to the cave since that night.

She poured the corn into the oil in a pan, put on a lid, and started shaking. So many close calls around life choices revolved around fate. And the man in her living room was better than any of her prior boyfriends. He was a keeper, and she was trying hard to make the relationship permanent.

When the popping slowed down, she poured the popcorn into a bowl, melted a stick of butter, and salted the corn after drizzling the butter over the top.

"Movie's ready and that smells amazing," Ian called from the living room. She grabbed a couple of sodas and the bowl before meeting him on the couch. The way to a man's heart and all.

* * * *

The next morning, she decided to work on the cookbook. Sunday and Monday were her veg days and the restaurant didn't open until

Wednesday, so she used Tuesdays for recipe development and projects. Like the cookbook. Or trying to save the farmhouse. Which she hadn't been making any progress on, even with Jon's cryptic discussion about how the company wasn't what it seemed to be. Therefore, the cookbook had won. Besides, she thought better while she cooked.

Hopefully, Barb wouldn't get herself into a pinch and need rescuing today, either. All she wanted to do was shuffle around the kitchen in her slippers and make food. She pulled out some frozen hamburger and put it in the microwave to thaw. Then she got the rest of the ingredients for a Korean rice bowl together. This had been one of Nona's favorite easy meals when she'd been in high school. She'd met a woman at church who'd been born in Korea. Her family had moved to the area after retiring from the Air Force. She'd told Nona that she'd adjusted some of her family recipes to be more "American" for her kids to accept the flavors she loved. This recipe had been one of the compromises.

Angie had loved talking to Mrs. Terrel about her native food choices. Those Saturday afternoon cooking lessons had been the first time Angie had considered a career in food. That she could be more than just a home cook.

Ian came and put his arms around her. "You look lost in thought."

"Lost in memory, actually. Are the Terrels still members at the church?" Angie should have looked them up when she came back home.

"I don't think so. You could call Maggie. She has a church directory." He poured a cup of coffee. "I haven't heard that name."

"Mrs. Terrel and Nona were friends. She taught me to cook some Korean meals years ago." Angie wiped her hands on a towel and refilled her own coffee. "Their kids were older than me."

"Is this one of the recipes?" He picked up the worn card on which a much younger Angie had carefully scribed the ingredients and steps.

"I was in high school. Back before I knew I wanted to be a chef." She sat down at the table and took back the card. "Funny how life leads you down just the right path at times. You look back and all the steps were perfectly placed to get you where you need to be."

"I'll drink to that." Ian lifted his coffee cup in a salute. "I thought I'd run to town today for supplies. Do you need anything at the store? Maybe come with me and do a bit of investigating?"

"You're funny. You know I don't plan these things." She saw his grin. "Well, not all the time. Anyway, I just don't know where to go on either the kidnapping or finding a way to fight the soybean plant. And when I don't know what to do, I cook." She picked up the recipe card. "I need to call Nancy and check on her. I know Estebe was talking to her about moving into one of his rentals. I'd feel safer if she wasn't in the same house that was broken into."

"You should call Felicia. She'll know."

Angie grabbed her phone. "You're right. I can't believe I didn't ask her yesterday."

"You've been a little busy." Ian stood and grabbed his laptop from the desk. "I'm going into the living room to play World War Two Remix for a while. Let me know if you need me to go get anything."

Angie nodded, then focused on the call. "Felicia, I'm so glad you picked up. How's Nancy? Have you heard anything?"

She listened as Felicia spoke. Then she stood and walked into the living room. "We'll see you in a few minutes, then."

Ian looked up from his laptop. "I'm not playing a game, am I?"

"Felicia and Estebe are coming over. They have some news about Nancy and the ex-husband. Mostly on the ex-husband." She leaned against the door frame and watched him. "It looks like the Scooby-Doo gang is being called back into service."

"That almost got you killed last time, when we started investigating the local chefs." He closed his laptop and leaned back on the couch. "Are you sure you want to get involved again?"

"No, what almost got me killed was winning one of the flights at the competition. It could have been anyone, and the killer didn't know I was investigating anyway." She pointed to the kitchen. "I'm going to make this Korean rice bowl recipe for lunch. You want to come help me while we wait for the other two?"

"Why not? My mom always said those that don't work, don't eat." He set his laptop on top of the bookcase out of Dom's reach.

"I always liked 'many hands make light work.' Same philosophy, softer delivery." She took his arm as he walked past and they went into the kitchen.

Lunch was almost done when Felicia and Estebe arrived. Dom went around greeting the newcomers with a nudge of his head to remind them to give him a few pets while they got settled.

Estebe took in a big whiff of air. "The food smells enticing. What are you making?"

"Just something I learned in high school. Go get washed up, and you two can set the table," Angie directed as Felicia came by to give her a quick hug. "Good to see you. I feel like I've been locked up for days."

"What are you talking about? I saw you in town yesterday." Felicia laughed.

Ian nodded to Estebe as they walked to the mudroom to wash their hands. "She wasn't supposed to be in town. She was supposed to be home, where she'd stay safe."

Estebe came back into the room, drying his hands. "And you expect Angie to listen when you tell her to sit? She is not a trained dog. No offense to Dom."

"Or me, I hope." Angie dished up the meat mixture on the rice Ian had just put into four bowls. Then she sprinkled each one with toppings. "All we'll need at the table are drinks and either a fork or chopsticks. I have both in the silverware drawer."

"I'll get both," Felicia volunteered. And for a few moments, everyone was busy getting the food delivered to the table. After they sat, Ian gave a short blessing.

"What do you have to share?" Angie asked.

Felicia pointed to Estebe with her chopsticks. "You go first."

"Nancy and her children are safely moved into one of my rentals. I matched the rent she had been paying, and she has a larger house with an actual back yard the kids can play in. I think their schools will change, but Nancy might wait until summer to do that." He took a bite of the dish. "This is full of flavor. Your high school self was a good cook, as well."

"Thank you." Angie beamed. "And thank you for what you did for Nancy. I think a lot of us are going to sleep better now."

"Her ex-husband is persistent, but this place has good locks and security." He smiled at Felicia. "Nancy is family. She should not be scared all the time."

"I did some digging on Charles Gowan," he went on. "His company is listed as the main contractor for the soybean plant designs according to the filings they just completed over at the courthouse. There is going to be a land rezoning hearing next month. We need to go and protest this. And have a lot of support or you're going to be zoned out of your Nona's house."

"On my list, but I'm not sure the company is playing fair with us. Jon seemed to think that the main contractor had some issues with prior developments and playing on the up-and-up." Angie took a bite as she considered the information. "Would that be on record? I mean, what the last project was the company worked on?"

"Somewhere." Estebe nodded. "I can ask my real estate attorney to do some digging."

"Won't they charge you?" Angie asked. She knew Estebe had probably already paid for Nancy's move and taken a big discount on the rent for the new house. He didn't need to be going further into the red for this wild goose chase.

"He owes me some time. It won't cost me anything, so don't get that look on your face." Estebe pointed to Angie with his fork. "I do what I want, I'm not being coerced into anything. I am a grown man and make my own decisions."

Angie laughed and held up a hand. "Okay, sue me for worrying about your over-the-top generosity. I'd appreciate you looking into this company. Maybe we can get rid of Nancy's problem as well as mine in one swoop."

Felicia held up her chopsticks. "I did my own research on Charles Gowan. He's a cad. He's been in six relationships in the last two years. And at least three had an engagement announcement in the local Napa Valley paper. From what Nancy said about their divorce timeline, one was three months before the divorce was final. I guess he was getting ready for the next Mrs. Gowen before the divorce was final. And there's rumors about his company and some financial issues. From what I heard from my friends who work in construction in the area, he's seen as a wild card. You don't hire him unless you need something done cheap and fast. He cuts corners."

"Jon said that his company gets rid of troublemakers. As in, they aren't around to be a problem anymore." Angie didn't look up as she spoke, instead focusing on moving around the rice in her bowl. "Did your contacts tell you any rumors about that?"

Chapter 14

After Angie's pronouncement, everyone kicked into high gear. By the time they finished lunch, they had a list of people to visit that afternoon. Felicia had brought her notes on the woman that Susan had mentioned in her diary. There were two that the group decided needed to be talked to about where Susan might have gone. It was agreed that Estebe and Felicia would delve into Gowan's company. Ian and Angie would talk to Susan's friends.

Ian finished making notes and looked up at the other three. "We need to keep Angie safe. If he's thinking about speeding up the process by eliminating her opposition for the project, he'll hit either her or the property. I'm going to ask Uncle Allen to have a deputy parked here to watch both Angie's and Mrs. Potter's place."

"That's overkill, don't you think?" Angie protested but no one laughed with her. The seriousness of the situation hit her like a punch in the gut. "You think he might do something to the house?"

"I've been looking into the past projects he was part of." Felicia pointed to the laptop screen. "Houses have burned down and made room for his projects before. Let's just take this seriously for a while. The worst that could happen if we're wrong is Sheriff Brown's personnel costs increase."

"I don't want to leave Dom here if there's even a chance. He might not be able to get out his dog door if something happened." Angie glanced over at Dom, who, instead of sleeping, was watching her intently. She knew he could feel the tension in her words.

"We'll bring him to the restaurant, and he can hang in the banquet room with Nancy's kids. I think she's bringing them along, just to be safe." Felicia shot Dom a big smile. "Who wants to go and play with some kids?"

Dom's tail thumped on the floor.

The group around the table laughed. "At least someone's good with the plan." Ian picked up his phone. "Let me call Uncle Allen and get him on board."

"We'll clean up the kitchen." Estebe nodded to Felicia. "The recipe is good. I would think this would be a good recipe for your cookbook. As long as the prep isn't too intensive, I could see many people making this for a weekday dinner."

Angie relaxed in her chair. The team—no, the family—she'd surrounded herself with made things easier to bear. Even when they were hard and scary. She smiled as she stood and took in the people she'd come to love in the last few years. "I'm going upstairs and getting ready for service tonight since we probably won't have time to come back here."

"You've got about fifteen minutes before we'll be ready here." Felicia picked up a bowl off the table. "Then we'll head into Boise to see what we can find. Should we plan on meeting at the County Seat at four?"

"I will call Nancy and have her start prep at three without me." Estebe pulled out his phone. "But we should try to be in the kitchen at four. Let's move it up to three thirty at the latest?"

"Sounds good. If we need to push off an interview or a stop until tomorrow, we'll have to do it. Service prep is important." Angie nodded.

"Saving the world has to be done in between everyday things." Estebe grinned. "Just like those superheroes in the movies. Peter still has to go to school and fight villains."

"I still think the Scooby-Doo reference describes us better," Angie added. "Besides, we're not saving the world here."

"Just maybe a life or two," Felicia added. The three of them went somber with the implications of that sentence.

"Uncle Allen says he'll send a car over now." Ian walked back into the room, tucking his phone in his pocket. He glanced around, feeling the tension. "What happened when I was gone?"

"Estebe tried to up our stakes to world saving." Angie smiled sadly. "But we're still just trying to keep River Vista clean."

"You guys and your pop culture references are going to freak you all out. Let's just say we're talking to some people and trying to figure out a puzzle. That way, life and death is off the table, at least until we have something to worry about." Ian moved beside Angie and gave her a hug. "Besides, Scooby-Doo never worried about saving the world."

"No, he was too busy hiding from ghosts, if I remember right." Angie let her head lean into Ian's comfort. Then she glanced at the clock. "I need to get ready. Ian, can you check on Precious and Mabel and maybe pack Dom's travel bag? He'll need food if he's staying with us during service."

As she ran up the stairs, she smiled at the way Ian always made everything just a little better. He added a touch of calm to the mix. When she got back downstairs, the kitchen was empty except for Dom. She grabbed his travel bag and stuffed a container of food, a water bottle for the road, and a few of his favorite toys. It was just like having a kid and getting them ready for a road trip.

Ian came in the back door, rubbing his hands. "It's cold out there. Estebe and Felicia took off for Boise to check on the filings at the courthouse first. They're hoping that leads them to the next stop."

"I'm ready to go talk to Susan's friends." Angie picked up the paper where Felicia had left the names and addresses. "I guess we try them at home first. I wouldn't have guessed that so many of these wives stayed at home. I mean, it's not the fifties."

"Maybe they like being homemakers. If I made more money, I'd like my wife to at least have the option. Think of all the things you could do?" He clicked on Dom's lead and took the backpack from her. "You ready?"

Almost as an afterthought, she grabbed both Susan's and her mom's diary and tucked them into her tote. Maybe there would be another clue she'd missed. "I'm ready."

She locked the door and hurried after Ian and Dom to try to figure out this puzzle. She shivered in the cold and for the first time, hoped that Susan was inside, warm and dry. If she was out in this cold for long, they would be looking for a body soon.

Angie recognized the first woman when she opened her front door. Tori Andrews attended several of the cooking classes at the County Seat. Angie stepped forward, her hand stretched outward to shake. "Mrs. Andrews, I'm Angie Turner and this is Ian McNeal. We're helping out with the search for Susan Ansley. Do you mind if we ask you a few questions about Mrs. Ansley?"

"Oh my, of course, come on in. We can talk in the kitchen. I always find it cozier than the formal living room. I'm not sure why we even have one since we don't do much entertaining. Mostly for family, you know." She held the door open for Angie and Ian to step through. "May I take your coats? I guess there is one good thing about having a formal living room, we can just set the coats there. Oh dear, am I chatting too much? My husband says I talk too fast when I'm nervous. I guess I could never rob a bank or anything, because I'd just keep talking and the police would find me right there."

Angie took off her coat and glanced around the ornate foyer. "We'd make a good pair. My go-to defense is not to say anything when I'm nervous. You have a lovely home."

"Well, thank you. Of course, it's mostly the decorator. He's a magician, you know. I mean, he really does card tricks at children's parties. I can't remember what his stage name is, but if you want a referral, I'll be glad to send him your name." She waved them farther inside the house.

Angie caught Ian's look of pure fear and almost laughed. The man didn't do well when people were discussing home decorating or other home art projects. "Mrs. Andrews, I'm afraid we don't have a lot of time, I have to open the restaurant soon."

"Well, of course, please follow me to the kitchen and I'll get you some coffee to warm up while we chat. And call me Tori. Mrs. Andrews is Tom's mother." She laughed at her own joke and hurried to the kitchen.

The room was decorated in a country theme, warm and cozy. Angie could tell the family spent a lot of time in the room. Children's books lay on the counters and graded schoolwork covered the fridge. Angie picked up a book, moving it to a pile on the island, where Tori motioned them to sit. "How many children do you have?"

"Just two, but they both love books. I think I've got a budding author in one. The other seems more like a lawyer. She fights me on every command and brings up examples of where her brother was treated differently. It's like a courtroom drama to get the dishes put in the dishwasher."

This time the woman's laugh was more natural and her speech had slowed. She set cups of steaming coffee in front of them. "I have croissants, too, if you're hungry. They're from the bakery in River Vista. I adore that place."

"I love Annie's." Ian sipped his coffee. "I've been spending my morning break over there with a few of the farmers who come into town for coffee."

"I've seen the old men crowded around the table in the back. It's cute seeing them in their overalls and farm coats drinking coffee and eating cupcakes." Tori giggled. "So it's a yes on the croissants?"

"Sadly, it's a no. Like Angie said, we're on a tight timeframe." He put his cup down. "We just have a few questions about Susan."

"Susan was a lovely girl. She came over a lot in the mornings. We'd talk about the kids, the houses, our husbands, and of course, the yoga group. Those girls give you a lot of conversation fodder. She and Jon so wanted a family, but they weren't having any luck. And when he—" Tori paused, and Angie could see the internal war going on inside on how much to say.

"We're not here for gossip, but if you know something that could help us find her..." Angie said softly.

"Jon had an affair. Susan never knew who, but she found texts from a woman on his phone. She even called the number and was going to confront her, but all she got was a voice mail. She was devastated." Tori tore off a small bit of croissant she'd gotten out of the package and took a bite.

"Did she confront him?" Angie asked.

"Yes, and he confessed. He said it was one time. He'd made a horrible mistake, but the woman wouldn't stop texting. That she'd threatened to tell Susan. He was relieved it had come out and he didn't have to lie anymore." Tori pushed the baked good aside. "I know he felt bad because he looked like hell the next week when we got together for a charity event just before school started."

"Did she forgive him?" Angie kept her questions short. This was Tori Andrews's story to tell.

"She said she did. But then she stopped coming over for coffee. The only time I'd see her was during yoga or in the planning meetings for the Cotillion." She sighed. "The event is this weekend, and it's not fair that Susan won't be there. Especially with all the work she did."

"When was the last time you saw her?" Ian picked up the questions.

"Let's see. It was just after Thanksgiving, so the first of December. The next planning meeting was a week away and she didn't attend. I called Jon that evening and he said she'd gone to her mother's house for the holidays. That she'd be back soon." Tori shook her head. "Then a couple of weeks ago, I read in the paper that she's missing? I went over to talk to Jon, but he was drunk and didn't make any sense. He said she just left. She wouldn't do that. Not with the event this weekend. She might have kicked his butt out of the house, but she wouldn't disappear. No way."

When Angie and Ian got into the SUV, Angie made some notes in a small notebook she'd brought. "When I met Jon last fall, he said his wife was dead. And that was why he was walking Timber. That must have been a total lie. Tori says she went missing the first of December."

"I wonder what date Uncle Allen has. That's a big span of time. But you're right, he might have lied to you to get your guard down. Never trust a random hiker at Celebration Park."

"You just don't like me walking there alone. But you don't get it." She reached back and rubbed Dom's head. "I'm never alone when Dom's with me."

"I think Dom sometimes lets his love of food distract him from sizing people up." Ian started up the car. "Where to next?"

Chapter 15

Angie read off the next address. "It's just a few blocks from here. And the Ansleys' house is just down that cul-de-sac. They're all together in this neighborhood. I guess they have more in common than just the yoga class."

"This is probably the nicest subdivision in River Vista. It's not surprising that a lot of professionals from Boise chose to live here." He glanced toward Boise and the foothills. "Before too long, this will all be one big town and River Vista will just be a suburb. I can't believe how much the area has grown since I've moved here."

"You should have seen it when I was going to school. You'd drive for miles before you'd even see a store between here and Meridian." Angie watched as they drove past the large houses with small yards. She pointed to a fake Tudor on the right. "There's the last one. Once we're done with this, I need to head to the restaurant."

"Do you think we've gathered any clues?" Ian parked the car on the street in front of the target house.

"We know Jon was having an affair." Angie rubbed Dom's head. "You have to stay here, boy. We'll head to work soon, and you can visit your favorite tree."

"He's going to kill that tree, you know." Ian stopped the engine and climbed out of the car. "And we know that Susan thought Jon was having an affair."

"No, that's not right. He confessed, remember? It was just a onetime thing according to him, but she wouldn't leave it alone. You don't think the woman went crazy and took Susan so she could be with Jon?" Angie studied the house.

"Then why hasn't she claimed her prize?" Ian shook his head. "No, something more than just an extramarital affair is going on here. Susan had to have found out something that someone needed to keep hidden. And the affair seems like it's common gossip now. Tori didn't blink an eye in telling you. She must have figured that if she didn't, someone else would."

They walked together to the front door, but before Angie could knock, it flew open. "There you two are. Tori told me you'd just left, so I expected you sooner. Come in, come in, we don't want to keep you from opening tonight. I do so love the County Seat. Marv and I eat there at least once a month. Okay, so maybe it's closer to once a week, but seriously, I don't like to cook and you're so close." A blond woman in a satin shirt and skintight jeans ushered them inside the foyer. "We can sit in the living room. Marv and I love having company over. He's a lawyer, but not in the same firm as Jon. Please have a seat. Can I get you some coffee or refreshments?"

"No, we're good. And as you already know, we're on a deadline. We're talking to Susan's friends. I take it you were on the cotillion committee too?" Angie perched on the white couch and hoped Dom hadn't slobbered on her pants or something worse. She'd hate to leave a mark on the white-on-white living room.

"Yes, I love working the events. I tend to do all of them. Silly, I know. I should leave some fun for the rest of the group, but at least I'm hitting my volunteer goals every year. I don't think Holly's hit any of the goals since she joined our sorority." A flash of anger hit the woman's eyes.

"Really. Holly isn't much of a team player, huh?" Ian asked, casually.

"I shouldn't speak ill of her. Apparently, she's just busy keeping her husband's business busy. I told Marv that Michelle Henricks is not his personal PR person."

"Who's Michelle?" Ian looked at the woman, confusion in his eyes.

She laughed, the sound throaty, like she was dressed in silken bedclothes. "I guess I thought you knew who you were interviewing. I'm Michelle Hendricks."

"He drove me here," Angie added, like that explained everything. "Anyway, Michelle, tell me about the last time you saw Susan."

By the time they'd gotten back to the car, Angie had a headache. Michelle had listed out each and every member of the yoga group, their families, and how they were tied to each other. Apparently, a lot of the men worked at the same place. The woman, none of them worked. They were officially housewives, but as Michelle had said, no one used that term anymore. Angie wondered whether any of these women would try to help at all if something happened to one of them. But of course, she already knew that answer. Susan had disappeared in broad daylight, and all they were worried about was whether the cotillion would go on with all this bad publicity. "She was more worried about this stupid dance than what happened to Susan."

"Seemed that way." Ian had turned the heat on full-blast, but he and Angie seemed to be the only ones who were cold. Dom slept soundly in the back seat. He hadn't even woken when they got inside the car. "Let's get you to the restaurant before you decide that going back and yelling at Michelle about her lack of empathy is a great idea."

Angie glanced back at the house as Ian did a U-turn in the street. "I wouldn't have yelled. Much."

"Okay then, besides what we think of Michelle, did we learn anything?" Ian kept his face turned toward the road.

"That she loves my restaurant?" Angie tried to think through the conversation. Except where Tori had been warm and fun to talk to, Michelle was all about Michelle.

"Yes, and they eat there a lot. But I was thinking: if Michelle loves doing the events, why was Susan even on the committee? I think Michelle could host a week at a summer lodge all by herself. Why did Susan ask to be on the committee?"

Angie shook her head. "You're thinking she's trying to figure out the other woman?"

"That's exactly what I'm thinking. Susan didn't want to be a party planner, she wanted to figure out what woman had the gall to burn a friend so completely by sleeping with her husband."

"How many people were on that committee?" Angie picked up her phone and dialed, putting it on speaker for Ian to hear.

"What are you doing?"

"I'm calling someone who speaks the language of the rich and famous. Felicia." Angie listened to the rings. Finally, she answered.

"Hey, Felicia, can you talk?"

"I just stepped out of the second law office." Felicia's voice was muted. "Did you find anything?"

"I was going to ask you the same question." Angie shrugged as she made eye contact with Ian.

"Shoot. I was hoping we could stop looking over our shoulder sometime this decade." She paused a second. "Looks like Estebe's coming out of the office now. We'll be heading back to River Vista. Maybe we can meet in the office for a few minutes to update everyone?"

"Sounds like a plan. We're on our way there. But I had a question. How many people are on event planning committees for these sorority things?"

"No more than three, four tops. Usually you're lucky if you're not working the event yourself. Everyone in that group is so busy doing nothing. I swear. Why?"

"The cotillion had four people. Holly, Tori, Michelle, and Susan. Well, five with them asking you to step into Susan's spot. Is it that much bigger of an event?"

The other side of the line went dead for a second, and Angie thought they'd lost the connection. "No, and I wasn't really needed when I did step in. I thought it was weird that Holly asked me to join, but I thought maybe Susan had been doing the work and the rest were just skating."

"You're saying they didn't need you?" Angie felt the lines furrowing on her face. This didn't make sense at all.

"No. I checked on the caterers and the event space, but that was two calls anyone could make. Why would Holly ask me to join if they didn't need me?"

"I don't know." Angie looked up and realized they were parking behind the County Seat. "I'm at the restaurant. I'll chat with you soon."

Ian stepped out of the car and grabbed Dom's lead. "I'll walk him for a bit, then get him settled in your office until Nancy and the kids get here."

"Thanks." Angie already had her keys out to unlock the back door. "People are going to start showing up soon, and I need to get the lights on and the doors unlocked."

She unlocked the restaurant doors and started flipping on lights as she walked through the building. The restaurant had become a second home for her. Somewhere she'd felt safe. Where she could invite others to join her for a chat. Maybe she was hanging on to the farmhouse too tightly. Maybe she could love another house just as much. But then she saw a picture of Precious and Mabel in the barn on a spring morning sitting on her desk. She'd caught the moment just before either of them had noticed her entrance and they were both sleeping.

It wasn't just her home. It was Nona's legacy. It was home to the zoo. And she was going to fight for it. Even if that meant putting her life in danger.

"Ms. Turner?" a young male voice asked from the doorway. She turned and saw one of Felicia's servers, a newer hire, Hank, she thought she remembered his name.

"Hello, Felicia is running a little late. Can you tell the other servers to start getting the dining room ready?" She smiled at the clearly nervous young man.

"Me?" His voice squeaked. "I've only been here a few weeks. They won't listen to me."

Angie laughed. "Yes, they will. Tell them that you talked to me and what I said. Everything's going to be fine. Leadership is earned one action at a time."

Hank looked sick, but he nodded. "Okay. I can do this."

Angie figured he was talking to himself, but she added on to the positive reinforcement. "Of course, you can. They were in your spot once too. The new guy, I mean."

She watched him leave, and then Ian came in with Dom. "Looks like Felicia's servers are all here. They're standing around talking in the dining room. Do you need to go give them directions?"

"Hank's going to do it." Angie motioned to Dom, and as soon as Ian took him off the lead, the dog went right to his bed, where he had a chewy toy waiting. "Good boy."

"He was a good boy. He did his business, and we came right back inside. I can't believe he gets cold with that coat, but he didn't want to spend any more time outside than I did." Ian glanced back out to the dining room. "Your boy, Hank, didn't seem too confident going out to deliver your message. Are you sure you don't want to supervise his delivery?"

"He'll be fine. Everyone has to step up one time or another. This is just his first time to assert his voice here. From what I remember when Felicia hired him, he's going to school for business or something. He's going to have to find his voice sooner or later."

"Trial by fire around here." Ian took a seat. "Can I make you a coffee? I'm getting me one. I'm chilled to the bone."

"Yes." Angie flipped through the online reservation system and matched it up with the book they kept on the hostess stand. "We're doing great for a Wednesday. And if we get some last-minute reservations or walk-ins, we'll be almost at full capacity."

Ian came back into the office with two cups he'd made from the pantry area where Angie had installed a Keurig for the staff. "Were you talking to Dom, or do I need to know what you just said?"

"No. Just talking to myself." She checked the phone messages and added a reservation from that. Then she made notes of the number of covers they'd have and at what time for the kitchen. Estebe liked to be prepared, especially if there was one busier time over another. She grabbed the sheet of paper and took a sip of the coffee. "Let me go post the dinner numbers, and I'll be right back. I need to review last week's financials for our accountant before I get dragged into the kitchen to cook."

Ian pulled a book out of his backpack. "Don't worry about me. I'm going to read for a bit, then run to the store for some groceries. Yes, I grabbed your list." He grinned at her. "Then I'll put them into your walk-in until we're ready to leave. Keep your staff out of my six-pack."

"If I thought you were buying a six-pack, I'd tell them." She paused at the door. "I'm kind of liking this arrangement we've got going right now."

He nodded. "Me too. My recliner at the apartment is more comfortable than this chair, but I want to hang with Dom for a while. And you know my landlady doesn't like pets in the apartment."

"You're sweet." She nodded. "Be right back."

She had just finished posting the numbers on a whiteboard at the back of the kitchen where Estebe could see it while he cooked when she heard the back door open. "Okay, who's here early? Are you here to work, or do you need a quick meal before we start cooking?"

When no one answered, she turned toward the back door to see a woman standing there, her eyes wide, taking in the kitchen. Angie stepped toward her. "I'm sorry, we're not open yet. If you want to call and see if you can get a seating tonight, I can give you the phone number."

"Is Nancy Gowan here?" the woman asked in a quiet tone.

Angie peered closer at the woman. "Sorry, we don't take visitors here in the kitchen. Again, if you want to make a reservation…"

The woman shook her head, interrupting Angie's words. "I need to talk to Nancy."

Then it hit Angie. This was the woman who had been with Charles Gowan. "You're Charles's wife. You need to leave here now. I'm not letting you even near Nancy, not after what he's done to her."

"You don't understand." The woman paused, reaching inside her tote bag.

A man's voice came from the door. Angie looked up and saw Estebe. "No, you don't understand. You need to leave here, now. If you want to talk to Nancy, you'll need to call and leave her a message."

Angie saw the woman calculating, then she apparently determined she couldn't take on both of them, and her hand came out of her tote empty. Angie wondered if there was a gun in there and if Estebe had just saved her life. She stepped toward the wall phone and picked up the receiver. "Leave now or I'll call the cops."

The woman scurried past Estebe, and he followed her outside. When he came back into the kitchen, she sank onto a stool, letting the phone dangle from its receiver. He came over and hung the receiver up on the charging station. "Are you okay?"

"I'm fine. Just thankful we never removed the kitchen phone." She stared at the door. "She's the new wife and was here to see Nancy."

"I think she was here to do more than see Nancy. Did you see her hand in the tote?"

Angie nodded. "I got that feeling too. Thanks for coming in when you did."

"Not a problem." He glanced at the door. "Since everyone typically comes in the back door, I need to make a sign telling them to come in the front. I'll have one of Felicia's staff serve as doorman until we open."

"I need to call Allen. He needs to know that the woman is making threats." She followed Estebe out of the kitchen and into the office.

"I was just about to come looking for you." Ian looked up from his book, then set it down when he saw Angie's face. "What happened?"

Estebe pointed to the desk chair. "Ian will call the police, but you need to sit down. You're shaking."

"What happened?" Ian demanded again, his gaze going from Estebe to Angie.

"Charles's wife came in the kitchen door to 'see' Nancy. I think she had a gun and she was going to shoot her, but I can't be certain. Estebe came in, and she decided she couldn't fight all of us so she left. We've locked the back door, so Estebe is going to put up a sign for the staff to use the front and assign someone to help let people in. And I'm calling the police." She stared at the phone, then at Ian. "Sorry, it's kind of a blur."

"Drink your coffee. I think you're going into shock. I'll call Uncle Allen and get him over here." Ian moved her cup closer. "I just let you out of my sight for a few minutes. When am I going to learn?"

"Not my fault people are inconsiderate and trying to attack my staff in my kitchen." Angie sipped the now-warm coffee. She wondered if she should get up and put the coffee in the microwave, but sometime during the discussion, Dom had woken and felt the tension. Right now, his head was on her lap and he wasn't going to let her go anytime soon. Not even just to the kitchen.

Ian pulled out his phone and dialed a number. When it was answered, he stepped into the hallway to talk to his uncle.

Estebe made a sign and took some tape. Then he disappeared out of the office.

Angie was almost alone right then. Or at least alone from human companionship. Dom was staring at her with large eyes. She stroked his back. "Don't worry, dude, I'm fine. A little shook up, but fine."

Felicia came running in the office with Estebe a few steps behind. "Are you all right?"

"As I just told Dom, I'm great. Relax. At least we know that Nancy's ex and his wife are behind the break-in. No way could that be a coincidence now." Angie took a sip of the coffee, then left her fingers wrapped around the warm cup. This was good. Calming. Maybe she could bottle this feeling.

"Angie?"

She opened her eyes and found everyone staring at her. "What?"

"We called your name several times. You weren't responding. Should we take you to the hospital?" Ian knelt beside her, his warm hands holding hers.

She looked down at him. When had she released the coffee cup? She took a deep breath. Then another. Blinking her eyes, she released Ian's hands and rubbed her face. "I'm fine. I guess I was a little more shaken up than I thought."

"I can handle service if you need to go home." Estebe studied her, his brown eyes filled with concern.

"No. I'm good. Maybe I should eat something, though. Get my blood sugar up?" She shook her head a little. "I don't feel bad. Maybe a little dizzy."

"Maybe you're pregnant?" Felicia asked, an evil grin on her face.

"Shut your mouth. That's not what this is." Angie looked up and saw Estebe come back into the room with a plate. "Food, that's what I need."

Ian pulled up a chair next to her. "I'll hang around, just in case."

Chapter 16

Angie had to talk to Sheriff Brown, and by that time, service had already started. She tried to start expediting, but Estebe shook his head. "Go home. We have it for tonight."

"You're going to be on your own on Saturday when Felicia and I both go to this cotillion thing. Maybe you're the one who should go home." She picked up a towel and wiped off a plate before setting it on the server's tray.

"I will be fine. You, on the other hand, look like you should be a ghost. Your color is bad. If you're staying, I'm feeding you again before you work." He studied her. "And you might as well bring Ian into the kitchen, as well. That way we know both of you have had a good meal."

"You know you're not the boss of me." Angie tried to straighten her shoulders, but Estebe was right. She was wiped out. She held a hand up to stop the words she knew were coming her way. "Fine, feed me, Seymour."

"I do not understand. What is a Seymour?" Estebe glanced over at Nancy, who started laughing. "Why are you laughing? Do you need to sit down, as well?"

"You'll never get the pop culture references, so it's really not even fun to tease you." Matt carried over a pot to the sink. "But Nancy, he's right. Are you okay?"

"I'm mad as hell." Nancy shook a pan on the stove.

From Estebe's look, Angie figured it was a little harder than necessary. She ignored the pan. "I didn't ask how you are. I'm so sorry. I know this isn't about me."

"No, you were the one who had to deal with that woman. It is about you. I'm just mad that I never figured what a jerk Charles was before it was too late. Before I was tied to him with three kids. Before he got me so far in debt that I've had to work three jobs to dig out. I was stupid for way too long." Nancy set the pan with the fish up in the warmer area. "Trout's ready. And I'm mad he brought this crap here, to my new home. To my new family."

"Family is family," Estebe said as he focused on plating the fish. "You are not the problem here. He is. Do you like the new house?"

"It's lovely, and we'll be out as soon as I know he's left town again." Nancy glanced at the next ticket. "Scallops going down."

"Heard," Matt responded.

"Do you not like the house?" Estebe passed the plate to the server. "I have others if you are not comfortable there."

"It's lovely, but I know you're cutting the rent for us. You deserve to have a renter who can pay full price for the home." She smiled at him. "I'm starting the strip for the next ticket."

"Heard," Matt responded again.

"You should have a house you love. I will find another one for you." Estebe set a plate on the warming station for the servers.

"I love the house," Nancy said, "but…"

"There is no 'but.' Having a tenant who loves a house means you will take care of it, not like those college students who just want somewhere to party. You can stay there as long as you want." He put his hand on the warmer shelf. "Nancy, we are family."

"Listen to the man," Angie said. "He seems to want to take care of all of us, so if he's focused on you, he's leaving me alone."

"Hey, now." Estebe turned from Nancy to Angie. "Go get Ian, and I will get your dinner ready. Then if you feel stronger after eating, you can cook."

"I'm glad I have your permission." Angie hurried out of the kitchen before Estebe could answer back or throw something at her. Ian was at the bar drinking what she assumed was a soda and talking on his phone. She went up and waited for him to finish the call.

"It's Uncle Allen. They haven't found her yet." He covered the mouthpiece of the phone. "Do you need something?"

"Estebe has told me to get you for dinner. He's feeding us at the chef table before he'll let me back on the line." She sank onto a stool next to him.

"You are the boss here, remember?" His eyes twinkled with humor.

Angie scanned the almost-full dining room. "Tell him that. Anyway, I'll meet you in there. I'm going to go check on Dom."

He nodded, then went back to his phone call.

Scanning the room, she moved toward the back and her dog. She just needed a check-in to get herself calmed down. Dom was good at telling her everything was okay in the world. She walked into the room, and the three children were lying in the front watching what appeared to be *Cinderella* on the screen. Dom lay with the children, three heads using him as a pillow.

He looked up and saw Angie, a doggie grin filling his face, but the only thing that moved on him was his tail. The oldest child looked back at Angie, a question on her face.

"Don't get up, I was just checking on Dom. If he needs to go out, come get me, I don't want you going outside with him."

The girl called back, "We know. Mom already told us we can't leave the building."

"Okay then." She paused a minute taking in the sight. Dom had already laid his head back down, and if she didn't know better, she'd swear he was watching the movie with the kids. She turned back to the kitchen and left the impromptu party alone.

Ian was already in the kitchen sitting at the table when she arrived. He took her hand. "Dom okay?"

"He's in kid heaven. I told them not to take him outside. That they should come in and let one of us know if he needs to go out." She sank into the bench seat.

"I'll take him out right after dinner." He kissed her head. "You should have taken Estebe up on his offer. You look beat."

"I am. After playing sleuth all morning, this happens, I'm not sure I can take another surprise." She leaned into him, and for a moment, things were good. Solid.

Estebe set soup bowls in front of them. "Potato soup to start your meal. You need the substance. You look tired."

"You gave me a sandwich in the office." Angie sat up and grabbed her spoon. "Why does everyone keep telling me I look tired."

Felicia came into the kitchen and sat at the table. "I'll take a bowl too, sweetie. So tell me what happened in your check-ins? They had to be better than mine. No one wanted to talk about this new developer. No rumors, no discussion, nothing."

"That's odd." Ian set his spoon down. "Nothing?"

"Nothing they would tell me." Estebe set a bowl of soup in front of Felicia. "I even told them I would be interested in putting some money into the development, but everyone told me the funding was already in place. Usually with such a big development, they are always looking for additional capital, even if it's just short term. This development, according to everyone I spoke with, is fully funded."

Angie sighed, running the spoon through her soup. "There goes next year's garden plans."

"Just because they have funding doesn't mean there aren't problems with the permits and land acquisitions. You need to have faith. Tomorrow before I come in, I will talk to my friend on the county land board. Maybe there is a way to block their petition. Is the land historic in some way?" Felicia asked.

"Not that I know of. Mrs. Potter's house was built for her when she got married. Nona took over the house from her mother, who moved into town when Nona married my grandfather. I'm not sure how far back the farm has been in our family." Angie scraped the last bit of soup out of the bowl with a piece of bread. "Can I have another one of these? I didn't realize how hungry I was."

"Your color is better too," Ian commented. "Food is your fuel. In more ways than one."

"I do love food." Angie watched as the kitchen door swung open. It was Nancy's youngest girl. She glanced around the room, looking for her mother.

"Celena, what are you doing in here? You need to go back and watch the movie with your sister and brother." Nancy nodded to the stove and Matt stepped up and took her place. She walked around and knelt down in front of her child.

"I told Elna I had to go to the bathroom. I wanted to ask you when we're going to California, Mommy. I want to see the sea lions." Celena had a teddy bear she held tight to her side.

"What do you mean? We're not going to California. We're going to Wyoming over spring break to see your grandparents, remember?"

"I know that, but Daddy said we were going to California when he called. He told me to get packed." She looked tired. "We packed everything to move into the new house, but then you unpacked my clothes. Maybe I should pack again for California?"

Nancy picked her up and gave her a hug. "When did you talk to your daddy?"

Angie could see the fear on Nancy's face, but she was keeping her cool around the kid, she had to give her that.

"Last week. He called and said he loved me and we were going on a trip soon." She laid her head on her mother's shoulder. "I'm tired, Mommy. Can you take me back to the room so I can sleep with Dom?"

"Yes, sweetheart." Nancy shot Estebe a look. "I'll be right back."

"The back doors are all locked, and the only way you can get to the banquet room is through the dining room. I'll alert the staff to make sure no one goes back there." Felicia stood and followed Nancy out.

"Out of the mouths of babes." Ian picked up his phone and stepped away from the table. "I'm calling my uncle. Maybe he has some advice for Nancy on getting a restraining order."

Angie finished her soup. Then she took her bowl to the dishwashing station. "Let's get service done. I think we've got a few things to discuss afterward. Number one being how we can make sure that Nancy and her kids are safe."

* * * *

By the time Ian, Angie, and Dom got back home, they'd made a plan on how they could get through service for the next week without Nancy. Estebe had set them up in a house in a gated community, so even if her ex could find them, he couldn't get inside the community without an invitation.

Ian shut off the engine and opened the door. "Let me get Dom out, and I'll do a sweep of the house. Keep the car locked to humor me, okay?"

"If I sit here long, I'm going to fall asleep. No one's waiting inside to hurt me. One, they wouldn't know that I took Dom with us, so they'd have to deal with him."

"Just humor me, okay?" He nodded to her purse. "And get your phone out just in case I'm not back in five minutes or someone besides me comes out of that kitchen door. Maybe we should move the car back a bit so he can't see you."

"Again, there is no 'him.' No one's in my house." Angie got her phone out and held it up. "Okay?"

"I'll be right back, and you can tell me I told you so." He leaned in and kissed her. Then he closed the driver's-side door and opened Dom's, grabbing the leash they'd put on him when they left the restaurant. "Come on, boy, let's go save the day."

Angie laughed, but she locked the car doors when he pointed to the lock. "This is getting ridiculous. Nancy's scared to death to let her kids outside at the new place. I'm stuck in the car until Ian clears the house of murdering strangers. What is going on with our world?"

She saw a flash of light behind her, and she turned to find its source. A dark SUV drove slowly by, then turned into Mrs. Potter's driveway. She texted Erica. *Are you home?*

No, I'm in Boise. I'm spending the night with a friend. Why? The response came back quickly. Erica must have had her phone close by.

I'm calling the police. Someone just pulled into your driveway. Angie dialed 911 on her phone, still watching the car. Two large people got out. She couldn't tell if they were male or female from the distance.

"Nine-one-one, may I help you?" a friendly, but serious voice asked.

"This is Angie Turner. I live off of Southside near Celebration Park? My neighbor isn't home, and a car just pulled into her driveway."

"Are you sure it's not them?"

Angie could hear the tapping of keys. "Positive. I just talked to Erica Potter, she's Mrs. Potter's granddaughter and is staying in the house and going to school at Boise State. She's in Boise, not at home. Well, I didn't speak with her, I texted her."

"I've got a car on its way. Stay inside your house and don't go outside," the dispatcher advised.

"My boyfriend, Ian McNeal, he's the sheriff's nephew, he's checking my house for strangers. I'm sitting out in the car."

Angie heard the sigh before the woman responded. Then the tapping resumed. "Is there a reason you think strangers may be in your house?"

"It's been a crazy couple of weeks. There's this developer who wants to buy my farm, and I'm not wanting to sell."

"Wait, you're part of the soybean plant development? You know that project will bring in a lot of new jobs, right?"

"Again, I don't want to sell my house. Would you sell your house?"

The woman laughed. "You haven't seen the shack I live in. I'd sell it in a heartbeat. But we're getting off track here. Just go inside the house and stay there. I'll make sure the officers come over as soon as they secure Mrs. Potter's house."

Angie saw Ian waving at her. Apparently, the coast was clear. She slipped out of the car, quietly closing the door behind her, and ran for the kitchen door. She pushed past Ian and closed and locked the door. She pointed to the laundry room. "Make sure Dom's inside and close his dog door."

"Who are you talking to?" Ian pointed to the phone.

"The police dispatcher. She's sending a car." Angie shoved the phone into his hands. "Talk to her while I take care of Dom."

He stared at her but picked up the phone. "This is Ian McNeal, who am I talking to?"

Angie found Dom coming inside just as she entered the laundry room. She moved his tail, then closed the dog door with a snap. Then she checked the lock on the back door. Still engaged. She sighed and then moved to the unused front door and repeated the process.

By the time she got back to the kitchen, Ian was all caught up with the happenings over at the Potter house. He held up the phone. "Kylie's staying on the line, just in case. The car should be here in just a few minutes."

"They haven't left?" Angie's stomach tightened. If they were still there, they might be breaking into the house. She tried to think positive. *Breathe, just breathe.* She closed her eyes. Ian's jab with his elbow jolted her out of her meditation. "What?"

"They're here. The cops blocked the driveway so no one can take off." Ian pointed toward the street. "Maybe I should go help."

The phone squeaked, and Kylie's voice came out loud. "Don't leave the house. I'll let you know when the suspects are in custody. Ian, are you listening?"

Angie tried to hide the grin, but Ian looked like a little kid who'd been told he couldn't go play.

He put the phone on speaker. "I heard you."

A few minutes passed, but finally Kylie came back on the line. "They have one of the two suspects. One escaped down the road. Please stay inside. I've dispatched another car to help with the search."

"If they come on my property, I'm going to freak out. Especially if they go in the barn. What about Precious and Mabel? We should have brought them inside so they're safe." Angie stared out the other window, hoping her motion-sensor light wouldn't come on and tell her that the other guy was nearby.

"Who are Precious and Mabel? Are they neighbors?" Kylie asked. "Maybe I should send another car if there are more potential hostages."

"Precious is a goat, and Mabel is a hen," Ian explained calmly. "Angie's just very attached to her zoo."

"I totally understand. I have an outdoor cat that I worry about every night when I feed him. Of course, he won't come inside and just live with us. He's got to be free." Kylie paused. "Hold on a minute, I'm getting a report from the second car."

Chapter 17

Once the dispatcher had reported that the second man was in custody, Angie grabbed her coat and flashlight and ran outside to the barn. The door was shut tight, which gave her some relief. She flipped on the overhead lights as she stepped in. Mabel was on her usual roosting place and opened one eye at the light.

"Sorry to wake you," Angie muttered to the hen. She heard Ian's chuckle behind her, and she turned to glare at him. "What? It's rude to wake her up just because I was worried."

"Yet we're still here in the barn." Ian was holding his phone in one hand, just in case. She couldn't see if it was still connected to Kylie and River Vista Dispatch, but when he held it up, she knew they were. "Go check on Precious so we can get back in the house and let Kylie get back to saving River Vista from bad guys."

A snort came over the speaker. "You're the most excitement I've had in weeks."

Angie smiled and turned toward Precious's pen. The goat was awake and watching her. She reached down into the pen to rub behind Precious's ears. The satisfied bleat told Angie that the goat was just fine. She was about to leave, when she saw something in the straw in front of Precious's pen. She reached down to pick it up, then jerked her hand back like something had bit her.

"Ian, you have your phone, right?" She turned toward him.

He pointed to the phone in his hand. "Right here. We're using it, remember?"

"Then whose phone is this?" She pointed to the black case almost hidden in the straw. "My phone has that purple case you bought me a few months ago, and I'm pretty sure it's still on the kitchen counter where I left it."

Ian walked over and took a picture of the phone. Then he glanced at the display. "Hey, Kylie, can you get a text on that line? I've got something you need to see."

Kylie rattled off a phone number to send the picture to, then she came back on the line. "One of the officers will be over there soon. Are you safe if you stay in the barn until they get there? Is there a second door? Are you sure you're alone? Maybe you should wait in the house?"

"Only one open door, unless you count the one in Precious's pen. All the other pens have their outside doors locked up to keep at least some of the draft out. The big doors are closed tight, as well." Angie shined the flashlight around the barn. "I never replaced the loft ladder, so unless this guy can jump twelve-plus feet straight up, I think he's gone."

Angie heard the tire tracks on the dirt driveway.

Ian turned toward the door and updated Kylie. "Help has arrived."

By the time the officer had questioned them again, and his partner searched the barn and the house, it was almost one in the morning. The cell phone was in an evidence bag in the police car. Ian was talking to his uncle as Angie drank another cup of herbal tea, hoping she'd be able to sleep. He hung up and went to check the lock on the door again. He nodded to the window.

"They're waiting for another car to show up to take over the watch. Uncle Allen apologized for not getting the car out here sooner. He believes that someone came on your property this afternoon and at least accessed the barn."

Angie snorted. "Do you think?"

"Angie, don't be like that. Allen is doing the best he can with limited resources. He had a car assigned here starting tomorrow as soon as Tony got back from his honeymoon. And he had cars doing drive-bys every two hours. These guys just got lucky." He went to the stove and poured hot water over a tea bag in a cup. "The vandalism idea was only a theory until they actually showed up tonight."

"Maybe we should move Precious to the goat dairy for a few days. I hate to upset Mabel's routine by moving her. I'm not sure she'd take the change well. And the dairy is way too busy for her." Angie stared at the tea in her cup.

"Someone will be here twenty-four-seven until this is over." Ian covered her hand with his own. "They'll be safer just where they are."

"I know they're just animals, but I love them. And I'm their human. I'm supposed to feed and care for them and protect them." Tears filled her eyes.

"And you do." He squeezed her hand. "You have the most spoiled zoo animals in the area."

"And yet some stranger was by Precious's pen today." She shook her head. "I feel so violated. And nothing has even really happened."

"Then use that feeling to fuel this investigation. We're going to figure out what's happening here. And I'm not letting you lose your home. I promise you."

She stood and dumped the tea out into the sink. "I love you, but you shouldn't make promises that are out of your control. I'm going to bed. Tomorrow's a busy day, and since Nancy's not working, I'm going to have to be on the line and expediting."

"Everything's going to be fine," Ian repeated.

The problem was, Angie wasn't sure even he believed his words.

* * * *

Thursday morning, a layer of snow had fallen during the night. Not much but just enough to make the world look bright and shiny under the sun that now sparkled the white ground and warmed the earth. When Angie woke, Dom wasn't in her room and she smelled coffee downstairs. Coffee and something baking. She got up and hurried to get ready for the day. If she was right, Felicia and possibly Estebe were downstairs making breakfast.

She smiled at the thought. The world could be coming to an end, but at least they'd have one last good meal because she was surrounded by people who cooked when they were nervous and who also knew that food made everything just a little more bearable. Even if someone was sneaking around your property when you weren't there.

When she finally reached the kitchen after a hot shower, she found out her count had been off by one person. Sheriff Brown also sat at the table drinking coffee. Everyone looked up when Dom went running to her side to say good morning.

"Let me grab you a cup of coffee. Go ahead and sit down. Allen will catch you up." Ian stood and kissed her on the cheek before leading her to the table.

"Good morning, Angie." Sheriff Brown—no, Allen—nodded to her. "Sorry about yesterday. I guess our theory of the houses being targets was on point after all."

"At least nothing was damaged, and you have two suspects in custody." Felicia nodded. "Have you made them talk yet?"

"Felicia, it doesn't work quite like that. All they've said so far was their lawyer's name and phone number. Funny, it's the same firm that Jon Ansley worked for, but in the criminal division." Allen sipped his coffee. "But their rap sheets tell us a lot about them. Local thugs who are hired out to harass people. They've been in trouble all their lives. Mostly petty stuff. They're known for arson. This is the first possible case we can pin on them."

"What about the phone? Did it belong to them?" Angie sipped her coffee. Knowing that the men were in jail was making her feel a little better about the safety of her house and of Precious and Mabel. She was keeping Dom with her as much as possible until this was settled.

"That we don't know. It's a burner phone. The good thing is, it has a few numbers we've been able to connect to the law office. I'm heading over there to talk to one of the partners this morning. They've got a little bit of explaining to do on all of these connections." Allen frowned. "There's one other number that the owner called twice a day. The first time is at eight a.m. They talk for thirty minutes, then he calls back at six p.m. We found out that's a burner phone too. We think it's attached to one of these guys, or maybe their boss."

"Sounds like it's during business hours. Maybe they're calling a local business?" Estebe said.

"It's too routine. And it happens on weekends, as well. And what kind of business uses burner phones?" Allen took the last bite of waffle and dragged it through the pile of maple syrup on his plate. "It's got me stumped. And now, the phone won't answer. I better get back to the office. My deputy is calling exactly at eight to see if he can get someone to pick up. Maybe they don't know their friends are in custody."

Angie waited for Allen to leave, then she looked around the table. "Are you all here to talk about the investigation, or did you think I needed some hand holding? If it's the latter, you all can leave."

"Don't be snippy." Felicia put a plate with a waffle in front of Angie. She put whipped cream on top and sprinkled mini chocolate chips over the top of that. "The syrup is warm."

Angie's stomach growled as she took a breath and took in the sweet maple smell of her breakfast. "Sorry, I get grumpy when someone is threatening the homestead."

"You get grumpy when you're hungry and under a lot of stress," Felicia countered. "I can fix one of those things, but not the other. Estebe and

I wanted to talk about service tonight. Should we hire a temp to cover Nancy's station?"

Angie thought about the question as she took her first bite of the waffle. It was so, so good. She shook her head. "Nope. We've been overstaffed since Hope graduated. Move Matt up a spot into Nancy's space, and let Hope cook on the line instead of just doing prep and grunt work. It's time for her to try her wings."

"Are you sure? I was under my mentor for years before he allowed me on the line." Estebe put a plate of bacon with a single fried egg in front of her. Then he sat down with the notebook where he wrote down all the staffing for every service since they'd opened. "We could add a temp to the line without much trouble."

"We need to show Hope we trust her. This is her trial. Besides, I know she feels bad about Nancy's situation, let her contribute. However, with Felicia, me, and now Nancy, you are going to need a temp on Saturday when we go to the cotillion. Maybe I should stay back."

"If I have to go, you do too. Besides, it's a great place to mingle with the River Vista rich and famous." Felicia smiled, reminding Angie of the Cheshire cat. "I redid your business cards so you can hand them out during the event. I have to handle the door for the event, so it's up to you to do the networking stuff."

"Great, my favorite activity. Maybe I should stay back and let Estebe go instead," Angie grumbled as she finished enough of her waffle to be able to put the bacon and eggs on the waffle plate. Ian took the empty plate from her and put it in the sink.

"No way. I like Estebe fine as a friend, but I'm not dancing with the dude. The only reason I'm going is to spend at least a bit of time dancing with my favorite girl." Ian kissed her head as he moved to the door. "Don't start talking the case yet. I've got to feed the zoo."

"She won't listen until she's done eating anyway, you might as well go now." Felicia jumped up as the oven bell went off. "There's my banana bread. I hope you all saved room for a slice."

Groans from the guys told Angie that they'd been eating for a while. No one passed up Felicia's award-winning banana bread. She grinned up at her friend. "Well, that's more for me and you."

It took about twenty more minutes for the table to be cleared and Ian to return from the barn. He opened his photo file and showed Angie the pictures he'd taken in the barn. "There's your girl, and the other one. One day I'm going to get them both in one picture."

They waited for Ian to wash his hands and then sit down at the table before pulling out the investigation notebooks. Ian did a summary of what they knew so far.

Estebe leaned back in his chair when Ian finished. "I think we have more questions than answers. And too many unconnected things. Except… does everyone think it's strange that Jon Ansley's law office is involved in all of these situations? I wonder if they handled Nancy's divorce too?"

Felicia's eyes grew wide at the thought. She picked up the phone. "Let me text her."

"You think it all ties together with the law office? Maybe Susan found out something she wasn't supposed to know. And we already know they are representing the soybean plant. If Nancy's ex is part of the same development company and used the law office for their divorce, they'd had information on her." Angie tapped her pen on the table. "It works, except for the body found in the park."

"Maybe that isn't connected at all?" Felicia looked around the table. "What if we throw that information out, then is everything connected?"

"I'll call Allen and see what he's found out about her. Maybe if we can separate that case out, all this will make more sense." He picked up his phone and stepped away from the table and into the living room. Dom rose from his bed and followed Ian out of the room, probably looking for popcorn or someone to rub his stomach.

Estebe turned his laptop screen toward the others. "Counting Jon, there are ten lawyers in the firm. Three partners who all went to the University of Idaho together. Each has his own specialty. One's criminal, one's corporate, and one's family law. They turned over the soybean company to the corporate partner, even though there is another attorney who could have taken the client."

Angie and Felicia stared at Estebe. "How did you find this out?"

He shrugged. "I asked when we were there yesterday. I told you I pretended I was interested in throwing some money at the project. I asked who was representing them. Chip Carson is their new attorney of record. From what I've seen, Chip hasn't done any legal work for the firm for years. He's more in charge of client development."

Ian came back into the room and set his phone on the table. "Allen says to remind you all that none of you are in law enforcement and don't need to be sticking your nose in these cases."

Angie waited for him to refill his cup and then sit down at the table. "What else did he say?"

"He said there was currently no information that linked the woman found in the park with the law firm." Ian sipped his coffee.

"Well, maybe that's a good thing. Now we can stop trying to add her into the puzzle." Felicia leaned against the chair. "Just a random death, then?"

"Actually, no, she was strangled. And he just got a hit on her prints. She wasn't the decorator's wife. I guess he made a mistake when he identified the body. And his wife was with her mom. The body is a college student who disappeared from her dorm six months ago." He looked around the room. "Her college is in Napa Valley."

The four of them fell silent.

Ian looked around the room. "Yeah, that's the reaction I had when Allen told me. And the other interesting point? She'd only been dead a few days when the body was found."

"Someone kept her for six months, then drove her across at least one state to kill her here?" Angie was putting together the pieces. "Wait, where did you say she disappeared from?"

"A Napa Valley college." Ian sighed. "And we happen to have a visitor from the very same place? Allen says there's no evidence yet tying Nancy's ex to the killing, but he is a person of interest. Especially after yesterday's incident with the new wife. And the fact they checked out of their hotel sometime yesterday afternoon, before the police could get there to question her."

Estebe put his hands on the table. "Hold up. You're saying that we think Nancy's ex-husband went from just being a royal jerk to being a kidnapper and murderer? Isn't that a bit of a stretch?"

"Not if you saw the fear in Nancy's eyes that night he came to the restaurant. Nancy isn't just avoiding him because they're divorced. She doesn't feel safe. And now, she doesn't feel like her children are safe, either." Angie stared at the black liquid in her cup and wished she didn't feel this way about another person. Especially the father of some pretty terrific kids. "What do we do now?"

Chapter 18

Dinner service went by without a hitch on Thursday. Hope stepped into her new role seamlessly, which made Angie proud that she'd built a strong team. One that could weave and bob with the changes life brought them. Friday morning, she was at home, doing what she loved and trying not to think about the soybean plant, Barb's missing daughter, or who could have murdered that poor girl from California.

Cooking eased her mind. Ian was working in the living room. He'd set up a mini-office in a corner and had put a sign on his office door in town with a cell number letting people know he could only be reached by phone for the foreseeable future. Angie had tried to get him to go to work, but he refused to leave her alone at the house.

Well, alone with a River Vista police officer and cruiser parked in her driveway. She'd taken today's guard a thermos of coffee and a basket of cookies, muffins, and a breakfast burrito as soon as they'd switched watchers. At least she should feed them if they had to waste their days watching over her property.

Angie figured the problem was over, especially with the guys still in jail, but Allen and Ian both had told her that she was being naïve if she thought the bad guys would give up with just losing their first-strike guys. When had her life turned into a thriller novel?

At least she wasn't in hiding with three kids, like Nancy was doing right now. Although that might have been easier. Angie stared out at the large barn that she'd played in as a kid. And the oversized garden plot that she'd already planted a crop of garlic in last fall. If she lost the farm, she'd lose a piece of herself along with the family history. The soup was bubbling, the casserole was in the oven, and she had an apple pie ready to go into the top oven as soon as she brushed the top with egg white to get a sheen on the crust. Her mom's journal caught her eye. She hadn't read for days, too involved in the drama that was her current life.

Angie poured herself a cup of coffee and sat down at the table. She was taking a minute, just for her. She opened the journal and got lost in her mother's high school days. She was still there when Ian came into the kitchen.

"It smells good in here."

Angie glanced up and at the clock. "I didn't realize I'd been reading so long."

"You needed a distraction." He went over and stirred the soup. "If you're going to bake this pie, you need to get it in the oven. By the time we eat and clean up the kitchen, it's going to be time to leave."

She stood and put the journal away. "It's funny how high school never changes. The things I complained about are the exact same things my mom wrote about driving her crazy. The principal didn't understand them. Sports got all the money, and the music department had to do bake sales. Same problems, different decade."

Ian poured himself a glass of tea. "Bleak was just saying the same thing last week when I visited. Of course, she's worried about the art budget. The girl has a natural talent for painting. I told Maggie that I'd help pay for her supplies if they wanted a benefactor. The girl's going to do something with that talent."

"I was kind of hoping she'd go into hospitality for a career. She's a natural with the customers. I bet she could run her own restaurant no problem right now." Angie got the egg carton out of the refrigerator and made an egg wash for the pie. "We need more female-owned businesses around here."

"The area can be a little patriarchal." He watched her as she finished and then slipped the pie in the oven. "Allen thinks the murder is tied in with all the other things we were discussing. And yes, he sees Charles Gowan as a big part of the problem. In fact, he'd like to interview him, but he's still nowhere to be found."

"Which means Nancy and the kids aren't safe yet." Angie took the casserole out of the oven and put a serving into a plastic container. Then she did the same with some of the soup. Finally, she packed everything into a basket with silverware and a muffin. "Tell the officer that I'm sorry I didn't get the pie done in time."

"There is no way I'm telling someone he would have gotten apple pie. He'll be happy with lunch, believe me. And if you have some pie for him tomorrow, he'll be surprised." Ian grabbed a couple of water bottles from the fridge. "I'll see if he needs to use the restroom. I can watch the neighborhood for ten minutes."

Angie set the table while Ian was gone. He came back in a few minutes later. "That was fast."

"I was just chatting with Herb. He says that they just sent a couple of cars out to the caves. It's the big news this afternoon. I guess there were a bunch of cars out there this morning, and one of the older women who lives down the road called in because of the noise."

Angie poured water into the glasses as they spoke. "She called in a noise complaint out there? I didn't think it was in city limits."

"The cave isn't. The fields on the other side of the road on the way up are in city limits. So when Uncle Allen gets called, he goes."

"Did they catch the guy in the act?" Angie giggled. "You know it's the place where all the high school kids have gone to make out since before my mom went to school in River Vista."

"I know the history. And no, no one was caught in the act. Although that might have helped solve this mystery." He glanced around the table. "Everything here? I'm starving. Besides, the kids need to have some fun."

"It's strange for people to be out there this time of year, though. Sit down and eat." Angie sat down and pointed to Ian's spot. "Although I have heard that the cave is warmer than the outside air in the winter. It's definitely cooler in the summer. The few times I was out there, it was blazing hot outside, but chilly enough in the cave I'd wished I'd worn jeans."

Ian pointed his spoon at her. "And who specifically did you go to the cave with?"

"A bunch of kids. Most of the senior band kids went after a football game one Friday. If I remember right, someone had an older brother buy a bottle of Annie Green Springs. It was nasty." She grinned. "My taste in wine has improved over the years."

"Well, we'll have to test that out one night when this is all settled. Maybe we can do a wine and cheese night with a few friends." He took a sip of the soup. "This is my favorite soup you make."

Angie grinned at him. "You say that every time we sit down to eat."

"What can I say, I love your cooking."

When they arrived at the restaurant, her office door was open and a garment bag lay on her desk. Felicia followed her into the office. "Good, I'm glad you're here early. Look at the dress and tell me if it will work for Saturday."

"I was just going to wear my little black dress." Angie opened the zipper and pulled out a silver dress that had rhinestones that sparkled in the office lighting. At least Angie hoped the jewels were rhinestones. Knowing Felicia came from a silver spoon background had made Angie question some of the choices her partner made lately. She glanced up at her. "It's beautiful, but just how fancy is this cotillion thing? Does Ian need a tux rather than just a black suit?"

Felicia slapped her hands together. "I'm so pleased you like it. No, the guys seem to get away with less than the women do. If you had come in a cocktail dress, no one would have said anything."

"To my face, you mean. Once my back was turned, I would have been getting a lot of flak from the others." Angie pulled the dress out of the bag to get a better look at it. "It's amazing. I probably need to do something with my hair on Saturday if I'm wearing something like this. My black strappy heels should work, right?"

"That will be perfect. And we have appointments with Sherry over at the Curl and Dye at one tomorrow. Are you going to be able to make it?"

Angie glanced up at her friend. "Sure, I'll just come in early to work on prep for Estebe. Should we hire a temp for tomorrow night? He'll be short two cooks."

"He says he'll be fine. I think he sees it as a challenge. He wants to show you he's up to the task." Felicia smiled softly. "I wish he was going with us, but he's stoked he doesn't have to play the game. Of course, he's sending me with a check for the charity we're sponsoring at the event."

"There's a fund-raising event too?" Angie tucked the dress back in the bag. "Should the County Seat donate?"

"Already done. We sent a donation when ticket sales were announced. That way we don't have to worry about doing anything tomorrow."

"You realize I don't read all of the accounting reports each week. I believe that's going to have to change." Angie hung the dress up on her coatrack and grabbed her chef coat.

"Actually, I count on it." Felicia grinned at the look on her friend's face. "Don't worry about it. It's not affecting the restaurant's bottom line, and we look good as a community member. I'll never put us at risk due to my spending."

"I was kidding. I didn't think you would." Angie sat down at her desk, laying the chef coat aside. "I forgot to check Susan's calendar. I wonder who did the accounting for that household. It had to be her, right? Maybe she found something odd and confronted Jon with the proof. Then he killed her in a fit of rage."

"We're back to thinking Jon is a suspect?"

Angie pulled her fingers away from the keyboard. "It's an easy decision to come to since it's always the husband. Wasn't there a book about that last year?"

"Maybe. I tend to read more romance lately. I need to check in with the front of the house." Felicia stood, but then paused at the corner of Angie's desk. "Look, I wanted to say thank you for going to the event tomorrow. I know I told you that I'd take care of the community schmoozing, but this is a really important night for River Vista. If we raise enough money, we can get a social worker here at the clinic every Saturday so people don't go without services."

"And I thought this was just so Holly would have a place to wear her newest gown." Angie opened her email program and scrolled down. "Stay here a minute and glance at this calendar. You might see something off more than I did."

"Sure, but I don't know what I'm looking for." Felicia perched on the edge of the desk. She leaned closer when Angie opened the calendar file. She pointed to the pages on the screen. "Susan used her calendar like a planner. She's made notes about everything in her life. See, there's her daily workouts and her weekly goals. She was trying a new recipe every week. That's cool."

"We're looking for something off." Angie scrolled back to August and started scanning the pages. "She's taken more than one of our classes?"

"I told you, she likes to cook. And learning new recipes is the fun part." Felicia pointed to an entry. "That's one of the cotillion planning meetings. She held them at her home. That's what made everyone suspicious when she disappeared. I guess Holly and her crew showed up for a meeting and no one was home. There's no way Susan would forget something like that. So Holly kept calling and kept pushing. Finally, she called River Vista Police to report her missing. She said if Jon wasn't going to do it, she would."

"Which, of course, made Jon look guilty around their friends." Angie didn't look up from the calendar. The woman had more appointments in a week than Angie did for a couple of months. She loved getting her nails done, that was for certain. "Man, Susan was a busy girl."

"In that crowd, if you don't have kids, you keep up with the salon stuff and volunteer. I know Susan worked with the women's shelter for years, helping women get clothes for interviews." Felicia pointed to an appointment. "Wait, she met with Soy Life Changes last week. It said it was a fund-raising meeting. Soy Life Changes that's a subsidiary of Taylor Farms. I saw it on the planning meeting notes. Why did she go back the next week?"

Angie flipped the virtual page. "There are two more appointments the next month. And then she misses her cotillion meeting a week later."

"You might want Ian to check with his uncle about when exactly Susan disappeared, but it looks like she met with the soybean plant people at least four times. And if they were fund-raising meetings, the number of meetings would have been one or two. One to say no and two, if they said yes and had a check for her to pick up. There's no way they would have had four meetings." Felicia stared at the screen and the last completed month of Susan's calendar.

A knock on the door sounded, and one of the servers poked her head inside. "Sorry to bother you, but we had some questions on the table assignments?"

"I'll be right out, Rachel." Felicia stood again but didn't walk away. "We have to find out why Susan was meeting with Taylor Farms and whom she was talking to. Maybe that was why she had to disappear. She might have found out something important."

Angie shut down the computer. "I just don't want to be the one to tell Barb that Susan isn't coming back. I really would have liked an entry that said, 'Running off to Tahiti with the pool boy since Jon's a jerk.'"

Felicia started toward the door. "I think there's just one problem with that theory."

"What's that?" Angie was buttoning her chef jacket as she followed after her.

Felicia paused in the hallway while Angie locked the office. "The Ansleys don't have a pool."

"Okay, then it was Holly's pool boy. Give me a break here, I just don't want to have to give Barb bad news." She paused at the kitchen door. "I know, wishes and horses."

Felicia laughed as Angie went through the doorway. "I have never understood that saying."

The kitchen crew was busy prepping. Estebe had music playing, an instrumental station that ran from the classics to versions of recent pop songs. Angie stepped over to her second in command. "Nice music. It looks like you've got things started. Where do you want me?"

"It's Nancy's night to pick, and this is her favorite station." He shrugged when he saw Angie's look. "What, just because she can't be here in body doesn't mean she's not here in spirit."

Matt called over from his section where he was chopping vegetables. "Estebe just likes to torture us. The only reason Nancy plays this music is she knows we hate it."

"It is nice music," Estebe argued. "And much better than that station you made us listen to last night."

"Hard rock will never die," Matt responded.

Angie shook her head. "Okay, children, where do you need help?"

Estebe grinned at her. "Go help Hope with the trout. I think she's a little confused on what a serving size is."

"Okay, that's so not fair." Hope used the back of her arm to wipe her forehead. "Totally true, but not fair."

"I'm on my way." Angie moved around the kitchen to where Hope was working. "Besides, you're my favorite. I'd rather spend time with you than the guys."

"Hey, that's not right," Matt called after her. "You know I'm totally your favorite chef of the kitchen."

"You have to be a real chef to be anyone's favorite," Estebe countered.

Angie took out her knife and set up a spot for her to work. Cooking was exactly what she needed. She'd started the day cooking, and she'd end it the same way. She called Hope over when she'd gotten settled and set up a demonstration. "So you start with your knife here…"

Chapter 19

Maggie was waiting in the dining room when Angie came out of the kitchen at the end of the service, sitting at the bar with Ian. She stood and held out her arms. "Angie, I'm so glad to see you tonight. Ian's been telling me all about what's been happening out at your place. I'm so sorry about the trouble."

"It happens, I guess." Angie gave Maggie a hug and then sat next to Ian. She nodded to the bartender, Jeorge. "Would you pour me a soda water, with a lime?"

"Yes, boss." Jeorge flipped a towel over his shoulder and quickly made Angie her drink. "I'm closing out the bar, so if you need something, just let me know."

"No problem, thanks, Jeorge." Angie sipped her water. "So, what are you doing here?"

"I'm Bleak's ride home. She's over there chatting with one of the waitresses she knows from school. I thought I'd give her some time to talk to Hope before I took her home. It's not a school night, and the girl works so hard." Maggie looked over at Bleak helping set up the dining room for tomorrow's service with a few other of the front staff. Pride shone on her face. "She came and talked to me about the trial. She's going to testify. She knows it will drive a wedge in her family, but she says it's the right thing to do."

"As long as she's happy, I'm happy. Just let me or Felicia know if I need to take her off the schedule. She's doing such a great job as hostess." Every joint in her body ached, but there was no way she was going to throw in the towel yet.

"Did you see she took out her piercings?" Maggie's voice dropped so she wouldn't be overheard. "I thought maybe you'd talked to her about them, but she doesn't even wear them at school."

Angie glanced over at where Bleak was standing. She looked normal. Not like the young vagabond Ian had rescued from sleeping in the alley months ago. She quickly turned back to Maggie before the girl could see her. "She looks great. You and Allen have been good for her."

"She's been good for us. I was so lonely before she came to live with us. Allen was always out on some call or the other. Don't get me wrong, he tried, but he's in law enforcement. I knew that was his dream when I married him. But I always thought we'd have a house filled with kids. Maybe once Bleak gets settled into adulthood, we should think about adopting a younger child. Now that I've done high school, elementary age won't be so scary." Maggie glanced at her watch. "We need to get home. We've got a movie to watch tonight still."

"What are you watching?" Ian asked as he gave his aunt a kiss on the cheek.

"A 'chick flick,' as Allen calls them. I'm loving getting caught up on all the ones I missed over the years." Maggie stood and called out to Bleak. "You about ready? I'm craving some popcorn."

Bleak grinned, then said goodbye to the others. She bounded over to where Maggie stood. "Me too. And Shelly just said this movie is amazing, so I'm looking forward to it."

Angie said her goodbyes and moved closer to sit by Ian. "I'm so happy for Maggie. She was a mess a few weeks ago."

"Apparently some daily sessions with Barb cleared up her fears. She talked to Bleak, got her to tell her about the trial and her concerns, now it's clear sailing until the next teenage crisis. But Maggie has a sounding board now. I think she'll be fine." Ian finished his soda. "I'm going to take Dom out for a short walk, and I'll meet you in the car in five. Okay?"

"Perfect." She watched as Ian made his way through the crew that was rapidly dwindling. Felicia came and sat down with her.

"Okay, so I texted you your salon appointment time and address. I'll already be there so don't worry about anything. And don't forget your dress in the office." Felicia ran through Angie's to-do list before the party. "Ian said you guys would be at the cotillion at seven. I think he's taking you out to dinner before, but don't say anything until he does in case it's a surprise."

Angie laughed at her friend's frankness. "Then you shouldn't have told me."

"I didn't mean to, it just came out." Felicia yawned. "I'm beat tonight. I'm shooing everyone out so I can lock up. And that means you too."

Angie stood, her hands in the air. "I got the message. I'll see you tomorrow night. Let me know if you need anything before I see you in less than twelve hours."

"It's a dance, not a trip. I'll be fine," Felicia said, pausing as she exchanged glances with Angie. "Okay, I totally deserved that. But I'm excited for our first formal event here in River Vista. This could be big for the County Seat."

"We're doing fine, but I'll be on my best behavior, unless someone brings up how wonderful getting the soybean plant is for the community, then I'm going to deck them." Angie headed to her office. "In a loving and sweet way."

"No wonder I don't usually invite you to these networking events," Felicia called after her.

Angie heard Estebe's laugh when Felicia asked him, "You do think she's kidding, right?"

Ian and Dom were in the car, and the car was near the steps leading to the back door when she came outside. Angie glanced over at the direction where the Red Eye Saloon's back door came out into the alley, but she couldn't see anything. She could hear the band blaring country music covers into the cold night. Friday and Saturday nights were Barb's biggest night. Even if Angie had some news, which she didn't, Barb wouldn't have time to chat now anyway.

She climbed into the car. Ian pulled out onto the side street, and they drove slowly out of town and past the front of the bar.

"Looks like Barb has a full house tonight," Ian said as the car moved past. Even in the cold of winter, patrons were standing outside the bar, talking.

Angie guessed they couldn't hear themselves inside with the music. She could hear the song perfectly outside in the car with the windows rolled up. "I'm worried about her."

"I know." Ian took the curve out of town that would take them over the railroad tracks and out toward the country. "She's a strong woman. She'll get through the surgery."

"There's the surgery. Then recovery. Then finding out about Susan." Angie wanted to add, "or not," but that just seemed cruel. If Susan was never found, Barb would go the rest of her life looking for her. That much Angie was sure of. "She's a nice person. She deserves some good news in her life."

"Maybe we'll find Susan alive and just out of touch. Like in one of those expensive rehabs where they don't let you talk to anyone until you've sobered up," Ian suggested.

"Did Susan have a drinking problem? Could that actually be what happened?" Angie sat straighter and pulled out her phone. "Maybe I can find some local rehab places and call to see if she's there?"

"At midnight? They really won't let you talk to her, even if you do find her. Besides, I didn't see anything in Susan's history that suggested she had a problem." Ian's voice sounded calm and solid in the dark.

Angie could feel Ian's gaze on her even though the light in the car was dim. She leaned her head back and closed her eyes. "What am I doing? I jumped on that idea, didn't I? Maybe tomorrow we'll learn something at the dance that gives us a clue about what happened. I'm still holding out hope for Susan running away with Holly's pool boy."

Ian chuckled as he pulled into the house. He waved at the new officer parked in the driveway where he could see both properties and then shut off the engine. "I'm going to go check in on our chaperone, then I'll be in. Do you need me to take Dom inside?"

"That would be awesome. I'm so tired that I'm going to grab a glass of water and see if I can get into bed before I fall asleep. Usually, I'm so wound up from an evening of cooking, I can't get to sleep. Tonight's the other way around. I feel drained." Angie thought about closing her eyes but wondered if she'd even get in the house on her own power if she did.

"I'll let Dom in first and take a look through the house, then I'll go chat with our new friend." Ian opened the door but glanced back at her, worry in his gaze. "Are you sure you're okay?"

"I'm fine." Angie opened the door, and the chill of the air slapped her skin. "If I was asleep, that air just woke me up."

Ian got Dom out of the car and followed her up to the porch. Angie already had the key in the lock, and when the door swung open, Dom bounded inside, bringing Ian with him. Ian got Dom to sit down so Ian could take off the leash, but then Dom ran to the mudroom and whined at the closed dog door.

"Sorry, dude, I need to open that for you." Angie followed Dom into the mudroom.

"I'm walking through before I go outside so don't turn off the lights, I'll get them," Ian called after her.

"Take him some cookies," Angie called after him. She unhinged the dog door, checked his water and food, then went back into the kitchen. There, she started to fill a thermos with coffee, using her single-serve coffeepot.

Ian came up behind her. "I thought you were tired."

She finished the coffee and turned, handing him the thermos and cookies. "Here. Now I'm heading upstairs. Make sure Dom comes in before you turn in."

"Yes, ma'am." He grinned at her. "You know we can take care of things without you, right?"

"My house, my work," Angie mumbled, but she smiled as she went upstairs. She didn't finish her thought until she was in her room, hanging up the dress for tomorrow in the closet. "At least for now."

* * * *

The next morning, Ian had already made a pot of coffee and warmed up a coffee cake. He had eggs and bacon out on the counter. She waved him down when he started to get up. "Sit, I can get my own coffee. She glanced out the window. The police cruiser was still there. "Everything okay this morning?"

"The zoo's fed, Precious says good morning, and I took out coffee to Fred, who's our new guy." Ian pointed to a box on the table. "And he brought this from Uncle Allen."

After pouring her coffee, Angie peeked into the box. "Donuts?"

"Yep. Fred had his own sack and had almost finished his coffee. So he was delighted for the refill." Ian grabbed a maple bar. "I've had one already, but I hate for you to have to eat alone."

"If I eat too many of these, I won't fit into the dress Felicia bought for me." Angie took a blueberry cake donut. "I have a hair appointment this morning. The time is on my email. What are you going to do?"

"I need to grab my tux from my apartment so we can get ready together when you're done. I'll drop you off at the salon and then do my errand. I should be back before you're done." He rubbed his face. "Bad timing for a party, but I guess we can see if anyone knows anything about Susan's disappearance."

"And I have to be charming and bring in more business to the restaurant. Felicia already told me that." She finished off her donut. "I don't know why she wants me at this one. She's our public relations person."

"People want to meet the person who's been developing all of these amazing recipes. Felicia may be the face of the restaurant, but you're the heart." Ian smiled at her. "It's just one night."

"If we weren't down Nancy, I'd feel better." Angie sipped her coffee.

Ian chuckled. "Yeah, but you'd still be complaining."

Just before they got ready to leave for the salon, Angie's phone rang. "Hello?"

"I'm glad I caught you. I need a favor." Barb's husky voice echoed in her ear.

Angie closed her eyes, hoping she didn't have to rescue Barb again from someone's house she'd broken into. "What can I do for you, Barb?"

Ian's eyes widened, and he stopped playing with Dom. They'd decided that he could stay at the house for the short time they'd be in town. And since they had their own police stakeout in the driveway. Even so, Angie had Ian tell Fred that Dom was in the house and where they were going. She wasn't taking any chances.

"I need to put someone down on these hospital papers as a contact person. The hospital called me yesterday, and I told them I'd have to get back to them."

Barb coughed, and Angie waited for her to stop before answering. "Of course, you can put me down. But I really think we might know where Susan is before you go into the hospital."

"You're a sweet girl, but I know there's no chance for us to find her alive now. It's been too long. The only thing that idiot Sheriff Brown is looking for now is her burial spot." She sighed. "I've resigned myself to that, and I had my attorney finish up the will. I might as well tell you that you and your friend are my heirs. You girls have been good to me, and I appreciate it. I pay my debts."

"You don't have any debts with me or Felicia." Angie rolled her eyes at Ian, who was watching her, and she saw his muscles relax. "And I wouldn't give up on Susan, not yet."

"You're a sweet girl, but I know what I know." Barb coughed again. "I won't keep you."

Angie was about to say goodbye, but she heard the *click* in her ear. Barb had already hung up. She set the phone down on the table. "I'm worried about her. She needs to go into this surgery with positive thoughts, not negative ones."

"Barb is a tough cookie. She'll be fine," Ian said, but as they left the house, Angie sent up a prayer hoping he was right.

Felicia was already at the salon, so once she was done, she sat with Angie and the stylist.

"I can't believe you all are going to the party. I tried to get my boyfriend to go, but he'd rather hang out at the Red Eye. I'm not sure he even knows any dance except line." The stylist, Tiki, grinned at Angie in the mirror. "I bet you'll be in gowns and your men will be in tuxes."

Felicia nodded. "Actually, I'm going stag tonight, so I'll have to steal Angie's date for a few spins around the room. Estebe won't kill him if he dances with me. I'm not sure of anyone else."

"I'm sure if they kept their hands off of you, Estebe will be fine with you dancing with other people," Angie said.

"I don't know. I had one client whose husband was so jealous, he didn't even like her doing her sorority stuff with the girls. She said he acted like a teenager when she even talked about other guys, even if they were married."

Tiki's eyes darkened a bit. "Then I heard she went missing. I bet that husband must have gone one step too far."

"You're talking about Susan." Angie exchanged a quick glance with Felicia. "You knew her?"

"Susan came in at least once a month. Sometimes I think she just booked her appointment so she'd have someone to talk to. Being a stylist is a lot like being a therapist. People tell you things." Tiki focused on trimming Angie's hair. "Not that I like to talk about my clients."

"No, I get it. I wouldn't ask you to go outside your comfort zone." Angie thought about how to frame the next question. "But Susan wasn't afraid of Jon, was she?"

Now Tiki broke into a grin. "No way. She thought he was cute, caring about her that way. She said he just didn't know how to show his love. Now, Jake, he wouldn't notice if I was dating the Bronco football team. He's so involved in his work. He runs a construction business."

"Jake's your guy?" Felicia asked.

"Yeah, he's not rolling in the money like a lawyer or doctor, but we get by." Tiki flashed a ring at them. "He bought me this just last week. He got it from Meridian Pawn Shop. I know because I found the receipt, but it looks just like the ring that Susan wore. I'm sure it's a cheap knockoff, but it's close, don't you think?"

Angie grabbed her phone. "Let me take a picture of it, and I'll ask her best friend tonight. I'm sure she'll remember the style. I'll take one of your cards so I can call you and let you know later."

Tiki held out her hand and let Angie take the picture. "Thanks. I don't really care, though. I'm just glad Jake decided to put some money where his mouth is. I've just been on him about spending way too much at the bar, which means he doesn't bring home a lot of money. He must have been saving up for this, though. I shouldn't be so judgmental."

Angie caught Felicia's gaze in the mirror. The ring didn't look cheap. And the wedding band had already been attached to the engagement ring. This might be the first clue in Susan's disappearance.

As soon as they left the salon, Angie texted the picture of the ring and the name of the pawn shop to Allen Brown.

A response came back quickly. A little too quickly in Angie's mind. And yeah, as she read the words, she knew she'd gotten into the stew with Allen.

"What did he say?" Felicia asked.

Angie held the phone up and read the message to her. "He says, you can't even stay out of investigating at a hair salon? What? Clues just fall into your lap. Let me do some checking."

"Man, he sounds heated."

Angie tucked her phone back into her purse. "This wasn't my fault."

Ian pulled up just then and parked in front of the salon. He climbed out of the SUV and walked over to them. "Your chariot awaits. Felicia, do you want a ride back to the apartment?"

"I'm good. I'll walk home." Felicia squeezed Angie's arm. "I'll see you tonight. Catch Ian up on what we found."

Ian looked from Felicia back to Angie. "I was only gone thirty minutes, forty tops."

* * * *

When they got to the party, Angie glanced around the room. Paper snowflakes dangled from the ceiling, and the décor was shiny white on white. She slipped off her coat and handed it to Ian, who gave it and his to the attendant at the coat closet. "Wow. This is beautiful. I can't believe they turned the VFW hall into a giant snow globe."

Ian took the ticket the attendant handed him and tucked it in his pocket. He took her hand. "You're the one that's beautiful. That dress Felicia gave you makes your eyes sparkle."

"You sweet talker." Angie leaned into him. "Maybe you could talk to your uncle and get him not to be mad at me?"

"He's not mad at you. You found a huge clue. Just because you were asking personal questions that were outside the scope of your job as a civilian, he's not going to hold that against you." Ian grabbed two glasses of champagne off a tray and handed one to her. "I wonder what he's found out about the ring?"

Angie sipped her drink and looked to see if she could find Felicia in the crowd. "I just hope that's not a designer brand that everyone bought that year. We need to find at least one good clue. Barb's counting on it."

She drew in a quick breath as she was pulled into a tight hug. As she could see Ian standing on the other side of the man squeezing her, she knew she wasn't in her boyfriend's arms. Besides, this cologne didn't smell like Ian.

Chapter 20

The odor reminded her of… Before she could finish the thought, she was spun around and Jon Ansley released her, tears rolling down his face.

"You found her ring. Here in town. That means something. It means she didn't leave me, not voluntarily. She has to be somewhere close by." Jon squeezed Angie's hand. He was dressed in jeans and what appeared to be a clean T-shirt. And he'd apparently showered recently, as his hair was still wet.

"Hi, Jon. I guess Sheriff Brown reached out to you about the ring?" Angie took a few steps away from the man and closer to Ian, who drew her into a protective hug, with his arm around her shoulder.

"He stopped by the house earlier. It's Susan's ring. She never took it off. She had it designed just for the wedding." He took two glasses off a passing tray and drank down one and then the other. "She was mad at me for something I'd done, or didn't do, so she designed this freaking crazy-expensive ring. I about had a heart attack when I saw the bill. But she loved the damn thing."

Angie saw he was shaking uncontrollably. She took the flutes out of his hands and then moved him into a nearby chair. "Jon, you realize this doesn't mean she's alive. They just found her ring."

"Actually, I don't care. I mean, I want her—no, I need her to be alive, but I have hope again. I haven't had hope for weeks. I thought I'd never know what happened to her." He leaned his head into his hands, then, running his fingers out through his hair, he stood and took in the crowd. "She might be here, watching."

"Why would she do that?" Angie glanced over at Ian, who looked as worried as she felt. Jon was acting just a little crazy.

He glanced up at all the snowflakes. "She made so many snowflakes for this thing. They'd be all over the kitchen when I got home, her hands would be cramping from using the shears. She loved this dance and the charity it supports. She'd be here if she could. Excuse me, I need to go looking."

Angie moved closer to Ian. He put his arm around her, apparently needing the support as badly as she did. She leaned into his chest. "Jon's taking this too well. He's going to fall over the other edge and get depressed when he doesn't find her tonight."

"I know. We should probably see if we can get him out of here." Ian started to move toward the hallway where Jon had disappeared.

"Let him go. Maybe he's right and Susan will just show up. Meanwhile, we've got others to chat with." She nodded toward Holly and her crew. "I'd like to know what they think about the ring being found."

Ian's phone rang, and he stepped outside the hall to answer. Angie stood by a table and grabbed some appetizers from the waiters who were passing trays. She watched the assembled crowd. Felicia was over talking to what appeared to be the catering manager based on the black suit with a label pin on the front. Either that, or the guy was taking his networking assignment seriously, like at one of those business chapter meetings where locals got together to talk marketing. Angie had attended one of those meetings, then told Felicia never again. No one actually talked, and fewer people listened. She'd come home with a pile of business cards she'd promptly thrown away.

No, Felicia was the PR part of the team. Angie loved talking to suppliers about the local food and their families and crews. You could learn a lot about people by knowing what was important to them.

Her gaze drifted over to Holly's table, where she stood with her husband. Few people actually sat; in fact, Angie only saw a few chairs at low tables near the sides of the room. They were filled with older guests, chatting and talking. They looked like they were having fun. Holly and her husband, on the other hand, looked like they'd just finished an intense fight.

Until someone walked up and started chatting with them. Then the demeanor changed and they were the perfect couple. Maybe Angie had just caught them in a bad moment. She watched as the other couple moved away from that table to meet someone else. Holly took three steps away from her husband, turned her back, and froze in place.

What the heck was going on with these people? She was watching the routine for a third time when she felt a touch on her arm. Ian held out his phone to her. "Uncle Allen wants to say something."

She took the phone, and due to the loudness of the room, she said, "Hold on a sec."

Once she was in the quiet hallway, she found a bench and sat. Her skirt flounced all around her and took up the rest of the bench. She patted down the tulle with a smile. Not her normal style, but she did feel like a princess tonight. She slipped off her heels and flexed her feet, trying not to groan in pleasure. Then she remembered the call. "What's going on, Allen?"

"My nephew reminded me that I hadn't properly thanked you for the lead today. I'm not really sure how you always seem to be in the middle of these things, but thank you for passing on the picture of the ring. That was good instinct."

Angie wondered how hard it had been for Allen to say that to her. "You're welcome. I just didn't think that Susan Ansley would have a ring that you could buy at the local chain jewelry store. This group is nothing if not about appearances."

"I've noticed that." He chuckled. Then she could hear someone in the background. "Hold on a minute."

Angie didn't mind waiting because it meant she didn't have to be in that room that was too hot and filled with people who didn't care if she was there or not because she didn't have an ounce of power. Or at least, not outside her restaurant.

When Allen came back on the line, he sighed. "Good news is we found the kid who hocked the ring. I'm going to have to have a chat with the pawn shop owner about thinking before he takes on buys. This kid is in Bleak's class."

"You're kidding? How did he get the ring?"

"His story is he found it. Out at the cave, he thinks. Or at the canal. They were checking to see if the ice was hard enough to walk on the patches of water still in Indian Creek when someone got the idea to go out to the cave. He admits to drinking a bit that night, and he's not sure when he found it, but he'd tucked it in his pocket and took it to the shop the next Monday to sell."

"So we think Susan was either climbing in an empty irrigation canal or hanging out at the local hookup spot." Angie rubbed her foot, trying to get rid of a cramp. Maybe she'd ask Ian to take her home. The night wasn't as magical as she'd hoped. "Neither one of those options sound like a woman who would also plan one of these events. It's pretty fancy for River Vista."

"Maggie dragged me to one of those cotillions a few years ago. You couldn't pay me to go to another one." Allen's voice sounded almost sympathetic. "Anyway, I thought since you were the one who found the lead, you should know it kind of drizzled out."

"Thanks for calling. I'd hoped it would be better news. Jon's here and he has his hopes up way too high." Angie knew it wasn't her business, but she was starting to feel sorry for the guy.

"I got that when he identified the ring. Now he's convinced that Susan's alive."

Allen kept talking but something he'd said had Angie thinking. She broke into his discussion about Maggie and Bleak with her thought. "Allen? How often do you get calls out to the cave?"

"In the summer? Almost every night and definitely every weekend. I've assigned one patrol car to do a drive-by every hour in peak times." He paused. "Why are you asking?"

"How often do you get calls out during winter?"

This time the pause was on the other side of the line. "New Year's Eve, yes, but mid-January? I don't think I've ever gotten a call out when it was this cold. And yet, I've sent guys out there three, maybe four times this last two weeks. I haven't been inside the cave for years. Is there room to hide a body there?"

"If they keep coming back, wouldn't it be more likely that Susan's still alive?" The cave was in a remote spot about ten miles south of town. Legally, it probably wasn't even in the River Vista area Sheriff Brown patrolled, but it was too far for any county offices to respond to an incident so it had unofficially been part of Brown's area of control for years. All Angie could think of was someone cold and huddled in the dark, damp cave. "Could she really still be alive?"

"We're going to find out," Allen Brown said, then he hung up on her.

When she went back into the party, she waved away a glass of wine. Felicia and Ian were standing together, watching her approach.

"You were gone awhile." Ian studied her. "And from the look on your face, Allen told you something. What's going on?"

"Let's get out of here. I need some air." She waved away the question. She'd tell them when they got into the car.

As they were walking out, Charles and his wife, Jane, stepped in front of the door. He pointed a finger at Angie. "I don't know what you're playing, missy, but you need to stay out of this fight."

"Which one?" Angie shot back and pulled out her phone. "The one where your wife is probably going to be arrested for harassing Nancy at work? I know you had a gun in your purse when you came in to 'talk' to her. What in the world are you thinking? That we'd just let you walk in and kill her?"

She dialed 911, and when the operator answered, Angie spoke quickly. "There's a woman here at the cotillion who has a BOLO out for her involvement in a possible failed kidnapping. Her name's Jane Gowan."

Jane's eyes widened, and she pulled on Charles's hand. "We need to get out of here."

"Hold on, what is she talking about? Calling the police won't do you any good. We haven't done anything wrong." He frowned at his wife.

"You don't know? You didn't tell her to do it?" Felicia stared at the couple.

"We have to go now." She dropped his hand and sprinted to the doorway.

He sighed and shook her head. He strode after her, muttering, "Women. She's such a drama queen."

Angie and Felicia stared at them as they left. Finally, Angie took a deep breath and without turning, asked a question. "Do you really think he didn't know?"

"Unlikely." Ian glanced around the room. "I guess we have to stay and talk to the police officer when they get here. Then let's go. I'm beat."

"Me too." Angie took his arm, and they walked out into the hallway to wait for the officer.

Ian glanced out the window. "He must have parked in the back. I can't see anyone in the front parking lot."

Angie wanted to follow Charles and Jane to their new living arrangement, but she knew the action would just cause one more lecture from Allen. And like he always said, it wasn't her business.

And besides, her feet hurt.

* * * *

On their way home, after stopping in Meridian for ice cream, Angie thought about Susan and Charles and Jane. They were all connected through the work on the soybean plant, but was that enough of a connection to mean anything in Susan's disappearance? If Nancy had been in the kitchen alone that afternoon, Angie was certain that Jane would have kidnapped her. Then another person would be missing. There was no way this was a random coincidence. She looked over at Ian in the darkened cab. "Have you heard from your uncle?"

"Nope. You've been with me since we left the cotillion. When would I have talked to him?" Ian rubbed his forehead. "Sorry. I'm tired and ready for this all to be done. Why would people act like this all the time? It has to be exhausting."

"Some people like drama in their lives. You and I are a drama-free zone." She laid a hand on his arm. "Did you have fun at the dance?"

"We got to leave early. The food was great. And I didn't have to talk to anyone except the police officer who took my statement. I'd call that a successful night." He turned the car into the driveway. Two cruisers sat there. "We've got a backup today for some reason."

One of the officers got out of his car and met them when they got out of the house. "Good evening, folks. Sheriff Brown thought it might be a good idea to have two officers on yours and your neighbor's house. Especially since we're still trying to track down the suspect from your break-in."

Angie looked from Ian to the new officer, trying to see what wasn't being said, but she couldn't decipher it. She pointed her keys to the house. "I need to check on Dom. Has he been quiet?"

"As a church mouse. I've been walking the property every thirty minutes or so, and he comes out to watch me. Sits on that back porch of yours, and I swear, I can hear his thoughts. Mostly, he gives off a vibe of questioning my competence. It's bad when a dog can make you doubt your effectiveness." The officer held out a hand. "My name's Mick. I've been to your restaurant with my girl. We loved it."

"Thanks, Mick. I'll have Ian bring you all out some cookies or pastries after we get settled. And some coffee. You're more than welcome to use the facilities too." Angie moved toward the porch, then froze. She pointed to a spot under the deck. "What's that?"

Mick moved in front of her and swore. "When in the heck did they have time to do this?"

Ian pulled Angie back. "You need to go sit in the car. In fact, move the car over to the barn and sit there."

Mick waved the other guy out of his vehicle. "Don't move the car. We're going to have to go through this entire property to make sure nothing else was tampered with."

Chapter 21

Angie folded her arms around herself and stared at the shape under her porch. Then her eyes widened. "We need to get Dom out of there."

"Not until the bombs are cleared." The other officer was on his walkie-talkie. His nametag said Devon, but Angie hadn't met him yet.

"You're sure it's a bomb? At my house?" Angie leaned against the car and sank to the ground. Tears fell down her cheeks.

"Technically on your deck. And it just looks like a bomb. It could be there to scare you."

"It's working." Angie closed her eyes and leaned her head back onto the tire.

"You need to get up out of the dirt." Ian knelt next to her. "You're getting Felicia's dress all dirty."

"I can't do it anymore. I can't fight. And I can't lose Dom." Angie let Ian pull her up into a standing position. She looked at Mick. "There's no way anyone got in the back yard without Dom noticing. What if we call him out the dog door and get him out that way?"

"He was pretty sharp when I was doing my rounds. He didn't let me get anywhere near the fence without him coming outside and watching me. I can't see him letting anyone in his yard." He glanced at the deck and the one bomb that had been found. "It's your call. If we leave him inside and the guy has a remote, we'll lose him anyway. Do you want to take the chance?"

Angie thought hard for two seconds, then she nodded. "I'll hate myself either way, but at least it's in my control this way. The other way, I'm just waiting for some jerk to ruin my life."

First, Ian went to the barn with Mick. They checked for trip wires, and when they didn't see any, Ian went inside to grab Dom's lead. Then they walked over to the fence as quietly as possible. Angie stood by the fence where she could see into the yard. Ian stood at the gate, ready to fling it open and get Dom outside.

"I don't see anything under the deck. Not like in the front," Angie said as Mick stood by her staring into the yard.

"Me, either. Are you sure about this? I hate to do this and make a mistake. The bomb squad is about forty minutes out." Mick focused his gaze on her.

"He's going to come outside anyway before they get here. One way or another, he's in danger. I need to get him to safety." Angie could feel the tears in her eyes, but she would not crumble again. "Besides, explaining dirt to Felicia is one thing. If I actually tear my dress, that would be a disaster."

"Your friend wouldn't care." Mick smiled at her. "But if you're sure, let's do this. I want to meet your Dom face-to-face."

Angie smiled and wiped her arm over her eyes. Her eyes probably looked like racoons by now. She glanced at the deck and the surrounding area one more time. There was still some snow on the ground in the yard, and there were no footprints that weren't made by her big-footed Saint Bernard. At least none that she could see. "I'm ready. Ian?"

"I'm right here on the gate and I have his lead ready to clip on him as soon as I get ahold of his collar." Ian smiled at her, his blue eyes twinkling. He'd been fighting back tears, as well.

"One, two, three—now. Call him out."

Angie tried to keep her voice from trembling as she called for Dom to come outside. If she'd been wrong, she was calling him to his death. She just had to have faith. "Dom, come here, buddy. Sweet boy, come see mama."

And as quickly as the words came out of her mouth, Dom flew out of the back door, his feet barely touching the deck steps, and he ran to the gate. Ian was there to catch him, and as he clicked the lead on, he slammed the gate closed. Angie ran over and gave him a huge hug, getting wet, slobbery kisses in return. Dom's tongue just kept growing. At least in Angie's mind. But she didn't care. Not now. He'd survived.

"Let's go get you two into the car, where we can wait for the bomb squad." Ian put his arm around her and moved her toward the vehicle. Dom trotted beside her like they were on their way to Celebration Park for a walk. Her gamble had paid off, and Dom wasn't dead. Angie wanted a beer. Bad.

Instead, she sat in the car with Dom and Ian and watched the house. Mick had told them they could move the car back toward the road, but Angie liked it just where it needed to be. Where they could keep an eye out for the house. A vigil, so to speak. She just hoped that no one had to die to make this vigil worthy.

Ian's phone rang just as the bomb squad was taking off whatever had been under her deck. They'd determined that instead of a bomb, someone had built a box to set under the deck to make it look like a bomb. A joke or a trick; either way, Angie was not amused.

"Hey, Allen, everything's fine here. Just someone playing a game or trying to scare Angie. What's going on with you?" Ian listened, and as Angie watched, his eyes grew wide. "Are you kidding? Is she okay?"

Angie glanced at Ian.

"No, we'll be there. I don't think Angie's going to want to leave Dom, so we'll bring him along, but he can wait in the car. See you soon." He listened for a few more seconds and nodded. Then he paused by the back door of the car, where Angie and Dom were sitting. He held out his hand to her. "Angie, we need to get changed and then head into town. Allen wants us there before he talks to her."

"I don't want to go anywhere except to bed. Wait, before he talks to who?" Angie stroked Dom's soft fur. She buried her face in his neck. She was bone-tired, and now that the scare was over, she felt like she could sleep for a year. He'd never been in real danger, but she felt like she'd taken a chance with his life. And she'd made a decision. She was done playing this game. A house was a house. But if keeping it forced her to lose or even possibly lose the people and animals she loved, she couldn't put them through it for her memories. She'd call her attorney on Monday. She whispered to Dom, "This will be over soon, boy."

"Dom will be fine. He was never in danger." Ian took her hand and squeezed it. "Susan. She's alive, but in bad shape. Allen found her in the cave. He said you were the one who pointed him there. When did you figure out Susan was in the cave?"

"Tell that to my emotions. I'm ready to break out in tears here." She studied him, trying to take in the new information. "Oh my God. Allen found Susan?"

"Yes. That's what I'm trying to tell you. She was in the cave. Allen said you knew it. How did you know she was in the cave? You never said anything to me." Ian's eyes were filled with joy and worry.

Worry, Angie knew that was about her. She needed to get back to the real world. She kissed Dom on the head and stood. "I didn't. All I said was it was weird him having to go out there so much during the winter. I never said it was because someone had hidden Susan there. Did she tell him who kidnapped her? Should I call Barb?"

"It's late, well, early Sunday morning. Let's talk to Susan first and Uncle Allen. He might not want this to get out." Ian took Dom's lead. "Come on, big guy, we need to go get changed, and then we're going for a ride."

Dom looked up at the sky, apparently checking to see if it was still nighttime. Then he shook it off and started to follow Ian into the house. Angie laughed at his confusion. "He's ready for the excitement, although he's confused on why we're doing it at night. I think my working late had messed up his sleep cycle. He's ready to play anytime I show up."

"He's just glad to see you. There's been a lot of change in his life, new people, new routines, the last few weeks. He'll be fine, but I bet he sleeps in the car during the ride." Ian held the door open for her.

"I'm not dumb enough to take that bet." She followed them upstairs and pulled out some clean clothes. Laying the dress on her bed, she sighed. Hopefully the dry cleaners would be able to get the dirt and dog slobber stains out of the fabric. Otherwise, Angie would have to buy her friend a new dress. She slipped on jeans and a sweatshirt, then checked herself in the mirror. Both her hairstyle and her makeup were a little too much for the casual look, but she didn't touch the hair. She wiped off the lipstick and eye color and took a clean tissue and wiped at her cheeks, hoping it would at least tone down the party look.

Ian smiled at her when she came downstairs. He was in jeans now too, having changed out of his tuxedo. "You still look lovely."

"But I don't look like I'm heading to some cotillion, right?" She pulled on her jacket and grabbed two water bottles to put in her tote. "I'm ready when you are."

"Too bad we didn't get at least one dance." He pulled her close and kissed her. Releasing her, he met her gaze. "I was looking forward to that part of the evening events."

Smiling, she kissed him quickly. "I was too."

It took almost an hour to get to the hospital and find the emergency room. When they entered the waiting room, Ian's uncle was sitting at a table on the phone. He held up a finger and finished the conversation.

"Who do you think he's talking to? Jon?" Angie glanced around at the stark, empty room. One couple sat in the corner, the man sleeping and the woman staring at the floor. They were waiting for news. Other than them, the room was empty.

"Probably." Ian put an arm around her. "These places always seem so cold and stark. Do they have to have everything white?"

"The chairs are a plastic blue." Angie knew what he was feeling. She felt like she was stepping into a sterile environment that screamed they weren't clean enough to be there. Even in freshly washed jeans and a top.

"Funny." He pointed to the other side of the room, where a coffee machine stood. "Want some coffee?"

"Please. I might just fall asleep standing here. It's been a crazy night." Angie pointed to a pod of chairs that circled a table. "I'll sit there, and if your uncle joins us, we'll have a table."

"I'll bring two cups of coffee for you. I'm going to scrounge for some tea." He headed over to the refreshments corner.

Angie sank into her chair, then pulled out her phone. She texted Felicia and told her what had happened. *Fake bomb at house. Now at hospital in Meridian. No one's hurt, but if you're up and still sober, can you come get Dom? He's in the car since I didn't want to leave him at the house.* She glanced over the text, hoping it wouldn't scare her. Angie glanced at her watch. Even if Felicia had had a few too many glasses of the wine, Estebe should still be at the restaurant cleaning up after the night's service. Maybe she should call the restaurant instead and have Estebe come drive Dom to Felicia's?

Before she could call, her phone beeped with an answering text. *OMG. Are you sure you're okay? Why at hospital? I'll be there as soon as possible. Estebe is driving.*

Ian set the Styrofoam cups on the table. He glanced at her phone. "Felicia?"

"Yeah, she's coming to get Dom for a sleepover. I don't want him sitting out in the car for long." Angie typed in a quick response to Felicia's answer. "She'll be calling when she gets here. One of us will have to keep their phone on them, so if we go into a no cell phone area, I'll stay outside until we get Dom taken care of."

"That dog is treated better than some kids." Ian pointed to the coffee. "You want some sugar or fake creamer?"

"Bring me two packets of hot cocoa if they have it. Chocolate will cover the taste of even bad coffee." She put her phone on the table and sipped some of the too-hot coffee. It really wasn't that bad, but with cocoa, she'd have even more caffeine and some sugar to keep her going for a while.

Ian came back with her cocoa packets, his tea, and his uncle. They sat down around the table and Allen leaned toward her.

"First item of business: Are you okay? I can't believe someone got by my guys and planted that fake bomb. Believe me, I'm going to have a chat with them."

Angie stirred the cocoa into both of the cups. "I'm fine. Dom's fine. The house is fine. I'm just tired of fighting this argument. Maybe it's time to just sign the paperwork?"

"Give up the house? Are you crazy?" Ian set his tea down, and some spilled on the table. "You love that house."

"I love the memories from that house. I love Dom and Precious and Mabel. I love you. The house just holds all the stuff and people I love. If I lost you because I was being hardheaded, I couldn't deal with it." Angie blinked away the tears.

"I'm not going to argue with you. Getting you out of that house would save me a ton of overtime, but don't make the decision tonight. You're tired. Things have been a little crazy. And you have some time anyway. The county board hasn't decided to rezone the area yet. I hear there's some issues with a bit of historical land they want to include in the project. You may not have to sell." Allen's phone beeped. "That's our signal. Put the house on the back burner. I want you to talk to Susan about what happened. I would typically have a female officer do this, and I'll be in the interview, so don't worry, I'll feed you questions if you need it, but I think she needs a soft touch right now."

Ian held his hand out for her phone. "I'll stay out here on Dom duty. I'll come back to the room as soon as I get him transferred over."

Allen glanced at her. "You brought your dog to the hospital?"

"I wasn't leaving him at home. Even with your guys on guard." Angie finished one cup of coffee and stared at Allen, daring him to challenge her.

"You're right, of course. And I apologize for not keeping him safe." Allen stood. "Are we ready?"

"What do you want me to ask her? Anything specific?" Angie bit at her bottom lip. "I don't want to upset her."

"You won't. Just ask her what happened. What was the last thing she remembered? Where was she when she was taken? Did she see her captor? Could she describe him?" He stood and nodded toward the end of the room. "She's in good shape, just dehydrated and dirty. And the room is dimmed because she's been out of the light for so long."

Angie nodded, thinking about what she knew about Susan's disappearance and what she'd want to know if she was investigating the disappearance. The scene between Charles Gowan and her earlier in the night flashed in her memory. She stood to follow and grabbed her cup. "I forgot to ask, did you find Charles and his wife?"

"We have some leads. That was brave of you to call her location in to the police. I would have expected you to jump in Ian's truck and follow them." He looked down at her as they were walking.

"Don't think it didn't cross my mind. I wasn't really dressed for a high-speed chase at the time." Angie smiled as they entered an elevator and Allen hit the button for the fifth floor.

"I'm glad you didn't. I've got all of my guys on some sort of event tonight. I didn't need you and Ian to get into some sort of altercation with someone who carries a gun in her purse." He watched the numbers change rather than look at her.

"That was the other reason. Charles didn't know about what she did at the restaurant. He was surprised when she freaked out about the cops coming. He wanted a team to come because he thought he was in the right. I wouldn't want to be a fly on the wall at their place tonight."

Allen didn't say much but held the door open for her as they reached the fifth floor. He showed his badge at the woman standing behind the nurses' desk and she nodded at him. Then they went into room 509. The lights were low, and there was only one bed in the room. A police officer in full uniform stood at one wall. Allen nodded to him, and the guy left the room.

"Who's there?" a small, quiet voice asked.

"It's Sheriff Brown again. And I brought a friend. Susan, meet Angie Turner. She owns a restaurant in River Vista." Allen spoke quietly and slowly.

"The County Seat. You're Felicia's partner. I went to a cooking class there last summer." Susan's voice got stronger.

"That's me. I'm sorry to meet you under such circumstances, but Sheriff Brown wondered if I could ask you some questions."

"So the frightened woman would actually talk? Is he from the fifties?" Susan's voice held a bit of a smile. "Yes, it's okay for you to ask me questions. But I have one for you first. And you need to be honest with me."

"What's your question?" Allen asked.

Angie figured it was something about Jon and his involvement with the kidnapping.

"What about the other woman? Did you find her too?"

Chapter 22

"What are you talking about? Was someone held with you?" Allen forgot his plan to let Angie ask the questions. He stepped forward, saw the wince in Susan's eyes, then stepped back away from the bed. "I'm sorry to be so abrupt. Should we still be searching the cave?"

Susan sighed, then looked out the window. "She's probably gone. All I know is someone was there before me. The guy had me in an area near the back of the cave. It looked like a small room, but I was chained to the wall. There was a bed with a thin blanket. One night, I reached under the mattress and found a pen and some wrappers. I thought it was just junk because I couldn't see very well. In the morning, the sun reflected through a rock pile. Just for a few minutes, then it grew darker and darker. I realized Abigail had written notes about her capture. She said this was the second place they'd held her."

Angie glanced at Allen, who was scribbling but not moving to call his officers to go back to the cave. Susan must have reached the same conclusion when he didn't leave the room.

"She's gone, isn't she?" Tears leaked from Susan's eyes. She wiped them away, quickly. "It's stupid being upset about someone I didn't know, but I thought maybe she'd escaped. And if she did, maybe I had hope."

She turned her face into the pillow.

"Are you okay? Do you need some water?" Angie moved to the bedside. Susan shook her head. "I'm just tired. Go ahead, ask your questions."

Angie went through the questions that Allen had led her to ask while he made notes about everything Susan said. As she was listening, she wondered if Abigail really was the girl whom they'd found in River Vista.

"I tried making noise, but no one heard. Finally, last night, I heard someone in the cave, and I was tired of being quiet. The guy hadn't come back for three days, so I figured if someone didn't find me, I was going to die of starvation or something."

"You keep saying 'the guy.' It was a man who took you?" Angie asked.

Susan hesitated before she answered. "I guess I figured it was a guy. He had disguised his voice with one of those vocal-alteration things. He was strong. He brought a whole case of water down by himself. It could have been a woman, maybe. Yeah, I guess. I'm not a very good witness, am I?"

Angie squeezed her hand. "You are doing great. I met your dog, Timber, a few times. He's a sweetie."

Her cracked lips formed a small smile. "I figured Jon would have given him away by now. He was always complaining about how he left fur all over his suits."

"I don't wear suits now, so it doesn't matter as much," Jon said from the doorway. He nodded to Allen. "Is it okay if I come inside?"

Angie glanced at Susan, who had moved toward the sound of her husband's voice. "Do you want him here?"

Susan nodded. "We've had our issues, but I'd like to see and talk to my husband please."

Allen cleared his throat. "Someone will be right outside if you need anything."

"Thank you." Jon touched Angie's shoulder as she walked past him. "Thank you for not giving up on her."

When they got into the hallway, Allen put on his hat. "Tell that nephew of mine to take you home. You've had quite an evening. Going to that dance would have been more than enough for me." He smiled at her as they walked toward the lobby.

"The woman you found in the park—that was Abigail?" Angie asked softly, hoping her voice wouldn't track back into the room.

"We haven't released a name because we are trying to find her parents, but yes. That was Abigail. I'll have to have the cave area tested, but I'm sure we'll find her DNA there. I can't believe what's going on. What are we looking at, some kind of serial kidnapper?" He frowned at her. "Sorry, just thinking aloud. But what made you ask about the captor? Do you have a theory?"

When she told him yes and what it was, his eyes widened. "Let me go check a few things out. I was serious about you going home. We might be able to finish up all these issues by morning."

Angie fell into Ian's arms as soon as they reached the waiting room. He'd been on his way to meet up with them, but then Jon had arrived, and the nurse had limited the number of visitors. "I figured Jon had more at stake."

"You're a sweet guy." Angie leaned her head on his shoulder. "Your uncle says we can go home. Did Felicia come and get Dom?"

"Yep. He was a little hesitant to go with her, until Estebe said the word 'popcorn.' Then he jumped into the Hummer. Good thing those vehicles have strong shocks."

Angie laughed as they made their way out of the building and walked toward the car. "Dom loves popcorn. I'll leave him there for the night. I don't want to disturb them again."

"Tomorrow's almost here anyway. I called someone to take over my Sunday school class tomorrow so we can sleep in. I'm beat." He started up the car and turned the heater on full-blast.

They drove in silence for a while, then Angie turned toward him. "I hope Susan and Jon can patch up their marriage now. I would hate for her to go through all this for nothing."

"Did she say if the captors told her why she was kidnapped? Or was it just one of those random things—wrong place, wrong time?"

"She didn't know. I had a few ideas I told your uncle about. I could be seeing unicorns instead of horses, but somehow it all fits." She leaned her head back on the headrest.

"Are you going to tell me?" Ian asked.

She tried to answer, but she fell asleep instead, thinking of dancing queens and kings and the rules of court.

* * * *

The next morning—well, afternoon, from her glance at the bedside clock—Dom lay at her feet next to her bed. She reached down and rubbed his head. "Hey, boy, I guess Felicia's here?"

He woofed lightly and then covered her hand in doggy kisses.

"I missed you too. Did you have fun at your sleepover?"

The bedroom door opened, and Ian stood in the doorway watching her and Dom. "According to Felicia, he chewed the arm of one of her leather jackets she'd left by the door and part of a shoe stand. But other than that, he was a good boy."

"He must have been anxious about all the activity last night. I should have sent along his chewy bones." Angie sat up on the bed. "What are you doing?"

"Coming to wake you up. It's time to eat. Lunch or brunch, whatever you want to call it at almost two in the afternoon, is ready." Ian slapped his hand on his leg. "Come on, Dom, let's leave the lady to get ready."

Dom, looking totally unsure that he should leave the room, huffed, then stood and went over to Ian.

"I'll be down in a few. I want to shower this fuzz away. I can't believe I slept so long."

Ian shook his head. "We didn't get out of the hospital until after three in the morning, so really you've just had a normal night's sleep. I just can't sleep past eight, no matter what. I'll see you downstairs."

Coffee was ready at her place at the table when she arrived in the kitchen twenty minutes later. She sank into her chair and sipped down half of the cup before looking up at Felicia, Estebe, and Ian, who were all watching her. "Okay, what did I miss?"

"Not much. Jon called earlier and said he'd be coming over as soon as he checked in with Susan." Felicia stood and went over to the stove, where she filled a plate with waffles. Then she put a pat of butter on each waffle and covered the entire thing with warm maple syrup. She set it in front of Angie, then repeated the action three times for the others.

Estebe moved around her and took a heaping plate of bacon out of the microwave. "This should still be warm. I talked to Nancy this morning—she and the kids are doing fine. No sightings of the ex or his current wife. I have a security team watching the house, but she doesn't know."

"Of course you do." Angie bit into a waffle and enjoyed the vanilla flavor mixed with the maple. "This is just what I needed after last night. I don't think I even tasted dinner. I was so worried about the dance. Did that go well?"

"After the police left, it was fine. I can't understand how River Vista can't have one event without having a police cruiser attending to chase away the bad guys." Felicia sat down with her plate of waffles.

"Sorry, I shouldn't have called nine-one-one about Charles and Jane." Angie sipped some orange juice that Ian had just set in front of her.

"That's not what I mean. It's not that you shouldn't have called—you did the right thing. It's just that we are not a normal little town. I bet other towns our size don't have dead bodies showing up in their parks." Felicia glanced at Estebe, who was staring at her. "What? So, I wanted a perfect night. What can I say?"

"Leave her alone. It's been a weird couple of weeks. Susan's okay, then?" Angie turned to Ian, whom she assumed had talked to his uncle.

"She's doing great. The team found the notes she mentioned and proved that the woman from the park had been held there. He didn't think it was for long, but it ties the two events together. He's looking into serials who keep their victims for a while. So far, he's got nothing." He finished his orange juice, got the pitcher from the refrigerator, and refilled everyone's glasses.

"That's a happy note for the breakfast table." Angie cut off another piece of her waffle, then set her fork down. "Was Susan molested? Is that the right word?"

"Actually, no." Ian frowned and glanced at his phone. "The kidnapper hit her on the head, tied her up, and then chained her to the cave wall. She was dehydrated but not assaulted otherwise. And so was the other woman."

"Abigail, we should call her by her name. She was a person," Angie said.

"Abigail was a college student in California. No signs of any torture or assault except for being tied up and dehydration. She wasn't killed by the kidnapper exactly—the girl had a peanut allergy. The coroner thinks she died because she was fed protein bars with peanut butter." Ian shook his head. "It's like the kidnapper was just collecting people to get them out of their normal world."

"Yeah, that's what I thought." Angie stood and went to grab her laptop. She opened it and found Susan's calendar. "When I asked Allen about this entry in her schedule, he said they verified it was the yoga class. It was the last place anyone saw her."

"I was in the class that day. Nothing weird happened." Felicia shrugged. "It was a Friday, so I left as soon as class was over. Susan was talking to some people at the juice bar."

"Look at the letter under the note. See the *J*?" Angie pointed to a squiggle under the entry.

"It could be a *J*, or it could be a swish from her note." Felicia stared up at Angie. "What are you seeing?"

"I didn't see it until after Charles said he didn't know about Jane going to the restaurant and looking for Nancy. Seriously, he was shocked." Angie used a piece of bacon to emphasize her words. "I bet he didn't break in to Nancy's house, either. I think his new wife did. Or at least, that's the theory I told Allen. He's checking into Jane Gowan's background and trying to track the couple down. I think when he finds her, she's going to be the one behind all this. Except for maybe hiring the thugs who tried to scare me out of my house."

"You think that was Charles," Estebe said. He stood and dialed a number on his phone. "Make sure you watch for a woman, as well. She was short, red-haired, a little on the heavy side."

Estebe paused as he listened to the person on the other side. "You're sure? Then go inside and protect them. I'll call Nancy and tell her to let you in."

Ian held out his phone. "She's there? I'll call Uncle Allen."

"Someone by that description just stopped their car next door. There's one of those Realtor ads on the side, it's a peel-off." Estebe held up a hand. "Nancy? There are two men at your door. Karl and Kent. Please let them inside and follow their instructions, okay?"

When he hung up, everyone stared at him.

"She didn't argue with you or question your orders?" Angie stared at him. "How did you get her to do that?"

"I'm her boss. She trusts me to lead her the correct way in the kitchen and in life. Why would she question me?" Estebe looked confused at the question.

Felicia laughed and hugged him. "You don't even realize how rare that is."

Ian came back to the table and set the phone down. "Uncle Allen is getting someone there. We might have just found Jane Gowan."

"If not, some Realtor is going to be questioning her choice of career in a few minutes when she's detained by police officers simply for trying to list a property." Angie took the last piece of bacon off the plate. "I'll clear the table if everyone is done."

"I'll help. We might as well be useful while we wait for news." Ian picked up plates and took them to the sink. "I wanted to run something by you anyway."

Chapter 23

Jon showed up right after Estebe dried the last plate. Felicia and Angie were huddled over a cookbook talking about a new dessert for the restaurant. When he knocked on the door, one of the police officers stood with him.

"Sorry, Dale, I forgot to tell you Jon was coming by." Ian opened the door and escorted Jon inside.

"Everything all right?" Dale glanced around the room, making sure no one was holding a gun on someone.

Angie stood and grabbed a box of cookies she'd set aside yesterday for the assigned watchers. "Everything's great. Do you want some cookies? I've got peanut butter, chocolate chip, and a few snowballs in the mix."

"Sounds great." Dale scanned the room one more time. "As long as you're all okay."

"We're fine," Ian assured him again. "Jon, do you want some coffee? It's been a long night."

"That's for sure." Jon sat at the table where Estebe had been earlier and ran a hand through his still-wet hair. He glanced over at Dom, who was on his dog bed, watching the new arrival. "I ran home and changed. I needed to feed Timber and tell him his mom was coming home too."

"She's going to love seeing him. When will she be released?" Angie set aside the cookbook and watched Jon's face. It seemed younger and somehow, more vulnerable. Which made him much more attractive than the man she'd met at the park so many months ago.

"Later today or tomorrow. It depends on how she does today." He pulled out an envelope of papers. "I wanted you to see this first. My boss came by this morning to let me know I'm welcome back at the firm. And to show me this. Taylor Farms has decided to go with another site in the area. The old processing plant has been determined to fit their needs better."

"You're kidding me." Angie eyed the documents warily. "Why the sudden change of heart?"

"Apparently, the developer, Charles Gowan, called them last night and told them that there had been some irregularities with the appropriations of this property, and they would be better off going the other way." He pushed the papers toward her. "Taylor Farms is offering you a small settlement for your time and energy. And of course, your neighbor would also get what they call a 'kill fee.'"

"Wait, you're going to pay me for not selling?" Angie laughed as she picked up the papers. Her eyes widened. "You're paying me *twenty-five thousand dollars* not to sell?"

Ian glanced over her shoulder and pointed to a paragraph. "I think they're paying you not to sue them in case the irregularities point toward them or their developers. Estebe, you know this stuff, look at the contract."

Angie handed the papers over to Estebe and looked at Jon. "I'm glad she's home, safe and sound."

"Almost home," Jon corrected as he stood. "And so am I. I've told her I'm going to be a better husband, a better man, for the rest of our lives. Look, I've got to get back to the hospital. I only agreed to deliver these today because I thought you needed some good news in your life for all you did for Susan and me. And I wouldn't say this since I'm actually representing my client, but as a normal guy who's been under a lot of stress in the last few months, I'm pretty sure that they lowballed you on the settlement. You might want to double that with your counter. And make sure Mrs. Potter knows the unofficial advice as well."

"I'll have my attorney look over the paperwork and get back to you." Angie nodded to him. "Go be with your wife."

He grinned at her and headed to the door.

Ian hurried to him and took his arm. "Could I talk to you for a minute?"

They disappeared outside, and Estebe set the papers down. "I don't see any issues with this contract. Legally, they didn't have to do this since you never agreed to sell in the first place, but Ansley's right, they're covering their butt in case you try to sue them for strong-arming you on the sale. Tell your attorney to triple the settlement offer. That way you'll probably get them to agree to something in the middle. Congratulations on saving your house."

Angie sank into her chair, tears filling her eyes. "I'd decided to give up. To let them have it in order to protect everyone I loved. If they'd hurt Dom or Precious or Mabel, I would have been devastated and blamed myself."

"You weren't the bad guy here. You were just fighting for your home. And that's never a wrong position to come from." Felicia gave her a hug. "Besides, there was no way the four of you were moving into the apartment with me. I'm definitely getting a cat."

Estebe put his arm around Felicia and pushed aside a lock of hair. "I was wondering if you'd consider moving, anyway. I think I have enough room in my home for you and a cat."

Angie heard Felicia's sharp intake of breath.

"You're asking me to move in with you? You know I'm a complete slob and I work crazy hours. Besides, I'm probably going to drive you crazy." She kissed him on the cheek. "And that's before I get a kitten who sharpens their claws on your leather furniture. It's a sweet offer, and I love you for it, but maybe after the kitten's house-trained. Especially since Angie and the zoo don't need a new place to live."

He shook his head and went down on one knee. He pulled a ring box out of his pocket. "This wasn't where I was planning on doing this, but fate brings you to where you are."

Angie stood and grabbed her phone, hunting for the camera app. There was no way she was missing this.

He took the ring out of the box and held it out to her. A marquis-cut diamond sparkled on a silver-colored band that Angie would bet was platinum. She saw Felicia's hands shaking as he gently took one of hers in his own. "Felicia Williams, will you marry me?"

Ian burst in the door just then. "The plan's all set for tomorrow morning." Angie shushed him.

Ian closed the door softly and then stepped toward Angie, wrapping his arm around her waist. "Sorry for the interruption, man. Go ahead."

"I will ask again, for Ian's sake. And to give you time to breathe." He grinned over at Ian. "Felicia Williams? Will you marry me?"

A heavy silence filled the kitchen as they waited for her answer. Angie had just started to lower the phone, wondering if recording the event had been a bad idea, when she heard Felicia's intake of breath. Not sharp this time, but the way the yoga teacher had taught the class the few times Angie had attended. She raised the phone again.

"Yes. I'll marry you."

Estebe slipped the ring on her finger and stood, pulling her into a kiss. Afterward, he chuckled. "I thought you were going to say no, and I would look like a fool, down on one knee."

"Never. My brain just needed to process the words. I wasn't sure you were speaking English for a minute." She leaned her head on Estebe's chest and held her left hand out to Angie. "I'm getting married!"

"I know." Angie snapped a picture of Felicia's ring hand, then one of the happy couple. She set the phone down and went to hug her friend.

Ian slapped Estebe on the back. "This calls for a celebration dinner. Who's hungry?"

"We just ate," Angie reminded him.

"Who cares? By the time we get somewhere, it will be dinnertime again. And we need some champagne to celebrate. It's been a really good Sunday." Ian squeezed Angie and then whispered in her ear. "It's all set for tomorrow morning."

"Almost all set," she corrected. She looked at Estebe and Felicia. "Want to help me out with one more celebration?"

* * * *

They were at Copper Creek eating dinner when Ian's phone rang. He looked up at Angie. "It's Uncle Allen."

Angie waited as he stepped away from the table to take the call. She sipped her wine, hoping this nightmare was really over and her theory had been right. Not because she wanted to be right, but because she wanted Nancy and Susan to be safe. And Abigail to have justice.

When he came back to the table, everyone stared at him.

"What?"

"Tell us what he called about." Angie set her glass down.

"Are you sure? I mean, it's your celebration dinner," he spoke to Felicia and Estebe.

They looked at each other, then nodded. "Family comes first. We want to know, even if it's bad news."

"It's bad news for someone." Ian grinned. "They caught Jane, and she told them that they'd never find Charles and he wasn't involved anyway. She confessed to kidnapping Abigail and Susan and dumping Abigail's body. She said they'd been in Charles's way. Apparently, she was taking care of his dirty work."

"She did this for him?" Angie shook her head. "She'd have to be crazy."

"Uncle Allen is betting on that. But since she confessed and they have her confession on tape, he thinks she's going away somewhere for a very long time." He grinned. "And they picked up Charles at the airport with a ticket to Mexico. Apparently he thought he needed a bit of a vacation from his wife."

"Does Allen have anything on him?" Angie asked after taking a sip of her wine. This was a great day.

"Charles definitely hired those guys to break into your houses. Both of them identified him, but they didn't know who Jane was. And according to what Jon told you, Allen thinks there may be more dirty deeds in the guy's past. He just needs to uncover them."

Estebe refilled everyone's glasses. "To justice, and to having the world back to normal."

As they clinked, Angie thought they needed one more good day to make the world a better place. She prayed they could pull it off. She held her glass up again after taking a sip and smiled. "To happiness."

* * * *

The County Seat had the front doors open when Ian and Barb stopped by right at 1 p.m. on Monday.

"Angie shouldn't leave this door open. It gives people the wrong idea, like the place is open or something. No one reads signs anymore," Barb groused as they came into the fully lit dining room. Bleak stood at the hostess station and nodded to them.

"Mrs. Travis, how nice to see you. Maggie sends her love and said to tell you that she'll be at the hospital waiting for you on the day of surgery." Bleak gave the surprised Barb a quick hug. "She's pushy like that. Always getting into your business, but sometimes it's kind of nice."

"Well, isn't that sweet." Barb squeezed Bleak tightly, then awkwardly patted her back.

"She really is amazing. She's taking me dress shopping later. I'm going to the winter formal. It's no big thing." Bleak wiped her face and the tears away as she stepped away from Barb. "Angie said I was supposed to seat you here at the window."

"You said we were here to pick up some meals to put in my freezer for after the surgery, not to eat lunch," Barb growled at Ian before she turned and followed Bleak. "Maggie is a very caring woman. You're lucky to have her in your life. But tell her she doesn't need to bother waiting at the hospital. I won't need a ride home for a few days, and I can call a taxi or an Uber, like you young people like to use."

Bleak laughed as she set down glasses and filled them with water from a pitcher that had been sitting nearby. "I don't think that will do any good, but I'll try. And yes, I am lucky a lot of people are in my life now. You are too."

As she walked away, Barb glared at Ian. "Don't tell me this is a 'be happy you're alive' intervention. I'm just having surgery, for gosh sakes. I don't need all this fanfare."

"Then just see it as a lunch." Ian grinned at her and sipped his water. "The menu's kind of set, but do you want a glass of wine or a drink?"

"I want a beer. In a freaking bottle," Barb groused.

Jeorge arrived by her side with a chilled bottle of the light beer Barb favored and a glass of soda for Ian. "If this isn't acceptable, I can list off what we have in stock."

Barb nodded and took the bottle. "This is just fine. Thank you."

Jeorge disappeared, and Bleak came back with a basket of rolls and a plate of loaded potato skins. She set both down and paused. "Do you want something else? More sour cream? More bacon?"

Barb shook her head. "This is fine."

"It smells wonderful. Thanks, Bleak," Ian added.

A couple walked past the window and came inside.

Barb placed a potato skin on her plate, then cut off a bite with her fork. She pointed to the people in the hallway. "See, I told you, no one reads the signs anymore. Now that child is going to have to disappoint them by letting them know the place is closed. A locked door does that just fine."

Ian stood and picked up his glass. "I think they're coming to see you."

He set his drink on another table and then added a chair next to Barb. When he moved out of the way, Susan and Jon stood in front of Barb.

"May I sit?" Susan asked.

"Sure, sit down." Barb's face paled. "You shouldn't be out. You just got out of the hospital."

Susan sank into the chair Jon pulled out for her and then pointed to the empty chair. "Please join us."

Jon shook his head. "I will in a few minutes for dinner. But right now, you need to talk to your mother. I'll be over at the bar if you need anything."

Susan nodded and turned back to Barb. She leaned toward the breadbasket and groaned. "I haven't eaten fresh bread in years. May I have a piece?"

"Of course. Don't eat too much, you've just had an ordeal."

"As long as it's not a protein bar, I'm good. I don't think I can ever eat one again." Susan laughed as she took a roll. "And calling it an 'ordeal,' well, that's an understatement. You've kept up on what's been going on?"

Barb nodded, handing her the butter. "Of course I have. I don't know if you remember, but Karen was my sister."

"And my aunt. I know, she told me before she died. I think I always knew. I mean, I have memories of you and me in a car going to get ice cream." She took a bite of the roll and groaned. "I'm never giving up bread again. This is too good."

Barb buttered a roll and took a bite. "The woman who runs this place is a very good cook. And a good person."

"Mom—I mean Karen—gave me a good life. You didn't have to worry about that," Susan said, setting the roll down and reaching for the other glass of water. "I just wish we'd been more connected."

"I was wild. I missed you, but I told myself you were better off. I'll understand if you hate me." Barb put a loaded baked potato on Susan's plate. "I know this is a lot to take in."

"I've had a lot of time to think about what's important lately." Susan put a hand on Barb's and met her gaze. "There's nothing I want more than to have you in my life. I'm here for you while you go through this. You have family."

"You don't need to…"

Susan squeezed her hand. "I know that. I want to. Besides, we can help take care of each other."

The kitchen doors opened, and Angie walked out with Estebe. He was carrying a tray with several dishes. She paused at the table and smiled at Susan. Angie reached down and hugged her gently. "I'm Angie. I hope you don't mind, but we've plated up the dinner family style. I thought it was appropriate."

Jon came over and sat down at the table. He put a glass of wine in front of Susan and a cup of coffee in front of his plate. "Are we ready to eat?"

Susan smiled at him and nodded. "Jon, do you know my mother?"

He nodded and reached over to shake Barb's hand. "I've met her a couple of times, but this is the first time I can say it's a pleasure."

Barb reddened, shaking his hand. "Sorry I broke into your house."

Jon stared at her as she dished up some of the mashed potatoes. She didn't meet his gaze.

"Barb, tell me about the Red Eye. What's it like to run a saloon?" Susan didn't miss a beat, dishing up a chicken marsala on her plate and passing the platter to Jon.

Angie and Estebe left the table and went back to where Felicia and Ian sat at the bar. "Set up plates, and I'll bring out the food." Estebe nodded to Bleak. "You're eating with us, right?"

"I can't miss a family meal." She grinned at Angie. "I love working here."

Jeorge got everyone drinks, and Angie kept an eye out on the other family who was eating together by the window. For the first time. From the laughter and smiles, it looked like Barb and Sunny were making up for lost time.

Felicia and Bleak were talking about her ring. And Jeorge and Estebe were chatting about next year's BSU Broncos team and their chances to break out for a championship.

Ian rubbed her arm. "Are you okay?"

She nodded. "Bleak had it right. This is a family meal. And I'm so blessed to have all of you in my life."

He leaned over and kissed her. "I think the blessing is on us and how you came into our lives. I love you, Angie Turner."

Angie kissed him, then they both rejoined the conversation. Life, love, and a future. It was a great Monday.

Recipe

When I was thinking about the recipe for this book, I wanted something from my past. A memory. The way a dish tastes or a memory of a meal stays with you. I made brownies while I was editing this and almost went with that recipe, since the rich chocolate taste is still in my mouth. Instead, I give you a childhood treat. Quick cookies were probably the first cookies I learned to make. And the ones I messed up, more often than not. The secret is in the chocolate mixture you cook on the stove. Cook it too long, and your cookies will turn into a crumble (that's really good over vanilla ice cream—not all failures have to be trashed). Not cooked long enough, and the cookies won't set. You want a soft ball stage for the chocolate. Drop a bit into a glass of water and reach in. If it turns into a ball, you're ready to stir it into the oats.

Quick Cookies

2 cups sugar
2 tbsp cocoa
1/2 cup milk
1/4 cup butter

Cook these ingredients in a heavy saucepan on the stove, boiling for 3–4 minutes.

Pour the chocolate mixture into a large bowl with the following mixed together:

3 cups oatmeal
1/2 cup peanut butter
1 tbsp vanilla
Optional: 1/2 bag of miniature marshmallows

Drop onto a greased cookie sheet to set.
Yum.

Love Lynn Cahoon?
There's plenty more!
Don't miss the rest of the books in the
Farm-to-Fork series
And be sure to try the
Tourist Trap Mysteries
And the
Cat Latimer Mysteries

And keep reading for a sneak peek
at
ONE POISON PIE
The first full-length book in
the newest series
from Lynn Cahoon:
The Kitchen Witch Mysteries
coming soon from
Kensington Books

Chapter 1

Karma sucks.

Mia Malone slapped the roller filled with cottage yellow paint on the wall. She'd missed another spot. Her lack of attention was one more thing on the long list of karma credits she could blame on her ex, Isaac.

If karma didn't smack down the lowlife soon, she had several ideal spells just waiting to be used on the rat. Maybe he'd like to develop a rash? Or be turned into a toad to match his true personality? A line of yellow paint dripped off the roller and onto the scratched wood floor.

She set the roller in the paint pan and with a rag, wiped up the paint before it could dry. Maybe a run would be more productive right now. She could burn off this pent-up energy tingling her fingers. Teasing her with all the curses she could inflict.

She took a deep, calming breath. Magic came back threefold. She needed to control her impulses, keeping her anger in check. As much as she wanted Isaac to pay for his betrayal, she didn't need any help in the bad luck department. Sighing, she sat cross-legged on the floor in the middle of the half-painted schoolroom and tried to envision her new life.

A noise echoed through the empty schoolhouse. *Had the door opened?*

"Mia," her grandmother called. "Are you here, dear?"

"To your left, Grans." Mia stood and dusted off the butt of her worn jeans, imagining dusting off Isaac and his bad energy at the same time. Keeping her karma clean seemed to be a full-time job since she'd left Boise.

Mary Alice Carpenter, tall and willowy, stood in the doorway to the foyer. The curl in her short gray hair was the only physical trait Grans and Mia shared. Mia stood a good five inches shorter than the older woman, and Mia's curves would have made her prime model material, oh, about a hundred years ago.

Besides her curly hair, she'd inherited power from her maternal grandmother. While her mother had turned away from the lure of magic, choosing instead the life of a corporate lawyer's wife, Mia had embraced her heritage.

Her grandmother took one look at her and groaned. "I knew he wouldn't stay gone. That boy is worse than spilt milk. You just can't get rid of the smell."

"I can handle Isaac." Mia gave her grandmother a hug. "You don't need to worry about him."

Grans's eyebrows rose. "Are you sure, dear? I've done a few transmutations in my time that might be quite appropriate."

Mia bit back a laugh and glanced around the large room. "Seriously, don't get involved. That part of my life is over. I've made a fresh start."

"You've bought a run-down money pit that's going to bankrupt you, just trying to keep the place warm." A second woman followed her grandmother into the room, shoving a cell phone into her Coach bag. "Sorry, had to take that. Apparently, my long-lost nephew is gracing us with his presence at my birthday party. Probably needs money."

"Adele, so nice to see you." Mia managed to choke out after a death stare from her grandmother.

Adele Simpson stood next to Grans and glanced around the room, noticeable disgust covering her face. "Mary Alice, *this* is what you fought so hard with the board to save?"

"The building should be on the historic register. You and I both know it would have already been protected if it sat in the Sun Valley city limits. Magic Springs is always an afterthought with the historical commission." Grans slipped off her down coat that had made her look like a stuffed panda.

Mia watched the women bicker. Adele, the meanest woman in Magic Springs, was the dark to Grans's light, and for some unbeknownst reason, Grans's best friend. She was also Mia's first and only client for her new venture. *So far*, she amended.

Gritting her teeth, Mia forced her lips into what she hoped was a passable smile. "Ladies, welcome to Mia's Morsels." She glanced around the room, sweeping her arm as she turned. "Currently, you're in the reception area, where staff and students will gather before classes and where we'll do most of the daily work scheduling. Here, customers will be able to sample dishes and peruse a weekly menu of available meals."

"You sound like a commercial," Grans chided. "It's just us. You don't have to put on the sales pitch."

Mia smiled. "Just trying it out. I've got a lot of work to do before I can even think about opening." She nodded to the half-painted wall. "Do you like the color?"

Her grandmother nodded. "It's friendly without being obnoxiously bright, like so many buildings. Daycare colors have swept through the decorating studios. I swear, the new crop of interior designers has no sense of style or class."

"Fredrick just did Helen Marcum's living room in pink." Adele sniffed. "The room looks like an antacid commercial. I swear the woman shows her hillbilly roots every time she makes a decision."

"I don't believe Helen's southern, dear." Grans focused back on Mia, closing her eyes for a second. "Color holds a lot of power. Pull out your books before you go too far. Although, if I remember, yellow represents the digestive system."

Mia loved listening to her grandmother talk about the representations of power. Being kitchen witches was different than being Wiccan, or what normal people would think of when you said the word 'witch.' They didn't wear black pointy hats or fly around the moon. Mia's magic was more about the colors, the food, the process of making a house a home. That was one of the reasons her career choice was such a natural extension of her life. Food made people happy. She liked being around happy people. Sometimes magic was that easy.

"You are not doing woo-woo magic stuff again, are you, Mary Alice?" Adele shook her head. "Next you'll be telling the girl to open on a full moon and wave around a dead cat."

Grans looked horrified at her friend. "I would never tell her to desecrate an animal that way. We've been friends for over forty years. You should know better."

"Oh, go fly your broomstick."

Grans and Adele had been the swing votes on the board allowing Mia to purchase the property, based on her pledge to save the building's history. The losing bidder had presented a plan to bulldoze the school and replace it with a high-end retail mall. Instead, Mia had a place to start over. Grans always said the best way to get a man out of your head was to change your routine.

Mia might have gone a little overboard.

Her arms and back ached from painting. Another two, three hours, the room would be done. Then she could move on to the kitchen, the heart of her dream. Right now, all she wanted was to clean up the paint supplies and return to her upstairs apartment for a long soak in the claw-foot tub. The unexpected visitors had her skin tingling, a sure sign nothing good was about to happen.

Catering Adele's birthday party had been an order more than a request, even though her business wouldn't be completely up and running for a month or so. The planning for the event had gone smoothly, like an aged Southern whiskey. The final prep list for Saturday's party sat finished on her kitchen table in the apartment. James, the chef at the Lodge, had allowed her time to prep in his kitchen tomorrow evening. By Sunday, she'd have a successful reference in the books for Mia's Morsels. Now, without warning, the triumph she'd hoped for was slipping through her fingers.

"Add one, maybe two more, to the guest list. Who knows who he'll bring from Arizona to help me celebrate?" Adele shoved a piece of paper toward her.

Mia glanced down. A name had been scrawled on the torn piece of notepaper: *William Danforth III.* She hadn't known Adele had any living relatives, let alone a nephew. "How nice. Are you two close?"

A harsh laugh came from the woman. "Close? I wasn't kidding about the money. He's checking on his inheritance. I'm pretty sure he thought I'd be dead by now."

"Now, Adele, at least he's visiting." Grans picked up Mr. Darcy, Mia's black cat who'd wandered into the room. He'd probably been sleeping in one of the empty southern classrooms where the afternoon sun warmed the wood floors. He curled into her neck and started purring. Loudly.

Unfortunately, during a late summer visit to Grans's house, Mr. Darcy had picked up a hitchhiker. The spirit of Dorian Alexander, who had been Grans's beau before his untimely death, had taken up residence with Mia's cat. A fact that weirded Mia out at times, especially at night when Mr. Darcy slept on the foot of her bed. Mia really needed to get Grans focused on a reversal spell. But this wasn't the time to be chatting about spells and power. Instead she focused on Adele and her party.

"I'm sure he's…" Mia stopped. What had she been going to say? That Adele's nephew was nice? If the guy had any of Adele's temperament, the guy would be a royal jerk.

Adele waved away her words, her hands showing her impatience. "Let me worry about Billy. You're serving beef tomorrow." The words weren't a question.

"I'd planned to serve squab with raspberry sauce and wild rice for the main course." Mia held her breath. *Please no last-minute changes—please.*

"That won't do at all." Adele watched as Mr. Darcy crawled up on Grans's shoulder. She reached out a hand to pet the cat, who hissed at her. Dropping her hand, she focused her glare on Mia. "My parents ran the Beef Council for years. You had to have known we had the largest cattle operation in the Challis area, maybe even the entire Magic Valley."

"I sent you the menu a week ago." Mia thought about the prep list she'd spent hours writing out last night. A list that would have to be completely revamped if Adele made this change in the menu. "I'm sure you responded."

"I've been busy. You should have called rather than sending paper." Adele stepped farther away from the hissing cat. "I don't remember everything. That's why I'm telling you now. Oh, and no cake, pie for dessert. Several different types, of course…you'll know which ones to serve with the beef. I've never liked cake."

"You already approved the menu," Mia repeated through clenched teeth. Apparently sensing her distress, Mr. Darcy jumped out of Grans's arms and walked over to Mia. He curled on her feet, watching the women.

"I doubt that. No matter, you need to serve beef. It's a tradition. I'm surprised you didn't know." Adele pulled out a beeping phone and after glancing at the display, focused on Grans. "We need to leave now if we're going to keep our court time."

Mia sighed. Trying one more time to win a battle already lost, she asked, "Are you sure you don't want squab?"

"The homeless eat pigeon. Porterhouse. Or whatever cut you think is best. You're the expert." Adele turned toward the door, pulling Grans along with her.

That's what you keep saying. Mia said, "I'll try, but the party is this weekend."

"I'm sure you'll do your best." Grans shook off Adele's grip and turned back to Mia. She planted a kiss on her cheek.

Mia followed them to the front door. Daylight filtered through the dirt-covered windows. Another item for her to-do list: hire a window cleaner. Mr. Darcy's soft footsteps padded behind her. "Thanks for stopping in," she called as they left the building. After the door closed, she added, hoping her grandmother wouldn't hear, "and ruining a perfectly good day."

If she was being honest, though, the ruination of her day had started with Isaac's call. She reached down to stroke Mr. Darcy. He meowed his wishes.

"Sorry, your dinner is going to have to wait. I've got to get to Majors Grocery," Mia told the cat, who looked horrified at the thought. She hauled the painting supplies to the kitchen. Her mind whirled as water rinsed the cheery yellow paint out of the roller and down the drain. Her detailed plan of attack for the event had disappeared with a flick of Adele's perfectly polished, bloodred nails.

Mr. Darcy wove through her legs as she stood at the sink. Finishing the cleanup, she laid the tools on a towel to dry and double-checked the lock on the back door. Then she climbed the two sets of stairs to the third floor and her apartment.

Christina Adams, the almost twenty-year-old sister of her ex, jumped up from the couch when Mia entered the apartment. "I thought you were going to paint this afternoon?"

"I thought you were coming to help just as soon as you finished lunch?" Mia studied the girl. Last month, Christina had returned to Magic Springs.

She'd shown up on Mia's doorstep with a police escort. Mark Baldwin, the town's only officer, had found her loitering in the small downtown park. Her long blond hair screamed cheerleader, but the bars in her eyebrow and her lip, along with the row of piercings in her ear, hardened the look.

Christina had been planning on starting college this semester after spending last year in Las Vegas, trying to make it as a dancer after some bad advice from her substitute dance coach. Now, after one more fight with the family, she'd tracked Mia down and asked if she could live with her for a while. Mia didn't have the heart to turn her away, even if Mia wouldn't be a part of the Adams family, now or ever.

She had the decency to blush. "I'm not really good at all that painting stuff. Maybe I could just help you with the cooking rather than the remodeling."

"Don't worry about it. I have a feeling we're going to have to pull an all-nighter if we want to finish prep before the party. And now we have to bake pies, as well." She went into the kitchen to get her list. "I'm heading over to Majors. Be ready to work when I get back."

Mia heard the television come on as her only answer. Training Christina to be a sous chef might be harder than she'd imagined. Running her fingers over the cookbook she'd left out that morning with the prep list, she remembered Isaac's call. Could there be another reason Isaac's sister had come to live with Mia? She locked her cookbook in the safe in her room. She'd been stupid before. Today she'd take paranoid.

Where was she going to get thirty servings of steak by tomorrow evening? And the side dishes had to completely change. Adele was paying for both grocery orders, no matter what Grans said.

She hoped the small country store had enough meat on hand. Or an idea.

As she opened the front door, she tripped over an envelope. The delivery service must have dropped it off late yesterday. They'd been busy in the kitchen, doing a trial run-through of the menu. The return address on the top was smeared, but the envelope was clearly addressed to Christina. Mia shoved the envelope into her purse. She'd give it to her when she got back. Or after the party, when she wouldn't mind losing her apprentice.

A dusting of snow had fallen the night before, coating the town in white. Magic Springs looked like a Dickens's novel Christmas. The roads had been plowed. Someone had run a small blade—probably on the front of a four-wheeler —over the sidewalks in front of the school and down the two blocks toward Majors. Small towns, Mia mused. No way had the city paid for this type of service. It had to be one of the homeowners in the village who donated their early morning service for the pleasure of driving their toy around the snow-covered streets.

Mia took a deep breath, trying to focus on solving her menu problems rather than being filled with the quiet beauty of the town. Beef. Maybe a garlic mashed potato? Or a scalloped? Or would Adele consider the menu too homey for her party? Would there be any way Majors could pull off an order of fresh asparagus? It was April, even though the town wouldn't acknowledge spring for a few weeks at the earliest. There had to be asparagus ready to harvest somewhere.

Stomping the snow off her boots, she pushed open the glass grocery slider. A bell rang over the door, echoing in the seemingly empty store. No cashier stood at the register; no shoppers filled the aisles. Mia glanced at her watch, five fifteen. The store closed early during the winter, but she'd just made it.

She grabbed a cart and headed to the butcherblock in the back. The meat case stood empty, and her heart sank. A bell sat on the top of the case, and she rang it once. No one came through the doors. Maybe Adele would just have to suck it up and eat the food Mia had planned to serve.

Mia could see her grandmother's frown. Again, she banged on the bell, harder this time, picturing Adele's unsmiling face each time she hit the silver chime.

"Hold up," a man's voice called from the back. "I heard you the first twenty times. I have my hands full back here."

Mia jumped back from the meat case. Her hand still reached out in front of her. She called toward the door, "Okay, I'll wait here."

That was dumb. Of course, she would wait. Now that she'd had some time to think, Mia pulled out a slip of paper and started making a quick shopping list. Peaches, asparagus, more butter, fresh horseradish, potatoes— she continued to write as she waited. Finally, she looked up from her list satisfied. She only needed to add thirty quality steaks. Maybe she should serve a soup too. That would give her more time to grill and prep the main course.

Loud voices were muffled by the swinging doors. Was that an argument? She inched closer, trying to see through the window in the door. Two men stood by a large metal table. One, dressed in a suit, shook a finger at the other. Now she could hear the actual words. "I'm not making this offer again. I'll wait and get the property for pennies when it goes to auction."

"I'm not losing this store. Majors has been in the family since the settlers came to Magic Springs. It's part of the community, the town's history. We're just going through a bad patch. Everyone is." The man dropped a box on the table. "I have a customer waiting for me. Unless you're here to shop, get the heck out of my store."

"You'll regret turning me down." The suit walked toward the door and caught sight of Mia watching. "Of course, you'd be here. Are you trying to ruin all my business?"

"I'm sorry, do I know you?" Mia stood back, stunned at the man's outburst.

"Why would you?" The man glared at her, then stomped around the counter and almost ran from the store.

Printed in the United States
by Baker & Taylor Publisher Services